MORGAN COUNTY PUBLIC
110 SOUTH JEFFERSON ST
MARTINSVILLE, IN 46151

P9-BBU-470

FIC
DAI
M

Dailey, Judy.

Animal, vegetable,
murder.

WITHDRAWN

ANIMAL, VEGETABLE, MURDER

AN URBAN FARM MYSTERY

Animal, Vegetable, Murder

Judy Dailey

FIVE STAR
A part of Gale, Cengage Learning

GALE
CENGAGE Learning

Detroit • New York • San Francisco • New Haven, Conn • Waterville, Maine • London

GALE
CENGAGE Learning·

Copyright © 2013 by Judy Dailey
Five Star™ Publishing, a part of Gale, Cengage Learning.

ALL RIGHTS RESERVED.
This novel is a work of fiction. Names, characters, places, and incidents are either the product of the author's imagination, or, if real, used fictitiously.

No part of this work covered by the copyright herein may be reproduced, transmitted, stored, or used in any form or by any means graphic, electronic, or mechanical, including but not limited to photocopying, recording, scanning, digitizing, taping, Web distribution, information networks, or information storage and retrieval systems, except as permitted under Section 107 or 108 of the 1976 United States Copyright Act, without the prior written permission of the publisher.

The publisher bears no responsibility for the quality of information provided through author or third-party Web sites and does not have any control over, nor assume any responsibility for, information contained in these sites. Providing these sites should not be construed as an endorsement or approval by the publisher of these organizations or of the positions they may take on various issues.

LIBRARY OF CONGRESS CATALOGING-IN-PUBLICATION DATA

Dailey, Judy.
  Animal, vegetable, murder : an urban farm mystery / Judy Dailey. — First edition.
    pages cm.
    ISBN-13: 978-1-4328-2691-8 (hardcover)
    ISBN-10: 1-4328-2691-3 (hardcover)
    1. Widows—Fiction. 2. Husbands—Crimes against—Fiction. 3. Seattle (Wash.) —Fiction. I. Title.
  PS3604.A3468A55 2013
  813'.6—dc23   2012047076

First Edition. First Printing: April 2013
Find us on Facebook– https://www.facebook.com/FiveStarCengage
Visit our website– http://www.gale.cengage.com/fivestar/
Contact Five Star™ Publishing at FiveStar@cengage.com

Printed in Mexico
1 2 3 4 5 6 7 17 16 15 14 13

ACKNOWLEDGMENTS

I would like to thank the following people who read and commented on *Animal, Vegetable, Murder.* Any mistakes, of course, are mine. My readers were Clara Chaney Brown, Teri Lynn Brown, Mary Buckham, Keri Clark, Dr. and Mrs. C. M. Cobb (organic farmers for more than eighty years), Deni Dietz, Anna Fahey, Marie Friedericks, Daphne Harris, Catherine Hendricks, Mike Munro, Connie Sais, Lucinda Smith, Joe Stowitschek, Theresa de Valence, and Wayne Ude.

This book would not have been possible without the support of my husband, Tom Dailey, and our writing dog, Gunner.

CHAPTER ONE

I tightened my grip on the axe handle and sucked in a deep breath. I can kill her. I know I can.

The rising sun warmed the air inside my backyard tool shed, causing dust motes to dance across the axe. Its blade sparkled, wickedly sharp but beautiful—and I was dithering again.

I had spent all week debating my choice of weapon. I'm a proficient shot, but I'd decided against my pistol. Gunfire at six in the morning would alarm my neighbors and prompt frantic calls to the chief of police.

The chief because he lives in my neighborhood, Laurelmere, a walled enclave of Old Money and Microsoft McMansions ten minutes north of downtown Seattle. Acceptable sounds in Laurelmere are the whack of a golf ball or the purr of a finely tuned Jaguar XF. Unacceptable sounds are babies crying, doors slamming, and gunshots. It's that kind of place, insulated from the distressing realities of everyday life.

Back to my choice of weapon. An axe, I'd decided. One swift blow, clean and sure. I didn't want to hurt her, never that, but I needed her out of my life.

After the first death, the next ones would be so much easier.

My victim watched me coldly from her wire mesh prison on my workbench. I hefted the axe, but her small black eyes didn't blink.

Last night she'd squawked plenty when I tossed the blanket over her head. She struggled fiercely as I wrapped it around her plump body. Her feet sprang loose and she tried to scratch me. I held her tight and shoved her inside the cage. This morning she seemed calm, even resigned.

Although I try to avoid anthropomorphizing my chickens.

Henrietta stared at me. I stared back. With a sigh, I opened the cage and stroked her speckled feathers. "I don't want to slaughter you," I said, burying my fingers in her downy chest. "But I don't have any other choice."

In February when Ken and I started our urban farm, we bought four mature hens because it was too cold for chicks. Ken planned to butcher the hens in August. He said we should eat only free-range organic meat. In theory I agreed. I didn't want anything pumped full of antibiotics and pesticides, especially not now.

But Ken was gone.

So I imagined myself setting down my weapon, reaching inside the cage, and pulling out Henrietta. I would need both hands to hold her neck against the chopping block. But then how could I swing the axe?

Impossible. It was time to stop kidding myself. I could no more kill a chicken than I could lay an egg.

With a mental apology to Ken and a bounce of heartfelt relief, I tossed the axe aside.

"In God's name, woman. Watch where you're slinging that thing."

I turned around to find my neighbor, Angus "Mac" Mac-Dougall, standing behind me. The axe had buried itself in the wooden floor six inches from his mud-stained boots.

"Don't sneak up on me, you blasted Scot."

Mac folded his arms across his chest and released a burst of stale cigarette smoke. At sixty-five, he was more than twice my age and prone to treating me like a child. He was a burly five-foot-nine, unshaven and probably unwashed. He wore denim overalls and a torn camouflage vest over a brown-edged T-shirt. Behind him, a fishing pole leaned against a bait bucket filled with undulating goop.

Mac and I were the social outcasts of Laurelmere. We had washed up here by accident, Mac when he retired and moved in with his millionaire son, I when my grandmother died and left me her house. Mac was cantankerous, not "gracefully aging in place." I was unemployed, not "seeking new opportunities for personal growth." We didn't play golf. We didn't practice yoga or meditate. And we weren't rich. Never had been and, God willing, never would be.

"Time to put this old gal out of her misery?" Mac jerked his head at Henrietta, who eyed him and clucked. "Stopped laying, has she? Change of life?"

I nodded. I picked up the axe and stood it in a corner of the shed, while Mac stuck a calloused forefinger under Henrietta's wing. She rubbed against his finger, ruffling the feathers around her neck. He scratched down to the skin. If she'd had the right equipment, she would have purred. Mac claimed a special rapport with chickens, but I thought they loved him because his hands smelled like fish bait.

"All my old hens should be headed for the stew pot," I said. "But I can't bring myself to kill them."

"You're too softhearted to be a farmer, Sunny. Why don't you let these gals hang around and buy yer eggs at the grocer?"

"I can't. I have six chicks being delivered this morning. Rhode Island Reds."

"Lemme see." Mac held out his hands and ponderously counted on stubby fingers. "That's four old hens and six wee replacements. Seems to me you'll be about five chickens over the line."

Mac was right. When the city council passed an ordinance allowing each household to keep up to five hens, they hadn't considered the problem of geriatric chickens. Good laying hens like Henrietta start producing eggs at six months and lay steadily for another two years. After that they're freeloaders, okay for eating bugs and turning weeds into fertilizer but not much else.

Except, of course, for chicken dinner.

"Why don't you help me?"

"Help kill 'em, you mean?" Mac took a step backward. "Nae, lass. They're my friends."

"But I thought you grew up on a farm. You know how to do it humanely."

"I'm not going to kill the old dears. That's final."

"Okay. I'll figure out something." I sighed. "When the chicks arrive, I'll stash them in the guest bathroom. That'll hold them for a while."

Mac's face crinkled into a grin, exposing tobacco-stained teeth. "Some farmer you are, Sunny. Chickens in the bathroom. My mam'll be turning in her grave."

"Yeah, right. Go catch yourself a nice fat trout for supper. You don't seem to have any problem killing them."

"They're stone cold, lass," Mac said. He gathered his fishing gear and left.

Still brooding about my chickens, I took Henrietta from the cage and tucked her under my arm. She clucked contentedly. We stepped outside the toolshed and surveyed my domain. The air smelled fresh and clean. The rising sun gilded the espaliered fruit trees that line my back fence. Bright red Sansa apples hung from their branches like Christmas ornaments.

Ken had built a trellis over our garden path so we could grow peas and beans in what otherwise would have been wasted space. Above me, string beans dangled within easy reach. Hummingbirds were busy in the flowers, pollinating as they moved from blossom to blossom. Tight rosettes of Devil's Tongue lettuce sparkled with dew, and foot-long cucumbers hung from their lattice frame.

For the chickens, Ken designed a wire-covered enclosure to protect them from predators. I move the cage every couple of months, so the girls can fertilize and debug a different part of the garden. Best of all, Ken fixed the door between the henhouse and the chicken yard so it opens and shuts on a timer. I never had to hurry home to lock them in at night, and I don't have to roll out of bed at the crack of dawn to release them either. Ken called our chicken yard the Coop d'Ville.

I wished for the hundredth time—the thousandth time—that Ken could see our little urban farm in its full, mid-August glory.

I set Henrietta inside the chicken yard as the other hens squawked impatiently, hoping I'd toss in a handful of cracked corn or a couple of slugs. After pulling a few weeds, I stuffed the pockets of my shorts with Stupice tomatoes. Mac had taught me to grill tomato slices for breakfast, although I passed on his perennial offer of homemade haggis. Sheep stomach and innards are so not my thing.

I sighed. Geezer that he was, Mac must feel lonely. I had resolved to bake scones and invite him to discuss potato scab over high tea when I heard a sharp crack and then a thud.

The Henriettas screeched and beat their wings. The hummingbirds darted to the tops of the cherry trees. I froze and listened intently, but I didn't hear anything more.

If Mac had stumbled, he would be cursing, loud, rumbling Gaelic curses. Something must have fallen from my roof, something heavy and important.

Well rats. I couldn't afford major repairs right now. Ken's life insurance company kept finding one more form that I had to fill out before they would honor my claim, and my checking account was sucking air.

I picked my way across a patch of garden that shimmered with rainbow-hued stalks of chard and lacy carrot tops. Past the corner of my house, I saw a man on the ground next to the woodpile.

He lay motionless, facedown, arms stretched wide. From the back he looked like a bank examiner or a Mercedes salesman, neatly dressed in an expensive pin-striped suit. Everything about him spelled dignified and formal—everything except the crown of his head. It was matted with gray splatters and oozed fresh blood.

"Are you okay?" I whispered, totally lame but all I could squeeze out.

No answer.

Should I try first aid or dial 911? I stepped closer. Close enough to realize the man wasn't breathing. Close enough to smell something worse than chicken manure. Close enough to see a torn photograph clutched in his fingers, a torn photograph of my husband, Ken.

Bile burned in my mouth. I didn't want anyone else to see that picture. I pulled it from the dead man's hand and shoved it under the ripe tomatoes in my pocket. Then I turned on my cell phone and called for help.

CHAPTER TWO

I have no idea how long it takes the Seattle Police Department to answer a 911 call. But I'm pretty darn sure if you add "Laurelmere" to the report, the response time is cut in half. While I listened for sirens, a swarm of questions buzzed in my mind. Who was the dead man and who shot him? What was he doing in *my* yard? Why was he holding a picture of *my* husband?

Every time I tried to come up with an answer, my brain froze and my teeth chattered.

Minutes later, a patrol car raced into my street followed by Medic One. Both vehicles rammed into the curb. Two uniformed officers, a man and a woman, leaped from the blue-and-white police car and sprinted down my walk. The gear hanging from their heavy leather belts clanked as they bounded up my steps. I met them on the front porch.

"Did you report a shooting victim?" the female officer asked as she slammed to a stop two inches from my nose. Not much older than Ken's daughter from his first marriage, she had translucent white skin, wholesome features, and a snub nose. Her name badge read P. J. Vanderhorn.

My stomach clenched. "Yes, I did."

Vanderhorn's eyes glittered with excitement as she scanned my front yard. "Where is it?" she asked.

"Not it, he. He's around the side of the house." I pointed and was surprised to see my hand shake.

"Make sure nothing's disturbed until the ME arrives," Vanderhorn told the male officer.

"Right."

Three EMTs carrying a stretcher and medical gear started up my walk. The policeman darted off toward the body and shouted for them to follow. Vanderhorn spoke into her radio. I sank onto my porch swing and felt the photograph crinkle in the pocket of my shorts.

I had been thirteen when I moved in with my foster mom in Kokomo, Indiana. The first day she took my picture with a Polaroid camera. I'd never seen one before, and the slowly developing images were magic. Now the picture I'd pulled from the dead man's fingers seemed to come into focus just like those Polaroids had.

The first thing I remembered about the picture was Ken's grin—impish, inviting. Then his clothes—a hot-pink gown topped with a red feather boa. Then his companion—someone whose hand rested on Ken's shoulder, someone whose image had been torn away.

OMG! Why was Ken in a dress? Worse yet, why did he look so darn happy?

Of course, the very first time I saw Ken, he'd been wearing women's clothes. We met at a Halloween party on Capitol Hill, the Seattle neighborhood best known for gay pride parades and small, hip boutiques. My costume was a vintage silk cocktail gown from my grandmother's collection. I didn't have any really great shoes to go with it, so I'd fallen back on my usual strappy heels.

As soon as we arrived at the pub, my girlfriends disappeared into the crowd. So typical. I had backed against the dimly lit bar, trying to appear indifferent to my conspicuously single state, when an older woman materialized next to me.

"Fabulous dress," she said in a husky voice. "Thirties?" She was wearing a sixties Chanel suit, crimson with white trim, and a matching pillbox hat.

"I think so. I love the detailing." I fanned the skirt so she could see the tiny pearl buttons that marched from neckline to hem. That's when I noticed her shoes—low-heeled, square-toed patent pumps—and her enormous feet.

Jackie O on steroids.

"Oh, man," I said and felt myself blush. She *was* a man. How could I have been fooled for even a minute?

He laughed, crinkling the fine lines around his eyes and mouth. I grinned back and started again. "Where did you get those fab shoes? I couldn't find anything that worked with this outfit."

"I own a specialty shoe store down the block."

We talked until the pub shut at two A.M. Ken wasn't fazed to learn I worked for a bank, and he absolutely, positively did not want to talk about mortgage foreclosures and the Great Recession. Hooray. He danced like a dream, laughed at my jokes, and escorted me home without starting a wrestling match on my doorstep.

Six months later we were married and I was living my lifelong fantasy—a husband, a house, and a flock of backyard chickens. I needed only one thing more for my life to be complete.

I smiled at the memory and tears started to well up.

And just like that, I realized what was bothering me about the picture of Ken. Besides the red feather boa and his incredibly poor fashion sense. The flowered curtains behind him proved the photo had been taken in our bedroom, taken after our wedding. The feather boa he wore had nothing to do with Halloween.

"May I have your name, please?" Officer Vanderhorn's voice jerked me back to reality.

"Sunny Day Burnett."

"Sunny Day? How's that spelled?"

"Just like it sounds. Two words. My parents were hippies."

"Okay." She scribbled rapidly. "What's your address, Ms. Burnett?"

"I live here."

"Really?" Vanderhorn raised a skeptical eyebrow and inventoried my outfit: green duck boots, sweat socks smudged with chicken droppings, grimy thrift-store shorts with tomato-bulged pockets, and a Nirvana T-shirt—my chicken-killing clothes.

"Do you have picture ID?" she asked. "A driver's license, maybe?"

"Of course I do," I snapped. "But this is my house. I inherited it from my grandmother."

I stopped and bit my lip. Vanderhorn's question was reasonable enough—I wasn't sure I belonged here either. My mother had been sixteen when she ran away from Laurelmere, sixteen years old and three months pregnant with me. By the time I was eight, we were homeless and living in a station wagon plastered with Grateful Dead stickers.

My explanation must have trumped my appearance. Officer Vanderhorn glanced at the street number on my house and wrote it down.

"Okay, Ms. Burnett," she said. "Where do you work?"

"I used to be a banker. But I was laid off at Christmas when the FDIC closed us down."

"Tough. Does anyone else live in this house?"

"No, my husband recently passed away."

"What was your husband's name?"

"Kenneth Dahl."

"I'm sorry for your loss."

Her sympathy, completely *pro forma*, triggered a familiar jolt under my ribcage. That's how the police had treated Ken's death from the very beginning—as a routine tragedy.

"Okay. Now, you said you believe the victim was shot. Do you own a gun?"

"A gun? You think I shot him?"

"It's just a standard question, Ms. Burnett."

"Yes, officer. I own a gun. A Glock .45."

"Where is it?"

"In the basement. In my gun safe."

As if by magic, another uniformed officer materialized beside me. "Secure the basement," Vanderhorn told him. "But don't touch anything."

"This is ridiculous," I said. "I haven't handled that gun in months."

"And it's licensed and registered to you?"

"It was my husband's gun. I haven't changed the registration to my name yet."

Vanderhorn scribbled busily. She glanced up. "Did you recognize the victim?"

I shook my head. "He's facedown."

"Did you move him?"

"Uhhh." I rubbed my eyes as visions of *CSI Laurelmere* danced through my head. I needed an explanation if the forensic guys discovered my shoe prints in the blood around the dead man—an explanation that didn't involve Ken's photograph.

"Did you move him?" Vanderhorn repeated.

"No. But I tried to find a pulse in his neck."

"Did you see anyone exiting the premises?"

"No."

"Tell me what happened."

I gave her a brief description of my morning, brief because I left out a few things: Henrietta, Mac, and the torn photograph.

"So about ten minutes ago you walked outside to gather eggs for breakfast. You heard a heavy thud and discovered the victim?" Vanderhorn tapped her pencil against her notebook. "That's it? You're sure?"

I nodded.

"Ms. Burnett, it's very important you think carefully about what happened here. You are practically an eyewitness. Anything you saw or heard could be a vital clue in identifying the perpetrator. Any detail, no matter how small, may be significant."

"I'm not a witness. I didn't see a darn thing."

"Except the body?"

"Well yes. Except that." My stomach clenched again.

Another patrol car screeched to a stop in front of my house, followed by a second ambulance with sirens blaring. Glancing up, I saw my neighbors standing in their doorways watching the spectacle, cell phones glued to their ears.

I was sure they were calling Horace Pennington III, head of the homeowners' association, to schedule another special meeting of the community council. Like keeping chickens, finding a dead body undoubtedly constituted a gross violation of Laurelmere's homeowner covenants.

The policemen had started to string yellow tape to block off my yard. One officer stood on the sidewalk, holding a clipboard and making notes. More patrol cars arrived to shut down the street. I spotted a news helicopter circling overhead and felt naked and exposed.

"What more can you tell me about the incident?" Vanderhorn demanded, her attention caught by a man and woman in an unmarked car that had been waved through the barricades. Clearly P. J. Vanderhorn wanted to hand the higher-ups a homicide neatly solved by her own insightful interrogation.

I recognized that level of ambition. I even identified with it. But Vanderhorn was going to have to shimmy up the greasy pole of promotion without my help. I wasn't going to tell her about Ken's picture until I knew what it meant.

"Ms. Burnett," Vanderhorn squawked. "Is there anything more you can give me?"

18

"Sure." I reached into my pocket, touching the edge of the photograph. I shoved it deeper and pulled out a ripe, red Stupice. "Have a tomato."

CHAPTER THREE

A chunky woman in her mid-forties climbed out of the Crown Vic, followed by a younger black man. The woman's pasty skin and beefy thighs suggested she had spent all of Seattle's two-week summer chain-smoking at her desk. A cluster of uniformed officers gathered around the newcomers, listening to rapid-fire instructions I couldn't decipher, and then fanned out along my street. Door-to-door interviews, I guessed.

The two plainclothes officers flashed their badges at the patrolman manning the yellow-tape barricade and signed his clipboard. They stomped up my pathway and climbed my front steps two at a time. Despite their casual attire—cargo pants, short-sleeved polo shirts, lace-up running shoes—they carried a daunting air of authority.

Snatching the photograph from the dead man and hiding it from the cops suddenly didn't seem like such an incredibly awesome idea.

Officer Vanderhorn jerked to attention as the pair stopped next to her.

"I'm Detective Sergeant Stanislaus." The woman offered her hand. "I'm leading the investigation." Stanislaus smelled of tobacco and harsh soap. Except for a thin silver band on the ring finger of her right hand, she didn't wear jewelry or makeup. Her short, ash-blonde hair looked like finger combing was all it needed and all it ever got.

"And this is Detective Wilson," Stanislaus added, jerking her chin at the man who followed her up the stairs. His hair was trimmed close to his scalp, his pockmarked face was shaven clean, and he moved smoothly as if gliding toward me on an upward escalator.

"Sunny Burnett." I shook Stanislaus's hand, which felt dry and hard, and nodded to Wilson, who paused behind her.

"You made the nine-one-one call?" Stanislaus asked.

"Yes."

"And you live here?"

"Yes."

"Okay. We'll need to talk with you, Ms. Burnett. Will you please wait inside with Officer Vanderhorn?"

"But I've already told Ms. Vanderhorn everything I know."

Vanderhorn straightened her shoulders and opened her notebook, ready to burst forth with her report. Stanislaus didn't even glance at her.

"I need to hear your story myself." Stanislaus's tight smile held a hint of pity. "You'll probably end up telling it a couple more times." She turned to Wilson. "The medical examiner's on his way. Let's check the scene." She reached into her jacket pocket, pulled out a pair of blue gloves, and snapped them on.

Detective Wilson left the porch. As Stanislaus followed, a long arc of water shot into the air in front of her.

"What the hell is going on?" I leaped to my feet. "You're wasting water. Turn it off."

The steam continued flowing.

"Make them stop," I shouted to Stanislaus.

I jumped the porch railing and dropped into my side yard next to the wooden tower that holds rain barrels for watering the front garden. Ken had built the tower to support four fifty-gallon barrels. Filled from the gutters, the barrels drain through a single hose, which produces a significant amount of water pressure. Ken had built an identical structure at the rear of the house for watering the back garden. The whole structure is in violation of Laurelmere's building covenants, but so far no one has complained.

The dead man still lay on the ground between the water tower and my woodpile. Several masked and gowned technicians surrounded him, hovering like chicks testing new mash, cautious but eager. Small flags had sprouted along the path next to blood spots and brain splatter.

I choked and looked up.

A young man in uniform had climbed to the top of the tower and opened the hose, shooting water into the strawberry patch in my front yard.

Detective Sergeant Stanislaus called to him, "Stop that."

"Yes, ma'am." With a barely discernible shrug, the officer turned off the hose. He braced his back against the side of my house, still at attention, and watched us.

"What are you doing?" Stanislaus shaded her eyes as she squinted at him.

"Ma'am. I'm draining these barrels. I thought the murder weapon might be inside, ma'am." He flushed painfully, another eager-beaver rookie certain to be slapped down.

"You think the killer escaped by climbing up the side of my house and over the roof?" I asked Stanislaus. "Who was he? Spiderman?"

"Ms. Burnett, that's not helpful. The weapon could have been tossed inside a barrel even if the killer exited through your front yard."

"So now we're looking for a seven-foot center with a great hook shot? Sorry. The Sonics left Seattle a couple of years ago."

"We need to check out every possibility."

"And every impossibility?" I stepped close enough to see the enlarged pores of her bulbous nose. "Each rain barrel has a fitted lid over a mosquito screen. Even if someone could have tossed a gun up there, it wouldn't have landed inside a barrel."

"Is that correct?" Stanislaus barked to the officer above her.

"Yes, ma'am. The barrels are covered, ma'am. But something up here smells really disgusting."

Disgusting? I bristled before I realized what he meant.

"I put chicken manure from my hens in the barrels," I said. "That way my plants are fertilized every time I water. That's what you smell—chicken manure tea."

"Right." Stanislaus wiped her nose on the back of her hand. "I'm sorry, Ms. Burnett, but we have to verify your statement. We're going to drain those barrels."

Again the officer on the water tower reached for the valve and again I yelled, "Stop!"

"Do you know what month it is?" I asked Stanislaus. "August. The driest time of the year. I've already used more than half of the water I collected last winter. The rest has to last until the end of September when it starts raining again."

A puzzled frown crawled across Stanislaus's leathery face. "Don't you have plumbing out here in Laurelmere?" she drawled, folding her arms across her ample chest and eying me skeptically.

"Of course we do. But city water costs money. Summer water rates are almost twice those of the rest of the year. Check your bill, Detective Sergeant."

Stanislaus scowled. "I can't afford to live in Seattle on a cop's salary, Ms. Burnett. And definitely not in this neighborhood."

"Well, I'm not going to be able to stay here if I have to use city water to keep my crops alive."

"Crops? So you don't have grocery stores in Laurelmere either?" Stanislaus shook her head. "I'm sorry, Ms. Burnett. But your property is now a crime scene. We will do whatever is necessary to locate and process evidence relating to that crime."

She cocked her head and stared at me quizzically. "Besides,

you seem a lot more upset about your rainwater than finding a murdered man in your backyard."

The air left my lungs. I wrapped my arms around my chest. "It's just—I'm scared. Everything's suddenly gone crazy. I can't bring the dead man back to life. I can't tell you who killed him. I don't know who he was or why he was in my garden. But I *can* keep you from wasting my rainwater." I hunched my shoulders. "I hope."

"Sorry, Ms. Burnett. You're going to have to let us do our job. Go inside and wait for me to interview you."

"No way. There must be something I can do to protect my farm. I'm calling my lawyer." I stomped away in my green rubber boots.

Well, as usual my exit line was ninety-nine percent bluster. I didn't have a lawyer, and I didn't know how to find one that specialized in small-scale water rights. Very small scale.

I was standing on my porch, helplessly watching my rainwater gurgle away when Horace ("call me Ace," which I suppose is better than "call me Hor") Pennington III emerged from his house across the street. He cleaved the crowd of bystanders on the sidewalk like the blade of a new plow, slapped a couple of policemen on the back, and talked his way past the yellow tape barrier. Ace, a highly successful criminal defense attorney for the filthy rich and their juvenile-delinquent children, was just the person to protect my constitutional rights. For the first time since I moved into Grandma's house, I was glad to see him.

Without hurrying, Ace strolled onto my porch and reached for my hand. Like the dead guy, Ace wore the standard uniform for an alpha male in Laurelmere: pearl gray suit, immaculate blue shirt, burgundy power tie. His polished shoes probably cost more than my pickup truck. Chemically whitened teeth flashed against his darkly tanned face, and his silver hair bristled to attention. In twenty years, he'd be the smirking hunk in a Viagra ad.

I was suddenly aware I hadn't shaved my legs for a week and my hair was twisted into a scraggly knot at the back of my neck. I tightened my lips against my crooked front teeth and wished I didn't feel so out of place in Laurelmere.

Without comment, Ace took a handkerchief from his pocket, a starched, pressed, monogrammed, and neatly folded white linen handkerchief. He handed it to me. "You have a smudge on the end of your nose."

I wiped while he surveyed the police activity with the territorial gaze of a rooster in a henhouse. "Looks like you've got a problem."

"Well, duh." I shoved the handkerchief into his hand. "You're a lawyer. Can't you make the police leave my rain barrels alone?"

"Is that why they're here? Rainwater violation?"

"No, of course not. Someone got himself shot in my yard. Some guy I don't know. It doesn't have anything to do with me, but the police seem to think they can destroy my whole farm anyway. I need an attorney."

"I'm more than happy to defend your property rights." Ace raised an amused eyebrow at Stanislaus. "Detective Sergeant, we submit to your good judgment. Is it really necessary to empty those barrels?"

Ah, the power of Laurelmere.

Stanislaus growled, she stammered, she stuck her hands on her hips. But the upshot was the young officer turned off the water, coiled the hose, and climbed down from my tower. So when Stanislaus told me that she needed to test my clothing for forensic evidence, I agreed peacefully until I remembered what lay under the ripe tomatoes in my pocket.

What to do? While I dithered—again—Ace relaxed against the porch railing, his hands in his pockets, a man clearly at ease in any situation. Stanislaus glanced at Officer Vanderhorn and ordered her to accompany me to the bathroom so she could bag my things.

"Yes, ma'am." Vanderhorn avoided my eyes. Apparently this job didn't hold the same glamour as browbeating a witness.

"No way." I appealed to Ace. "Why do I have to strip down? Don't they need a search warrant or something?"

"Now, Sunny," Ace said in a soothing tone and put his arm around my shoulders.

I wanted to snarl and bite his hand, but I shook him off instead.

"You and I both know you have no involvement with this death," Ace said. "But, as your attorney, I advise you to cooperate with the investigation. This way we'll have a written record the police couldn't find any forensic evidence connecting you to this unfortunate incident should you be brought to trial."

"Brought to trial? Me? Because of my rain barrels? But—"

Stanislaus rolled her eyes. "We're talking murder here, Ms. Burnett. I need your assistance."

"I don't trust cops." I folded my arms across my waist. Thank goodness my T-shirt wasn't dripping chicken blood. If I had succeeded in slaughtering Henrietta, I'd be headed for the chain gang.

"But you can trust me, Sunny. I'm your attorney."

Ace again. I couldn't shake the feeling he was trying to give me a secret message. Well, as my foster mom in Indiana always said, "Why buy a dog and bark yourself?" He was my attorney, so I'd listen to him. At least for now.

"Okay. You can have my clothes."

Stanislaus smiled briefly. She turned toward Detective Wilson and shouted, "Let's get a GSR on her, too."

"GSR?"

"Gunshot residue," Ace said. "To test whether you fired a gun recently."

"But—"

"I advise you to go along with that as well."

"Why?"

"Here's the thing, Sunny. If the test is negative, then it proves you didn't fire the weapon that killed the man in your yard."

"But what if it's positive?"

"All that means is that you touched someone or something with GSR in the past couple of days, not that you fired the murder weapon. We can work with the test results, whatever they are. Again, you have to trust me."

I hesitated. Somehow testing for chemicals sounded more serious that some guy sniffing around my chicken-killing clothes.

"Honey—I mean Sunny. Your husband trusted me. That should be reason enough."

Why did Ace mention Ken? Did he know about the photograph? I studied Ace's face—tanned and bland—without finding a clue.

"Okay, Detective. I'm completely and totally innocent. Let's do whatever tests you need to prove it."

Stanislaus nodded to Wilson. He left the porch to confer with one of the crime-scene technicians.

I heard a commotion, like the rapid-fire chittering of a thousand pissed-off squirrels, coming from next door where Mac lived with his son's family. Oh great, the police must be questioning Mac's daughter-in-law, Nasreen. She and her husband both worked in IT. Except for making millions of dollars in salary and stock options, I had no idea what they did. Nasreen cut back to part-time during the summer, ostensibly to be with their thirteen-year-old son, Pete, who was one of those scary smart kids Seattle spawns like salmon.

In reality, Nasreen seemed to spend most of her time maintaining the Laurelmere Twitter-bitch network. We all followed her, we couldn't afford not to. I could just imagine this morning's tweet: IF CHICKENS WEREN'T BAD ENUF, NOW SHE'S DIGGING UP DEAD GUYS TOO.

After Detective Wilson disappeared into my backyard, a crime-scene technician trotted past us to a white van, which had appeared among the phalanx of vehicles in front of my house. Every one of them was idling, spewing carbon toxins into the air. When this was all over, I was going to email the police chief and make a formal complaint.

I just hoped I wouldn't be emailing him from the county jail.

While we waited for Wilson to return, Stanislaus sketched a map of my property in her notebook. The tower holding my rain barrels figured prominently. An outline marked the body of the dead man. She penciled in Xs for his eyes.

"That's wrong." I pointed to the sketch. "He's on his stomach. You can't see his face."

Stanislaus sighed like it'd already been a long day. She closed her notebook and folded her arms over her chest.

"I think I've heard of you, Detective Stanislaus," Ace said.

"Detective Sergeant," she snapped.

"Ah yes." He turned to me. "Detective Sergeant Stanislaus is the darling of the prosecutor's office. When it comes to violent crimes, she has the highest close-and-convict rate in the state. Isn't that right, Officer?"

"Yep." Stanislaus scowled, signaling the discussion was closed.

"Did you recognize the victim?" Ace asked me.

I shook my head. "But he must be from around here. He was wearing a suit and tie like yours. Plus, I didn't see a strange car and nobody in Laurelmere would walk more than ten feet if his life depended on it."

Whoops. Maybe it had.

"I might know him," Ace said. "Do you want me to have a look, Detective?"

She scowled. "I don't need your help, Counselor. We've already ID'd the victim."

"And?"

"And we won't release his identity until the next of kin have been notified. You know that. SOP."

"Okay." Ace shrugged. "So, he was wearing a suit and tie, huh? For sure he's not Mac, right Sunny?"

I glared at Ace, trying to beam "Shut up" into his thick skull. No such luck.

"Didn't I see Mac call on you this morning? Is he still around?" Ace rocked back on his heels and smiled at me smugly.

Finally I understood why Ace was involving himself in my problems—to get revenge on poor old Mac. When Mac retired and moved into his son's basement, he'd bought a rowboat even older than he was. He kept the boat hidden in a thicket of alder two hundred yards from the Laurelmere golf course and went fishing every morning. In the beginning, the community had been in an uproar. Floating fiberglass palaces were okay, but honest wooden rowboats were not.

But Mac wasn't as much of a dumb rustic as he pretended. The issue came to a climax when the oldest and richest residents of Laurelmere asked Ace, their self-anointed leader, to call a community meeting and ram through a change to the home-owner covenants that would outlaw rowboats and, surprise, surprise, chickens.

Just before the meeting, Mac reminded Ace those same documents once forbade "Jews, Negroes, and Orientals" from buying homes in our community. If Ace Pennington brought up rowboats, Mac would bring up Laurelmere's history of discrimination and invite the media to a free-for-all.

The wind left Ace's sails in an exasperated hiss. Now the oldest and richest didn't exactly tolerate Mac and his fishing pole or me and my hens, they simply turned their noses upwind and pointedly didn't see us.

Apparently, Ace had decided entangling Mac in a murder investigation would be a great way to get even. That bastard.

I was seething when Detective Stanislaus turned to me. "There was someone else at the scene this morning?"

"My neighbor." I sighed. "He's a harmless old guy. Retired. He goes fishing every morning at daybreak and stops by to say hello. He left long before I heard the shot. I didn't see any point in dragging him into this thing."

"That's not your decision to make, Ms. Burnett." Detective Stanislaus opened her notebook and turned to a fresh page. "I need this man's name and address."

Ace glanced at the crime-scene technician who was walking toward us with a duffel bag hanging from each shoulder. "I can give you that information, Detective. Let poor Sunny have her hands tested so she can get cleaned up."

What was this "poor Sunny" business? He made me feel like a homeless kid again and I didn't like it.

"No, I can tell her." Rapidly I reeled off the information Stanislaus wanted. "But Mac's harmless," I repeated, frowning at Ace. "Just a retired guy who likes to fish."

"Harmless?" Ace chuckled in that irritating, know-it-all manner of lawyers and FDIC examiners. "I don't think so. Angus MacDougall is a retired policeman from Scotland. I assume he is also an expert shot."

Someone inhaled sharply. It could have been me.

"Scotland Yard?" Stanislaus repeated. "You're kidding me."

"No, Scotland the country. He's from some little village out on the moors."

Having dealt with Mac strictly in his persona as the world's oldest living fisherman, I'd forgotten he was a cop. But hey, maybe he could help me figure out what to do with the photograph of Ken. Unlike that weasel Ace, Mac didn't care about protecting Laurelmere's reputation as an exclusive community.

But first, I had to get my hands tested and then figure out how to strip in front of Officer Vanderhorn without exposing the picture.

I stuck my fists in my pockets. My tomatoes were ripe to bursting.

CHAPTER FOUR

The crime-scene technician sat across from me at my kitchen table. He was thirty-something, with a short, neat beard and horn-rimmed glasses. He smelled clean and fresh like newly washed sheets drying in the sun.

He took my right hand and began to swab the webs of skin between my fingers. I asked what he was testing for. In college I'd been a struggling chemistry major before I realized finance came as easily as breathing and chose to go the whole MBA route. Even so I was surprised and dismayed by the long list of chemicals in gunpowder, and by how many of them I could have touched.

"Nitrates?" I repeated, pulling my hand away. "Nitrates are in fertilizers, even chicken manure which I have in abundance. Lead? I'll bet ninety percent of the paint in this old house is lead based. Soot? I burn firewood for heat. I touch soot every time I dust."

Although I don't dust all that often.

"I wouldn't worry, Ms. Burnett." The technician took my hands again. His fingers were firm and cold. "Mr. Pennington is one of the best defense attorneys around. I'm sure he will be able to explain away whatever I find."

"But the thing is, I'm completely innocent."

He swabbed and nodded, nodded and swabbed. He'd heard it all before.

"Did you find anything incriminating?" I asked when he released my hands.

"I'm not allowed to tell you or your lawyer the results until I've filed an official report with the prosecutor's office," he answered in a loud, formal voice, clearly meant to be overheard by Officer Vanderhorn, who was pawing through the hand towels in my guest bathroom. Then he winked at me and whispered, "Don't lose any sleep over it."

"Thanks." I got up and stepped to the bathroom door. "What are you messing with now?" I asked Vanderhorn. "I had this bathroom set up as a brooder for my baby chicks."

Vanderhorn dropped the commode lid back in place. "What kind of toilet is this anyway? It's weird."

"Weird? It's European. The tank on the wall fills with water from my rain barrels. To flush you pull on the chain."

"Oh, yeah? That's cool I guess." She beckoned me inside. "I have to take the clothes you're wearing."

"I'll need something to put on. There's a robe hanging in the upstairs bathroom."

I waited for Vanderhorn to retrieve my robe so I could hide Ken's picture where she had already searched, under the stack of towels. But she just nodded to another officer who was stationed by the front door. I heard him tromp upstairs.

We stood in awkward silence until the cop returned with my robe, which had "Hilton Hotels" embroidered in gold thread over the left breast, a reminder of the days when staying at luxury hotels had been a routine part of my banking career.

The officer handed the robe to Vanderhorn and returned to his post. She shut the door to the guest bathroom with us inside much too close together. With no options left, I faked a stumble against the edge of the cabinet and crushed the tomatoes in the pocket of my shorts.

"Oh, dear."

Smiling apologetically, I scooped up a handful of goop and held it out to Vanderhorn. The rich smell of ripe tomatoes filled the small room. The meaty flesh oozed through my fingers. Dark red fragments of tomato skin clung to my hand like plastic wrap. Crimson juice bled onto the floor.

Vanderhorn wasn't a farm girl. She edged away as if tomatoes were radioactive.

"Why don't I dump this mess in the kitchen compost before I give you my clothes?" I offered.

"Yeah, okay."

She stood in the doorway watching while I emptied both pockets into the stainless steel pail next to the sink. I dug around in the warm stew of coffee grounds and eggshells to find a lettuce leaf to cover the picture and, I hoped, protect it.

Back inside the bathroom, I heard Detective Sergeant Stanislaus try to persuade Ace to leave. As my attorney, Ace insisted, he was entitled to stay and protect my interests. After Vanderhorn bagged my clothes, I scooted upstairs to shower and shave my legs. My hair is always a mess in the summer, a tangle of brown curls impossible to tame. I fluffed it dry while swearing I'd get a professional cut as soon as Ken's insurance company sent me a check. I swiped on lip gloss—it was too hot for makeup—and pulled on a sundress and sandals.

Ace met me at the bottom of the stairs. He smiled broadly, his eyes wide with appreciation.

"I'm going to need a retainer," he said.

Not appreciation, greed.

"A retainer? But I'm your neighbor." What I meant was, I'm your poor widow neighbor who's out of work.

Ace raised an eyebrow. He could do a lot with a single eyebrow.

"Okay," I said. "How much?"

"At my firm for a case of this complexity, five thousand dollars is the standard minimum."

"Five thousand dollars? No way. I don't need the whole darn

firm, Ace. Just you. And now the cops have decided to leave my rain barrels alone, I probably don't need you either."

Ace sighed patiently, as if I were sitting on death row and asking about long-term health care. "You never know what's going to come up in a murder investigation." He leaned against the wall and studied me. "How about a hundred dollars?"

I stared back. "How about five dollars?"

"Okay, done." Ace held out his hand, palm up.

I found my purse and pulled out five ones as crumpled as if they'd been used to stuff a turkey. He took the money and we shook. I now had an attorney on retainer. But I wasn't sure what Ace wanted to protect: me or the gilt-edged sanctity of Laurelmere?

The police pretty much ignored me. I paced the back deck so I could keep an eye on my garden while the cops searched for the murder weapon. Before he left for work, Ace found homemade lemonade in the refrigerator and poured me a glass. He set up a chair for me on the deck in the sunshine, plumped the pillow, and made sure the iced pitcher was nearby.

Maybe I could get used to having an attorney on retainer.

Nine hours later, around six P.M., the last of the photographers, fingerprint experts, and forensic examiners packed up their gear and drove away. Jack Rabbit, the guy who was supposed to deliver my baby chicks, never did show up. I'd given his name to George, the security guard at the entrance to Laurelmere, but I assumed Jack Rabbit hadn't been able to penetrate the yellow-tape cordon around my house.

As the sun flirted with the horizon, I sat on my back deck with a half-empty glass at my elbow, feeling exhausted and violated. They're only doing their job, I told myself when the forensic guys tramped across my garden, tore apart my woodpile, and frightened my chickens. "I'm glad Ken isn't here to see this," I muttered when an officer carted away the bloodstained bricks from the path where the murdered man had fallen.

But I was kidding myself. In the three months since his death, I had never missed my husband more than I did right now. Plus, I had about a million questions to ask him.

As soon as the last official vehicle departed, I retrieved Ken's picture from the compost bin. Acid from the tomatoes had bleached his fuchsia-colored gown, but his smile was as bright as ever. I blotted the photograph dry with a tea towel and propped it against the coffeemaker.

I tried to study it objectively like a detective would. What could Stanislaus learn from this picture?

Well, my first guess had been right. The picture had been taken in my bedroom. Grandma's wallpaper, nosegays of faded red roses, was instantly recognizable. So were the curtains I'd made after we were married. Ken and the other person had been standing against the wall opposite our mirrored closet doors, admiring themselves.

And that other person? Everything about him/her had been torn away except for a forearm wrapped around Ken's neck and a hand draped over his shoulder.

Another man, I decided. Without question. The hand was large with hairy knuckles and close-cropped fingernails.

Was he the dead guy? I tried to remember what his hands had looked like. Big? Hairy? I couldn't be sure. Stanislaus, of course, could make a side-by-side comparison. If I gave her the picture.

So, being completely objective, if I were Stanislaus what could I conclude from the photograph?

That sometime since our wedding on Valentine's Day, Ken and some another guy had dressed up in women's clothing and posed for a picture in my bedroom. *Our* bedroom.

And, objectively speaking, that was way too creepy.

The whole thing had to be some kind of joke. Like Ken wearing a dress for the Halloween party where we'd met. Maybe he and the other guy were trying out for a part in a play or trying to fool one of their friends or . . .

I couldn't think of anything else, but there had to be a reason my husband was wearing those clothes. A reason that didn't have anything to do with the murder.

I decided that showing Stanislaus the picture would just confuse the murder investigation. In the interests of justice, the best thing I could do was forget all about it.

I stuck the picture between the pages of *Urban Homesteading*, the bible of city farmers, and put it with my cookbooks in the kitchen. I pulled a T-shirt over my sundress, then went back to my garden and started repairing the damage the police had done.

Dragonflies were swooping in lazy circles over my corn patch when Ace strolled into my backyard a few minutes later. "Here's the retainer agreement and the receipt for your five dollars." He thrust some papers in my hand.

"How much would it cost if you end up defending me against a murder charge?" I asked as I studied the fine print on the retainer agreement.

"It all depends," he said. "If you decide to plead not guilty?"

"Of course. I'm not guilty."

"Well, there's a lot of factors to consider. My time, the time of my associates, the firm's overhead, private investigators, expert witnesses, travel expenses." He stopped and examined me critically. "And with you there'd be the cost of new clothes, haircut, makeup, maybe a style consultant."

"Do you always insult your clients?"

"I'm just trying to be realistic here, Sunny."

"Okay, okay. How much total?"

"Easily a hundred thousand dollars. Minimum. Could be twice that much."

"A hundred thousand? I don't have that kind of money. What can I do?"

"Well, lots of my clients take out a mortgage on their home or sell it or dip into their retirement savings to pay for their defense."

"And if you lose the case?"

"You still have to pay me. I don't mount a criminal defense on a contingency basis."

I shook my head. "And we call this a justice system. Justice for the rich, maybe."

"Yeah, well. Speaking of which, have the cops identified the man you found yet? I didn't see anything on the news."

"I guess Stanislaus managed to contact the next of kin. She told me his name before she left. It's a guy I never heard of, but apparently he lives—lived—in Laurelmere."

"What's his name?"

"Lank Lungstrom."

Ace paled. "Lank? The dead guy was Lank Lungstrom? Are you sure?"

I nodded. You don't forget a name like that.

Ace dropped into the chair next to me like a sack of compost. "I can't believe it."

"You knew him?"

"He was a member of our poker group."

Oh, the infamous poker group.

The day after Ken moved into my house, Ace invited him to join a weekly poker game held in Ace's basement entertainment center. I encouraged Ken to go, happy that he'd made friends in the neighborhood. After I was in bed, Ken would stumble home, buzzed on pizza and Red Bull. He'd shower, slide between the sheets, and we'd make love until dawn.

"The poker game," Ace repeated. "What did Ken tell you about it?"

"Nothing." Overhead, a dragonfly caught a mosquito. I glanced at Ace. "What does the poker game have to do with Lank's death?" I asked, not sure I wanted to hear the answer.

"You really don't know about poker night, do you?"

"No."

Despite the warm air, I was becoming chilled. I sat on a deck chair, folded my hands across my stomach, and closed my eyes. I wanted to close my ears, too. I was starting to have visions of strippers, lap dances, and lines of coke instead of pizza and Red Bull.

Ace scooted his chair closer. I felt his breath against my ear, smelled mouthwash. Felt crowded. "You know Ken liked to dress up, didn't you, Sunny?"

"Dress up?" I straightened so fast that my head clipped his chin. "What do you mean?"

Ace studied me as he rubbed the side of his jaw. "Ken liked to wear women's clothing. You know that, right?"

"You lying bastard." I stood, pushed back my chair and threw my glass of lemonade at Ace's crotch. "Take that back."

Okay. I knew Ace was telling the truth. I had the darn picture after all. But I wasn't going to admit anything. Especially not to Ace.

"Damn it, Sunny. Have you gone crazy?" Ace grabbed my napkin and rubbed at the wet spot on his fly.

I heard a loud creak and glanced up. Mac's daughter-in-law, Nasreen, had opened the window of her office. The office was a morass of computers, monitors, printers, scanners, and writhing electrical cords. Even in the dead of winter, humming electronics had kept the room temperature close to a hundred degrees until Mac's son installed a climate control system just a bit more sophisticated than the one used by reconnaissance satellites. The only reason Nasreen ever needed to open her window was to spy on her neighbor—me.

If the Laurelmere Twitter-bitch network found out about Ken's picture, I'd have to shoot myself.

I gave Nasreen a finger wave to let her know I knew she was eavesdropping. Unabashed, she nodded but she didn't shut the window. I scooted closer to Ace.

"Tell me what's going on," I said, trying to keep my voice soft and calm.

"Look what you did to my pants. I can't believe it."

"Your pants will be fine. What do you know about Ken?"

"Well, I met him about three years ago."

"Three years ago? I thought you met him after we got married."

"Sorry. No." Ace wadded up the napkin he'd used to dry his pants and tossed it over the side of the deck. What a jerk. It takes paper months to decompose.

"I first met Ken when I bought a pair of shoes at his store," Ace said.

I knew all about the store, Ken Dahl's Specialty Shoes. Mental head slap: that should have been a clue to Ken's interests. "Ladies shoes?" I asked. "Size sixteen or seventeen?"

"Yeah. Black leather with a T-strap. He stocked quality stuff."

"Forget the shoes. Tell me about Ken."

"We got to talking and I mentioned my weekly poker games."

"What's so great about playing poker at your house? Besides the transcendent joy of being in Laurelmere, of course."

"Well. Ah . . . Dressing up. That's what the poker games were about." Ace's voice was harsh, as if the words were being forced out of him. "It wasn't just Ken. We all did it."

"You dressed up, too? Good God!" I rocketed out of my chair and stared down at Horace Pennington III, scion of Laurelmere and personal attorney to the very, very rich—and to one poor wannabe chicken farmer. "You all dressed up? How did it start? How did you meet? Why—"

Ace shot a glance at Nasreen's window and held up his hand. "Whoa. Quiet. Sit down before you fall down."

Well, to make a long story short, four guys from Laurelmere had hooked up on the Internet through a chat room for men who liked to wear women's clothing. Plus, they all bought shoes from Ken. "So naturally when Ken married you and moved into your house, he joined the poker group."

"Naturally." I sank into my seat.

"We're not gay, nothing like that."

"Right." I knew Ken wasn't gay. I knew that for sure.

"We've all been married," Ace continued. "The problem is that dressing up around the house gets pretty boring after a while, even if your wife is okay with it. But none of us wanted to go out in public either. Except for Ken, we're all pretty prominent people."

"Isn't cross-dressing a violation of the homeowner covenants?"

Ace leaned back in his chair. "Give it a rest, Sunny."

Shadows were creeping over my deck, the dragonflies had closed up shop, and I still didn't know what to do with the photograph hidden on my bookshelf. If everyone in Laurelmere knew about Ken's predilections, I might as well telephone Detective Stanislaus and tell her the truth. But I didn't want to admit that I had removed evidence from a crime scene. I didn't think Ace could protect me from the consequences, even if he wanted to.

I considered mailing the picture to Stanislaus anonymously, but no. The tomato stains would give me away. I turned to my attorney-on-retainer to ask his advice, but his fingers were beating an impatient tattoo on the arm of his chair.

"I want you to call Mac," he said.

"Why? Is he a cross-dresser, too?" I couldn't imagine Mac wearing a skirt. A kilt, maybe, but that didn't count.

41

"No. I want him to investigate Lank's murder. And Ken's death." Ace gave me a speculative look. "I never believed that Ken got drunk and killed himself. Did you?"

"No, never." I surveyed my vegetables, the fruit trees, the greenhouse, the hens, the worm bin—each one a reason for Ken to drive home safely. And then, of course, there was me.

"I think the person who killed Lank is targeting the poker group," Ace continued. "A few weeks before Ken died, someone tried to run me off the road. He came up right behind me, turned on his high beams, and hit my right bumper. He was going at least eighty or ninety miles an hour. He pushed me across the shoulder. Thank heaven my brakes were working. I stopped with one of my front wheels over the bank of the Skagit River. Another two feet and I would have gone straight in."

"What did the police say?"

"They thought the same thing I did—drunk driver, road rage."

"We have to tell Stanislaus."

"No, not yet. I don't want to talk about the poker club unless I have to. Not just because of me, but my friends might be hurt. Mac is the perfect solution."

"Because he's not 'prominent'?" I made finger quotes around the word.

"You know what I mean."

"Yeah, I do know what you mean, and I think it stinks. You tried to force Mac to move out of Laurelmere because of his rowboat. Now you're in a jam, and you want him to rush over to rescue you and your 'prominent' jerk-off friends."

Before Ace could answer, I stood up, bumping his chair. "Good-bye."

I reached for the screen door.

The moment I touched the handle, a boom thundered overhead. Chunks of shattered bricks bounced off my roof and showered the deck. Ace pushed me facedown on the wood planks and threw himself on top.

A moment of utter silence was broken by sirens, car alarms, and squawking chickens. Someone screamed. The air was filled with an acrid yellow haze that scoured the back of my throat.

Ace's belt buckle dug into my butt. I heaved him off and struggled to stand. He jumped from the deck, ran to the corner of my house, and looked across the street.

"What happened?" I wheezed.

Ace scrubbed his bristly scalp with the knuckles of both hands and shook his head. "My house just blew up."

CHAPTER FIVE

Angus MacDougall sat in his basement apartment with his grandson Pete. Mac was drinking a pint of Belhaven and watching soccer, and Pete was totally engrossed in his iPhone. Ever since Pete turned thirteen, his mom, Nasreen, had started conducting random urine tests. He had failed the last one and was confined to quarters until it came up clean.

A loud KA-BOOM sounded. The television picture crackled. The overhead lights flickered. The stack of dirty dishes in the sink clattered. Pete jumped up. "What the hell!" he shouted.

"Wait here," Mac said.

"But—"

"You'd be no bloody use." Moving on sheer reflex, Mac chucked his tankard into the kitchen sink. He grabbed an electric torch from the hall closet and flicked it on. He ran outside where the last traces of daylight still lingered and halted on the sidewalk to assess the threat.

An alarm was going off inside Ace's house, a shrill, anxiety-arousing burglar detector. Car alarms rang in all of the vehicles parked at the curb or in neighboring driveways, a cacophony of outrage that screamed, "Not in Laurelmere. Not in Laurelmere." People spilled from the adjoining houses and clustered in the street: nannies herding children, maids with dust cloths in their hands, cooks holding spatulas, and dogs barking frantically.

Smoke poured from the roof of Ace's house. Mac recognized

its distinctive acrid odor and yellow tinge. A terrorist attack? Here?

The outside walls of the house appeared intact, but the windows were shattered, blown outward by the blast. Pieces of brick chimney were scattered in a forty-meter radius. Bad luck had dumped most of them on the windshield of Sunny's truck. As he ran past, Mac checked the pickup—cab and bed—and confirmed it was empty.

But try as he might, Mac heard no agonized screams, saw no severed body parts.

Thank you, sweet Jesus.

It was no guarantee, of course, that the house had been empty when the bomb went off.

He pulled his sleeves down to protect his arms and trotted to the front entrance. The heavy wooden door hung open at a crazy angle, held by a single hinge.

"Wait! Don't go in there."

Mac glanced over his shoulder and saw that bloody wanker, Horace Pennington III, racing toward him from Sunny's house.

"Get away, ye daft bastard." Mac picked up the cracked stump of a two-by-four the blast had tossed into a rhododendron bush like the proverbial matchstick. He pulled the neck of his undershirt over his nose and mouth, and propped the door open with the board. Shouting, "Hello," Mac entered the house and stopped. He listened intently, straining to catch any moans or cries. "Hello, anyone there?"

Over the shriek of the alarms, Mac heard sirens approaching.

Excellent. If he found anyone inside, there'd be an EMT for backup. After five years of retirement, his first-aid skills were rusty. He stepped into what had been a marble-lined foyer and peered through thick dust. A draft swept into the foyer past him and out the door.

Praying the breeze wasn't fanning a fire overhead, Mac followed the draft and found a wooden stairway that curved around on itself and led to the second floor. The treads and risers seemed intact. Moving quickly, Mac climbed the stairs, careful not to let his full weight—fourteen stone—fall on any single step. Parallel to the stairs, a hole ran the height of the house from roof to basement like God had taken a drill bit six feet in diameter and sunk it through the structure. Pieces of plaster hung from broken lathe, the joists were cracked, and electric fires sparked and died between the studs. The wind, stronger now, ruffled his hair and filled his nose with ash.

The damage was a textbook illustration of a directed charge. Whoever had set the explosion was either ex-military—or had a functioning Internet connection.

Hanging onto the banister, which felt remarkably solid, Mac looked down the hole to the basement. He aimed his torch into the blackness. The beam lit up pink and red fragments dangling from protruding nails. They waved at him like bloody fingers. After a breathless moment he realized they were pieces of cloth and possibly feathers. Maybe that's what the explosive had been wrapped in, some kind of garish bedspread or blanket.

He shouted into the darkness. "Is anyone there?"

And heard an impatient yell from the foyer. "Mac. Get down here."

He righted himself and glanced over the banister at the first floor. At the bottom of the stairwell, Ace stood scowling up at him. A tight knot of cops, EMTs, and firemen ebbed and flowed through the foyer like trout feeding in a shallow stream. Abruptly, the house alarm stopped.

"Come down, you old fart," Ace bellowed into the sudden silence, his voice still pitched to be heard over the alarms. "The whole place could cave in on you." Ace motioned imperiously, like Mac was a wayward butler or a tweeny caught smoking in the bushes.

What a pure goon, Mac thought without moving.

"Could anyone be up here?" he asked.

"No."

"Are you sure?"

"Positive." Ace tapped his wristwatch. "The cook goes home at six, the gardener doesn't come on Tuesdays, and the cleaning crew finished by noon. That's it. There's nobody around but me."

"Someone had to set the explosive in the basement. I'd better check—"

"Come down. The arson squad has the basement under control."

Mac looked into the hole again and saw flashlight beams crisscrossing at the bottom of the shaft.

"Okay." As the rush of adrenalin subsided, Mac's hips started to stiffen. Descending the stairs turned out to be harder and slower than racing up. He felt too old to be a hero, an assessment reflected in the carefully averted eyes of the young men with bomb-sniffing dogs who climbed past him to the second story.

"Who's in charge here?" Mac asked when he was still three steps from the ground, still high enough that Ace had to look up at him.

"Captain Anderson," one of the firemen snapped.

"Where is he? I need to see him." Mac took the last steps and planted himself firmly against a marble wall. It felt cool and solid against his back. He was on the verge of hyperventilating. He tried to calm his breathing. The crap hanging in the air wasn't doing his lungs any good.

"Outside." A tall slender man in uniform stepped into the foyer from the kitchen. His dark hair was shot with silver, his face lined. He pointed at Mac. "Now."

Recognizing don't-fook-around-with-me authority, Mac complied.

Outside, some of the car alarms were still bellowing like cows at milking time. The firemen had erected barricades around the perimeter of Ace's home. Police officers had arrived and were handling crowd control. A shrill Asian woman in oversized glasses jumped up and down, waving to attract Captain Anderson's attention. Mac guessed she was a reporter. He also guessed the captain had no intention of talking to her.

"What did you say your name was?" Anderson asked, turning his back on the reporter.

"Angus MacDougall. Call me Mac."

"What were you doing in the building, sir?"

"What d'ya think? Someone might have been trapped. I feared the whole boggin' thing might blow."

"I don't know where you're from, Mr. MacDougall, but here in Seattle we leave the heroics to properly trained personnel. You're lucky we didn't have to rescue you, too."

As Anderson lectured him, Mac watched the reporter bounce closer to the captain's back. A uniformed officer stepped in her path and deflected her as neatly as Beckham would have.

"Bollocks, man. Don't ya know what yer dealing with? TATP. Triacetone triperoxide."

Captain Anderson's eyes sharpened; he stood taller. "What do you know about TATP?"

"London, 2005. I helped clean up after the terrorists' attack in the tube."

Anderson frowned. "Tube?"

"The underground. The subway. That's what them bloody buggers used, TATP. You'd not forget a smell like that."

"You have ID?"

"Back at the house." Mac jerked his head. "I live across the street."

"Don't move." Anderson glanced around the yard and motioned to a sturdy, middle-aged woman standing just inside the barricade. She wore a pair of cargo pants that looked like they'd been wadded in a ball and kicked downfield by a squad of monkeys. As she approached, Anderson said, "Tell your story to Detective Sergeant Stanislaus." Without waiting for a reply, the fire chief disappeared into the house.

Detective Stanislaus coughed, wiped her mouth with the back of her hand, and suggested they find a place to talk. Mac offered his basement apartment. She skillfully steered him through the mass of hysterical neighbors and jabbering media. As he led her down the stairs to his front door, he noticed a pack of black sedans glide into the street and stop. Each was filled with men in navy-blue jackets.

Stanislaus followed his gaze. "The Feds."

Mac shot her a questioning look.

"The FBI. They'll take over the whole case if they get a chance." She jammed her hands into her pockets and scowled.

Mac liked the detective. He liked her square build, her no-nonsense approach to crowd control, and her smell—old cigarettes smoked clear down to the fag end. She smelled as stale as the pub in Glasgow where he'd spent his formative years. It was a welcome scent, an honest one. No one in Seattle admitted to smoking, yet he saw cigarette butts everywhere. Must have been dropped by the wee fairies. The city's smug hypocrisy drove him crazy.

They settled in his living room, which reeked of fish and chips. His daughter-in-law, Nasreen, refused to serve her family anything he caught, so most nights he ate a fry-up sitting in front of the telly. Pete, of course, hadn't obeyed orders and waited for Mac to return. Just as well. Mac didn't want his grandson to watch Stanislaus question him. It might undermine any authority he had with the boy.

"Fancy a pint?" Mac asked, retrieving his beer mug from the sink and opening the cooler.

"No. I'm on duty." Stanislaus sat in his recliner, adjusting the controls so her back was ramrod straight.

"Tea? Coffee? I've got a packet of that Starbucks instant somewhere." Mac hefted the electric kettle in her direction.

"No."

Detective Stanislaus drew a small recorder from the pocket of her cargo pants and set it on the coffee table. Mac dropped onto the couch opposite her, sloshing some beer on the tabletop.

"Got a towel?" Stanislaus asked.

"Got the next best thing." Mac pulled out the tail of his shirt and smeared the beer around.

"Do you mind if I tape our conversation?"

"S'right," Mac grunted, bemused at sitting on the other side of an interview. He was in no hurry to start talking. He'd spent the walk back to his apartment evaluating his position. He might be old and retired, but he wasn't a gormless fool, not quite yet. Over here in America, away from his own patch, the cops had no idea of who he was. All Stanislaus and Captain Anderson knew was he'd been the first man at the bomb site. And that he'd identified the explosive. It was a classic scenario—bad guy hanging around the crime scene offering to help the police. Unless Mac moved nimbly, he'd be the prime suspect.

"So, Mr. MacDougall, let's start at the beginning. Where were you when you heard the explosion?"

"I was watching football on the telly and it were just after the start of the second half."

"Football? In August?"

"You folks call it soccer."

Stanislaus nodded.

"So I was watching American soccer—or trying to. Your teams are crap, you know. Pure crap. I've been a member of the Tartan

Army my whole life, so I know crap when I see it. And why do you Americans give yer football clubs such daft names? The Houston Dynamos. That's something heavy that spews out a lot of noise but not much forward motion. Is that what you want a football team to be?"

The detective rubbed her eyes. She looked dead knackered. "If we can get back to the explosion, Mr. MacDougall."

She wasn't easily distracted, not by beer, not by football, not by sheer exhaustion. Mac took a long swallow of Belhaven and leaned back on his couch, trying to find a position that eased the growing ache in his hips.

"I ran outside. I knew right away what had happened. Once you smell TATP, you'd know it anywhere."

"How do you know what TATP smells like, Mr. MacDougall?"

Mac pushed himself up, awkward on his arthritic knees. He picked up his empty stein. "It's a long story, Detective. Sure you don't want a drink?"

"I'll have tea. Two sugars, no milk."

Mac plugged in the kettle. *A long story and a long night. I hope I can satisfy her.*

He winced. The last time he'd worried about satisfying a woman had been years ago and half a world away. But it had been a hot summer night, just like this one.

An hour later, the lingering smell of TATP—or maybe just the memory of the smell—kept Mac loitering about the steps of his son's house watching Detective Sergeant Stanislaus and the last emergency vehicles drive away. The FBI cars remained, quietly dominating the street. A thumping bass from Pete's bedroom assured him the little bugger was okay.

Stanislaus had seemed satisfied by his tale of the bombing, but totally uninterested in anything else. After she left, he realized he'd hoped she'd hang around, swap war stories, share a pint or two. But clearly she didn't consider him a colleague—just an old berk trying to be a hero.

After the bombings of July 7, 2005, Mac had almost changed his mind about taking retirement, but Margaret's condition had worsened while he was away mopping up in London. Like always, Mac went where he was needed most, so he returned home to nurse his wife until she passed. And now—now he sat on the steps of a house fancy enough to be the gamekeeper's cottage at Balmoral Castle and he had nowhere to go. No one who needed him.

Except maybe that bloody wanker, Ace.

Ace had just stepped onto the sidewalk that led to Mac's apartment. And he was still making that rude gesture.

CHAPTER SIX

After chunks of Ace's house stopped dropping onto my deck, Ace sprinted home. I quickly checked the Henriettas. They were clucking hysterically but seemed unharmed. A couple of tomato plants had taken direct hits, but the wire mesh over the chicken yard had protected the hens from falling debris. With a whispered thank-you to Ken, I dashed into my kitchen. I called 911 and grabbed my fire extinguisher. By the time I ran down my front steps, sirens were converging on our street from every direction.

Dense clouds of yellow smoke poured from the roof of Ace's house. Alarms were going off all around me. Trying to find a safe place, my neighbors ran back and forth between their homes and the street like chickens with their heads cut off.

"Get away," Ace shouted as I ran onto the sidewalk in front of his house. "There may be another explosion."

I froze. "Was anyone hurt?" I called back.

He shook his head. "The house was empty."

"What happened? A gas line exploded? Or did someone try to blow your house up?"

"I don't know."

"Your house and my yard. Is someone trying to kill both of us?"

"No. Believe me, Sunny. None of this has anything to do with you."

Wrong. But I didn't see any point in continuing to argue with him at the top of my lungs, so I waved my fire extinguisher. "I want to help."

"Get away. There's nothing you can do."

I backed up against my brick-battered pickup truck and measured my dinky extinguisher against Ace's smoldering Tudor façade. He was right. There was nothing I could do.

All the windows facing the street had blown out, and shards of glass were scattered across his lawn. The air smelled of toxic chemicals. I pulled the neckline of my T-shirt over my mouth and tried to inhale as little as possible.

Two fire trucks screamed to a stop in front of Ace's house, followed by a Medic One van and several patrol cars. Firemen trotted past me carrying long, heavy hoses. One stopped and ordered me to go back home. I turned and saw my neighbors clumped on their porches, holding cell phones to their ears. Those with headsets were gesticulating wildly. I sensed we were headed for another contentious meeting of the homeowners' association.

I felt my pickup truck rock and glanced into the bed. Pete was there, hunkered down amid broken glass and hunks of shattered bricks. He held his iPhone at arm's length, pointing it in the direction of Ace's house. Pete had inherited soft brown eyes and girlish lashes from his Iranian mother, Nasreen. His lanky limbs, smattering of freckles, and the hint of auburn in his glossy black hair had come from his father's side of the family. And brains? Masses of them from both parents. Genetically, the kid was programmed to be the next Bill Gates—or Osama Bin Laden.

Standing on tiptoe, I leaned into the truck bed and said, "I thought you were under house arrest."

"Yeah, whatever." Pete's attention went back to his phone. "I couldn't miss this. It's super cool. Mom won't mind."

"Yes, she will. You'll be grounded for life if you don't get home before she knows you're missing."

"Nah." He didn't even glance at me.

The kid was too big for me to haul away and too little to stay here. I tried one last time. "If anything else goes off, you could get hurt."

"Shhh. There won't be another significant explosion."

Pete sounded so sure of himself that I didn't question how he knew. Instead I asked, "What are you doing with your phone?"

"I'm streaming to my webpage. Go check it out. It's massive."

I heard a screech. "Peeete!" Like a sonic laser, Nasreen's voice burned through sirens, car alarms, ringing cell phones, and blasted my truck. "Peeete! Come home now."

"Yeah, yeah, yeah." With a shrug, Pete wedged his phone between the roll bar and the back window and climbed down, careful not to bounce the truck. He winked at me and ran home, darting around the police barricades like a small brown eel.

I heard more explosions inside Ace's house. A length of half-timbering crashed into the adjoining yard, just missing a fireman. As I watched him brush sparks from his uniform I was seized with guilt. I should have given Detective Sergeant Stanislaus the picture I took from the dead man's hand.

Ace said the murder had nothing to do with me, but he was wrong. The explosion and the murder had to be related—same place, same day, same off-the-wall craziness. Plus both were linked to the poker club, the club Ace refused to tell the cops about. I still felt squeamish about Ken being a transvestite, if that's what he was. My stomach still clenched every time I thought about his picture, but I couldn't let my feelings get in the way of a murder investigation.

Should I tell Ace I was going to break my promise? Should I give him a chance to warn his "prominent" friends?

As if in answer, a finger of fire sprouted from Ace's roof. I didn't have time to see what the killer planned to do next. I had to level with Stanislaus.

Five minutes later, I was watching the scene from my bedroom window. My nose itched. I rubbed it and came away with blood on my fingers. My whole face had swollen from Ace knocking me to the deck. The taste of burned wood lingered in my mouth and throat.

I'd called Stanislaus and left a message saying that I had important new information. I didn't say what. I didn't want anyone else picking up her messages and learning about the poker club.

My cell phone rang. It wasn't Stanislaus and I didn't recognize the number, so I didn't answer. I checked my messages. I had forty-seven, none from Stanislaus. I keyed in "delete all."

As the adrenaline drained away, I began to feel cold and isolated, an air bubble trapped inside an ice cube.

I pulled my grandmother's down comforter from the linen closet and wrapped it around me. Still, my fingers and toes felt rigid. Little splinters of ice seemed to dangle from my body.

The first responders had set up an array of arc lights on the perimeter of Ace's lawn. They cast shadows that danced and swayed just beyond my line of sight. I glimpsed someone at the end of the street trying to get past the police. The darting figure reminded me that Jack Rabbit, the chicken delivery guy, hadn't shown up. Tomorrow I would call him and arrange another meeting, but not tonight. Tonight I was too cold to move.

As I tightened the comforter around my shoulders, I remembered huddling under a blanket in my family's station wagon on Thanksgiving, watching the rest of the world through an ice-frosted window. We'd gone to a mission for supper, but my parents refused to spend the night in the shelter. Maybe, as they said, the shelter wasn't safe.

Maybe they needed to be on the street to score.

What I needed—a Thanksgiving dinner with all the trim-mings—hadn't mattered that night, but it mattered now.

No one except my doctor knew, but I was four months pregnant. I wanted to stay in this house and put down roots. I wanted to give my baby a safe place to grow up in. I wanted to cook her a turkey dinner with mashed potatoes and gravy every Thanksgiving of her life. But I couldn't live here with a killer on the loose. Unless Stanislaus caught the guy who was responsible for all this death and destruction, I'd be homeless again.

I found myself clenching my fists so hard that my fingernails were digging into my palms. I opened my hands and called Stanislaus. Again, no answer.

Trailing the comforter behind me, I drifted downstairs to the kitchen bookcase and found *Urban Homesteading*. I took out Ken's picture and studied it. Nothing had changed. His smile still beamed from ear to ear.

Squeamishness gone, I found myself sobbing. Poor Ken. I had loved him so much. I thought he loved me. But if he loved me, how could he keep this kind of secret from me? Maybe he thought I wouldn't understand. Well, I didn't. But maybe I could have—if he'd explained, if he'd given me a chance.

I dried my eyes. I put the picture back in the book and stuck it in the kitchen bookcase to await the call from Stanislaus. After the fire engines drove away, I checked the locks on my doors and windows and went upstairs to bed. I tucked the comforter around me, thankful beyond measure for the roof over my head and four solid walls between me and the killer.

Pounding on my front door woke me up. It sounded like a bull elephant heaving a battering ram. Instinctively I reached for Ken.

The banging continued. Stanislaus? Or the killer? I checked the clock. It was past midnight. And probably killers don't knock.

I slipped into Ken's bathrobe and my scuffed bunny slippers and descended the stairs. I grabbed a heavy vase from my grandmother's sideboard and cracked open the front door. Ace stood under my porch light, his hands behind his back, shifting from one foot to the other, like a first grader who needed to pee.

"You scared me to death," I said, setting the vase on the hall table. "What do you want?"

"I need a place to stay."

"Hmmm." I looked past him. Wisps of smoke drifted from the broken windows of his house. A couple of uniformed officers guarded the yellow-tape perimeter, and several dark cars idled at the curb. A nasty smell hung in the air.

"Do the police know why your house blew up?" I asked.

"No."

Okay, this would have been a good time to tell Ace that I had called Stanislaus about the poker club. But I didn't because a thought hit me. Maybe becoming Ace's new best friend wasn't the most prudent idea in the world. If the Cross-Dressing Poker Club (I'd started to think of it in capitals) was the killer's target, what Ace needed was a place with armed guards and full-time security. What I needed was to lock my door and go back to hiding under the covers.

"Seattle is full of four-star hotels," I said. "Why don't you stay at one? You can call for a reservation."

"Sunny, please."

"I'm sure you'd be happier if you moved into a hotel." I was babbling now. "Valet parking, room service, mini-bar, fluffy bathrobe, in-room Jacuzzi, dirty movies. I don't have any of those amenities."

"You have fresh eggs." Ace nudged my door with his shoulder. "Besides, I need to keep an eye on my property. Your house is perfect."

"You're worried about looters in Laurelmere?"

"I wasn't worried about bombers and look what happened."

"Still, you can't stay here."

But in spite of my better judgment, I felt myself weakening. His natty plaid shirt and khaki pants were rumpled and stained, his silver hair was laced with a fine web of ash, and he had a black smear on the side of his nose. He could have starred in a heart-wrenching public-service announcement for homeless men at the Union Gospel Mission.

But darn it, no matter what had happened to his Tudor palace, Ace still had more money than God. He could get his house rebuilt bigger and better than before. Instead of pestering me, he should be picking out massive Swedish appliances or diamond-studded chandeliers or a bidet with gold-plated fixtures.

My halfhearted protest came too late. Ace had already wedged one foot in the crack. He was slowly inching the door open. Okay, this was another moment when I could have told him about Stanislaus, the picture, and breaking the promise I'd made to him. But I didn't. Instead I asked in a voice as sugar-laden as freshly picked corn, "If you're going to sleep over, would you like to borrow a nightgown?"

Ace shook his head. He pointed to my feet. "I want bunny slippers just like those."

"I don't keep extras."

He took a step past me, stopped, glanced back at the trail of sooty footprints.

"Sorry. That's no way to repay your hospitality." Ace stripped off his shirt, pants, socks, and shoes, standing on one leg and then the other. He folded them into a careful ball with the ashes trapped inside. I braced myself, but he wasn't wearing a pink bra or lacy thong, just a soot-smeared undershirt and a pair of plaid boxers with a polo player on it. He dumped his clothes into a wastepaper basket and collapsed on the couch. Out of loyalty to Ken, I tried to avert my eyes while he undressed, but oh man, it'd been a long time. Every inch of skin I could see was firm and nicely tanned.

How about the inches I couldn't see?

"I talked to Mac," Ace said.

"Huh?" With an effort I forced my eyes to the oil still life that hung over the fireplace. My grandmother had painted it. Red and yellow zinnias in a vase. Colorful, but thankfully no sex appeal, none at all.

"He said he'd help us," Ace continued.

"Us? There is no us. Did you tell him about the poker group?"

"Yes and no."

I understood. Yes to testosterone, no to feathered boas.

"Mac thinks there's something dodgy about the explosion."

"Dodgy?"

"Mac's word, not mine. Apparently it was too small. Also it was a directed charge, whatever that means. I didn't understand about ninety percent of what he said, but I think he's going to start investigating tomorrow. He'll need your help." Ace stretched and scratched his bristled head. "I'm going to bed now. Do you have any brandy?"

"Back up a minute. Mac needs my help to investigate the murder of your poker-playing buddy? What about the police?"

"I'm not going to tell them about the poker club. That's final."

Another good time for me to say, "Too late. I've already called Stanislaus. So nah-nah-nah." But I didn't.

He stood and rubbed his eyes, smearing soot across his checks. "You can help Mac chase down the Laurelmere gossip. The dirt sweet old ladies won't tell the cops about people who are acting peculiar, having affairs with the gardeners, snorting coke behind the rhodies, stuff like that."

"If Detective Sergeant Stanislaus wants to know about the dirt in Laurelmere, all she has to do is follow Nasreen's Twitter-bitch feed."

"I think it's going to take more than a hundred and forty characters to find the guy who shot Lank Lungstrom."

"Okay. But why focus on Laurelmere gossip? Do you think the killer lives here?"

"All of the poker players do. Or did. Plus the security guards don't let just anyone through the gates. Uninvited guests have to show ID and sign in. If the killer-slash-bomber came from outside Laurelmere, the cops would already have his name from George or one of the other guards."

"How about climbing over the fence?"

"And juggling a loaded gun? Or a bomb ready to detonate? I don't think so. The police chief agrees. He said the cops checked the perimeter fence and didn't find any trace of an intruder."

"Helicopter drop?"

"Get real."

"Okay, the killer lives in Laurelmere. I'll accept that as a working hypothesis. But I still don't see where I come in."

"People will talk to Mac if you're with him. You're one of us."

"That's so untrue. I'm nothing like the people who live in Laurelmere. I don't care about money or golf or what the neighbors think. All I want is to live a simple life, raise my chickens, grow my tomatoes, and watch the dragonflies in my backyard."

Ace stepped closer to me. He smelled of sweat and smoke, not a fragrance that Ralph Lauren would be in any hurry to brand.

"Give it up, Sunny. You belong here. Your grandmother lived in this house for more than fifty years."

"But my mother lasted only sixteen."

"Well, there is that."

"Did you know my mother back then?"

"She babysat me every Saturday night. In fact, the police decided I was the last person to see her before she ran away."

"You?"

"Yeah. Apparently Jessica put me to bed with a sleeping pill dissolved in my bottle. By the time my parents returned home and discovered she was gone, she had a six-hour head start."

"And that, ladies and gentlemen, is Jessica's parenting style in a nutshell—with an emphasis on the nut."

Ace grinned. "So you're going to help Mac talk to the neighbors?"

"No." I may have stamped my foot.

"How old are you anyway, Sunny? You look about sixteen in your bunny slippers, but sometimes you sound like your grandmother."

"I'm thirty, but I don't see what that's got to do with anything."

"You have potential." He lifted a lock of my hair. "I think you'll clean up good."

I brushed his hand away. "Don't touch me, you patronizing pig."

"If that's the way you feel, I'm going to bed. Where do I sleep?"

"By yourself."

"Well, duh. Where's the guestroom?"

"Follow me." Scuffing my bunny slippers furiously, I stomped upstairs.

CHAPTER SEVEN

At seven o'clock the next morning, I was sipping my second cup of coffee and frowning at the *Seattle Times.* I had carried the newspaper inside, scanning the headline through the transparent wrapper: "Bombing, Police Suspect Terrorism." The newspaper account referred to Ace as a prominent local attorney, who requested his name not be used.

I tossed the paper on the breakfast table where it flopped like a dead rat encased in plastic. A full-color picture of yellow smoke rising from the hole in the roof of Ace's house dominated the front page, proving that the photographer had weaseled his way closer to the scene than I realized. Below the wreckage was a picture of my house labeled "Murder Site." My name, of course, was printed in full. Guess the reporter figured out I wasn't prominent.

As far as I was concerned, the darn paper could just sit there until hell froze over.

After Ken died, I had started seeing a grief therapist. I was numb with shock, and she kept saying, "Tell me how you feel. Tell me how you feel."

I hated those sessions. I knew how I felt—like part of my soul had been ripped away. But expressing my feelings wouldn't make any difference. Ken would still be dead, and I would still be half a person. Then one day I answered, "I feel like shit."

That's the day I stopped needing a therapist.

Now, however, her question was relevant. How *did* I feel?

Part of the answer was easy: I felt invaded. Invaded by the dead man, Lank Lungstrom, who'd picked my yard to die in. By the police who turned my house and garden upside down. By Ace who bullied and cajoled his way past my doorstep and was sleeping in my guest room.

And now I had been invaded by the media. They were trespassing on the small, secure, nontoxic world Ken and I had created with our own two hands.

And I felt not just invaded, but scared.

What would I do if someone blew up *my* house? Even if I survived, with no job, no garden, no chickens, I'd be destitute and out on the street again.

I needed to come up with a plan that would keep me safe while Stanislaus did her thing. Like hanging a big banner in my front window that said, "I sleep with a sharp axe." And I definitely did not want to walk around Laurelmere, helping Mac interrogate my neighbors. I might as well paint a flashing bull's-eye on my back.

Detective Stanislaus hadn't returned my call yet. Maybe she'd jailed the killer overnight or found his body in Ace's bombed-out basement, and I could go back to normal life and figure out how to butcher my old hens.

Maybe not.

I turned on my cell. Even after my magic "delete all" trick last night, I discovered fifty-two new voice-mail messages in my inbox and even more texts. The most recent was from Daphne, my best friend from the bank. Like me, she'd been laid off at Christmas. Unlike me, she had a husband and medical insurance. We jogged through the Arboretum together every Sunday morning at six A.M.

Daphne's text said: "Call Jessica pls she called me ten times makes me crazy!!!"

My phone started ringing. I recognized the number. Another

invasion was about to begin. With a sigh, I pushed Talk.

"Baby, I saw the paper. You need a lawyer, and I found you one. You're due in his office at nine forty-five this morning. Better get a move on. Wear heels and something nice and feminine."

The only person in the world who would issue marching orders before saying hello was my mother.

"Hi, Jessica." I didn't call her Mom. That word was reserved for my foster mother in Kokomo, Indiana, who had taken me in when I was eleven. Mom washed my face, combed nits from my hair, and fed me the first home-cooked meal I'd had in years.

"Listen, baby. This attorney, he's the best defense lawyer in Seattle. He's one of Lawrence's golf buddies, so he agreed to see you right away, but strictly as a favor to Lawrence. You've got to be there on time or the deal's off. Get a pencil and I'll give you his address."

Lawrence Lee was Jessica's husband, not my father. Besides being wealthy, Lawrence was hard-working, colorless, and silent, a perfect example of the bling inherent in cost accounting.

"I don't need a lawyer. Thanks anyway."

"Of course you do. If you think a public defender will be good enough to get you out of this mess, you're sadly mistaken. Your father went that route and look what happened to him."

"Buddy got caught selling heroin to a cop from the back of his station wagon in broad daylight in downtown Indianapolis. It's hard to come up with a viable defense for that level of stupidity."

"It was entrapment, pure and simple. The public defender was in cahoots with the cops, I'm sure of it."

I didn't bother to feed her the next line in our script, which was, "Wrong."

After my father ("Buddy") went to prison and I went into foster care, my mother hitchhiked back home to Seattle. Jessica didn't tell anyone about me, not even after my grandmother signed her into the Betty Ford Center. It took seven years, several relapses, and untold dollars, but my mother emerged clean and sober. I admired her for kicking the habit—it was a real achievement. But it left her with the illusion that she had a lock on truth with a capital T.

Especially when it came to ruining—whoops!—running my life.

"Look, Jessica. One of my neighbors is an attorney. I've got him on retainer, but I'm pretty sure I won't need him. I just found the dead guy. I don't know anything about him."

Okay, so I lie to my mother. Who doesn't?

"One of your neighbors? A man?"

I could feel her antennae quiver.

"Yes, Horace Pennington the Third is a man."

"That name's familiar. Have I seen it in the society pages?"

"According to Ace, you babysat him. And left him alone for six hours with a sleeping pill dissolved in his formula."

"Oh, I remember Ace. Cute, but really demanding."

"He hasn't changed a bit."

"Is he single again?" Jessica was nothing if not persistent.

I ground my teeth and told another lie. "I don't know."

Even though my mother didn't approve of Ken ("too old, too many ex-wives, too much of a free spirit"), she had been hit hard by his death. She wanted me married and pregnant. Having totally messed up her own life—and mine—Jessica was dying to become a grandmother and have a shot at screwing up the next generation.

Not that I was bitter or anything.

"What firm is Pennington with?"

I told her and she said, "I guess that's okay. Let me know if you need help paying him. I could always take the house off your hands."

"Taking the house off my hands" was the opening of another

well-thumbed script with no applause lines. Once my grandmother found out about my existence, she left her house to me,
free and clear. I'm sure she had been motivated by guilt as
much as love, but every time I walked in the door, I felt like she
was giving me a wrap-around hug.

Jessica was still furious. Of course, my real estate taxes are
only a little less than the rent on a chateau in the south of
France, so Jessica might end up with it after all. She firmly
believes that she and Lawrence belong in Laurelmere and I
don't.

I'm sure the community council agrees, despite her crazy
past. Like a shower of holy water, being filthy rich washes away
a multitude of sins.

"Good-bye," I said.

"Wait a minute. I'm coming right over. You need my help."

I flipped my phone shut. It rang again. This time it was Jack
Rabbit, the chicken delivery guy.

"I tried to drop off your chicks yesterday, but no go. They
wouldn't let me through the police barrier. What the hell is going on in Laurelmere?"

"Someone died and—" I caught myself as tears welled in my
eyes. I'd thought I was dealing with the murder just fine, but
Jessica's call must have softened me up.

"Who died?"

"A guy named Lank Lungstrom."

A moment of silence and then Jack said, "That's too bad."
His perfunctory tone was as bracing as a splash of cold salt
water. "I can't drive your chicks to Seattle again."

"I'm happy to pick them up. I need a road trip right now."

"My spread's in Orting."

"No problem. How about if I plan to arrive around noon?"

"Okay." He gave me directions to his farm and hung up.

Orting is a small rural community in southwestern Washington about two hours' drive from Seattle—far enough, I hoped, that my house hadn't been featured on the front page of the local rag.

I managed to dress without waking Ace. I told myself that I was being considerate, but sometimes consideration is just a synonym for cowardice. I wasn't going to let Ace spend another night in my guest room, but I was pretty sure I wouldn't be much better at being an evictor than I had been at being an evictee.

If that was even a word.

After Ace touched my hair last night, I knew he would take over my life if I let him stay. Maybe his late wife had enjoyed living with a masterful man who bossed her around, but I hated it. I wanted to be treated like an equal, not like a childish twit in bunny slippers—not even when I was acting like a childish twit in bunny slippers.

Maybe especially then.

My hope, probably futile, was when I got back home with the chicks, Ace would be gone. Best case, he'd leave behind a nice thank-you note and a pound of Fran's caramels with gray salt. Worst case, a pile of dirty towels and beard stubble in the bathroom sink.

Before I left, I fixed up the guest powder room for the chicks. I put a sturdy cardboard box across the sink, high enough to benefit from the heat lamp if it turned cold at night. Then I filled the chicks' water dish and poured crumbles into their feed bowl. After hatching, chicks can survive forty-eight hours without food or water, but by the time I got my new girls home, they would be ravenous.

The windshield of my truck had been smashed by bricks pinwheeling from Ace's house. From bitter experience I knew if I made a claim, my insurance company would pay and then drop me. And forking over the money for a new windshield was out of the question.

Mac owned a VW van as old and disreputable as his rowboat, but it ran.

After scattering some grain and vegetable scraps in the chicken yard for the Henriettas, I walked next door to Mac's basement apartment. Across the street, the ruins of Ace's house were even more dismal in broad daylight—charred beams, burned furniture, and an ugly smell that clung to the structure like a toxic fog. A patrol car spewing carbon emissions idled at the curb, and the yellow tape strung from tree to tree fluttered weakly in the morning air.

I knocked softly on Mac's door, not wanting to wake the geeks asleep upstairs. Mac's son was a software engineer at Nintendo, his Iranian daughter-in-law a software engineer at Boeing. The geeks mainly talked in bits and bytes, and Mac was mainly unintelligible. Their complete and utter lack of communication probably explained why they all got along living in the same home. That and the fact the house had five bedroom-bathroom suites, two complete kitchens, and a home theater big enough to shelter a boatload of Somali refugees.

Mac opened his door and agreed to drive with me to Orting if I'd fill up his tank.

"Couldn't we just siphon the gas out of my pickup? I filled it yesterday."

Mac eyed me speculatively. "Siphoning gas is a good way to poison yerself, lassie."

"I just spent fifty dollars on gas. I don't want to leave it in a truck I can't drive."

Mac fished around in his pocket and pulled out a tattered wallet. "My treat. You can pay me back in eggs."

"Fine, get your keys."

"Don't get yer knickers in a twist. I want me breakfast first. And Pete's coming with us."

"He's still on mommy probation?" I asked.

"Yep."

"Well, find him. We don't have time to eat. Jessica is on her way over."

"Then get yer skates on, lassie. Let's go."

CHAPTER EIGHT

"Stop yanking on it, lass. You'll ruin the mechanism." Mac pried Sunny's fingers from the seatbelt. Like everything else in the VW van, the passenger restraint system was covered with a sheen of oily dirt. He snapped the latch into the buckle. "It wants a gentle touch."

"I don't have any confidence in a seatbelt older than I am."

"You gonna beg off the trip?"

Mac hoped not. He needed to question Sunny if he was going to keep her safe. And he knew he could keep her safe, even if he was old and retired. Even if he was still aching from his burst of heroics last night.

"No." Sunny sighed. "I guess I really should pick up the chicks. Anything's better than sitting around waiting for Stanislaus to call." She pulled her cell phone from her pocket and propped it on the dashboard, where it remained stubbornly silent.

Mac half turned and called over his shoulder. "Pete, got yer seatbelt on?"

Pete, totally engrossed in his iPhone, grunted. Nasreen had amended his house arrest to include Mac's van, but Mac wasn't sure the kid ever knew where he was except in virtual space.

Mac turned the key in the ignition. After just enough hesitation to make life interesting, the motor started. He glanced at Sunny and raised his eyebrows. In thirty years as a cop, he'd learned to start an interrogation quietly, like a sly old fox stealing into a henhouse, whiskers a-twitching.

"I thought the detective already talked to you," he said. "What's going on?"

"I remembered something last night," Sunny answered. "Something important. I left Stanislaus three messages, but she hasn't called me back."

"Something important, eh?" he repeated slowly. The van lurched over the speed bumps that littered Laurelmere's cul-de-sacs like land mines. He waved to George, the security guard, as they passed through the gate.

Sunny bit her lip and nodded without looking at him.

Mac let the silence drag while he pulled onto SR520. Behind him, some young hotshot in a BMW hooked and zoomed around the van. Mac merged into the carpool lane of I-5 and groaned.

Traffic was miserable. Typical Seattle, he thought. You've got these thundering great highways going this way and that and still folks get where they're headed no faster than if we all were driving oxcarts. And to hear the environmentalists bleat on about climate change, we're dropping as much shite as a pair of oxen, too.

Meanwhile his brakes were making a noise like a mouse trapped in a piccolo. It would be hard to question Sunny under these conditions.

For a moment, Mac longed for the old interview room in Prestwick: scarred table, battered chairs, three generations of fear and sweat and nicotine coating the walls. A place where a man could get the job done.

"Ace asked me to investigate Lang Lungstrom's death," Mac said. A tractor-trailer tried to squeeze him on the right. Mac gunned the engine and shot past. Anything to keep from using the brakes. "He promised you'd cooperate."

"Ace has no business making promises for me."

"He's yer lawyer."

"But not my keeper."

"I'm just trying to help, Sunny."

The van passed under the freeway lid in downtown Seattle. Sunny cleared her throat. Mac couldn't see her face, but she didn't sound happy. "I don't want you or Ace messing with the police investigation. Stanislaus seems to know what she's doing. I think we should just let her get on with it."

"Lovely idea, lass."

The van exited the tunnel. Mac blinked as his eyes adjusted to the glare created by sunshine bouncing off the canyon of office towers. Ahead of him, Mount Rainier floated serenely in a wash of clouds.

"I wouldn't pin my hopes on that detective," he said.

"What do you mean?"

"The FBI showed up last night while Stanislaus were questioning me."

"The FBI? That's good, right? They always get their man?"

"That were the Mounties, lass. And as for whether it's good or not? That depends. If the Feds believe they're fighting terrorism, they'll consider naught else."

"But Stanislaus—"

"My guess, based on thirty years of policing and politics? She's been pulled off the case. Or *pushed* off mebbe. Budgets are tight. The local cops aren't going to spend time chasing an investigation that's been taken over by the Feds. That's why Stanislaus hasn't returned your calls."

"That's crazy. Lank Lungstrom wasn't a terrorist."

"Could take the FBI a while to figure it out. In the meantime . . ." Mac concentrated on driving and let her work out the implications.

After a few minutes, Sunny responded. "So, let's say you're right. Stanislaus is off the case, and the FBI thinks the murder and bombing are part of a terrorist plot. But what if they're wrong. Then what?"

"The killer, if he's smart, will go to ground. Mebbe they find him, mebbe not."

"And if he's not smart?"

"If he's not smart," Mac paused to watch her face, "or if he hasn't finished what he plans to do, there could be more deaths."

"In Laurelmere."

"Aye, lass. In Laurelmere. That seems to be ground zero."

Sunny huddled in her seat, her shoulders hunched, chewing her bottom lip as she thought. Finally she straightened. "Okay, if Stanislaus isn't going to investigation, you have to. How can I help?"

"Tell me about Ken."

"Ken? My husband Ken? Why? What do you want to know?"

"Ace thinks Ken's death was the start of this whole thing."

Sunny rubbed her forehead and knuckled her eyes. "And I think Ace is wrong."

"Tell me anyway."

"Okay. Long story short: Ken and I met at a Halloween party. We hit it off. Love at first sight and all that jazz. We were married on Valentine's Day. Meanwhile, my grandmother died and left me her house. Everything was going great. We tore up the backyard and created an urban farm. Then in May, Ken had an appointment with a supplier. He owned a store on Capitol Hill, Ken Dahl's Specialty Shoes. On the way home from the meeting, he drove off the road, flipped the car, and died instantly. His blood alcohol limit was way over the line." Sunny's voice broke. "You know all this."

"I knew Ken died in a car accident. Why does Ace think his death is linked to the murders?"

"You should ask him."

"I'm asking you, lass."

Another sigh. "Three things. First, Ace claims someone tried to kill him by running him off the road. It happened a couple of weeks before Ken died. Second, Ken had been sober for nine years. I don't know why he'd suddenly start drinking again. Third, Ken was part of Ace's poker club. So was Lank Lungstrom. And the explosion happened in the basement where they met to play."

"Tell me about the poker club."

"Well, that's the thing." She glanced out the window and called out, "You just passed our exit."

Ten minutes later, Mac drove the van down a tree-lined lane. Jack Rabbit's farm was a beautiful sight, like a smallholding back home, a barn and house tucked under a grassy hill and shaded with towering maple trees. The barn was in fine shape, but the house needed fresh paint and a new roof. Plywood covered a couple of upstairs windows, and the porch sloped away like an old codger crawling home from the pub. The only sign of life was a massive black dog that lolled in the sunshine next to a padlocked shed.

Mac approved of farmers who put their animals and machinery ahead of their own comfort. He was looking forward to meeting this Jack Rabbit, even though Rabbit's name made Mac think his mam must have hated kids.

Mac stopped the van in the driveway and honked his horn once. The dog twitched its ears but remained supremely indifferent to their presence.

Sunny stopped fixing her face to tug on Mac's arm. "Don't honk. That's rude."

"But—"

"Hey there." Jack emerged from the barn with a shout and a wave. He was older than Mac had expected, maybe mid-forties, although Mac had a hard time judging age in the States. As far as Mac could tell, Americans fell into two categories—grossly overweight or fitness obsessed. In either case, they looked younger than folks at home.

And acted younger, too, what with their electronic toys and canary-yellow Hummers and cell phones that did everything but pee for them.

Jack fell into the fit category—good teeth, an overabundance of glossy hair, easy stride, and capable hands. Sunny straightened her clothes before she opened the passenger door. So that's why the lass was primping. Mac felt absurdly irritated.

But not as irritated as Jack, who clearly had hoped Sunny would make the trip by herself. After Jack gallantly helped Sunny climb out of the van, he asked, "Would you like a tour of the old homestead? It's been in my family four generations."

"I'd be thrilled," Sunny said. Mac groaned, but no one asked his opinion. Mac prodded Pete who shook his head without lifting his eyes from his iPhone or unfastening his seatbelt.

Fifteen minutes after they arrived, Mac was good and sick of listening to Jack and Sunny natter on about farming. You'd think Jack owned a couple of thousand acres instead of this tiny place back of beyond. They went to inspect the henhouse, but the smell of chicken droppings was as overpowering in that small, sun-beaten building as one of those goopy French cheeses.

"I'm going to wait in the van," Mac told Sunny.

"Fine, whatever." She was enthralled by Jack's arrangement of nest boxes for his hens.

Mac rousted Pete from the backseat of the van. "Let's take a walk."

"I'm starving," Pete said. "Can I order a pizza?"

"To be delivered out here? Is that some kind of joke?"

"No, Grumps, I'm really hungry. I found a place in Orting. They take credit cards. Two large pizzas for the price of one if you order before five. Give me your credit card and I'll call it in."

"Nae. We'll eat when we get home. And yer coming for a walk with me."

Pete squirmed in his seat. "I'm watching *Captain America*."

"Ya must have seen that twenty times." Mac grabbed Pete's shirt. "Come on, out of there."

"This isn't fair."

Without answering, Mac headed across the fields toward the woods. Pete bobbed behind him like the tail of a kite, his gaze fastened to his iPhone.

The path to the woodlot was surprisingly clear and wide with well-defined ruts and a smattering of new gravel. Mabbe Jack harvested Christmas trees and sold firewood during the winter.

Mac had wandered only a short ways when he realized the stand of fir and maples around the perimeter of the woodlot was not very wide, only twenty yards or so. Enough to give the appearance of a dense forest from the highway or the barnyard, but now he discerned a clearing in the middle of the trees, a clearing big as a soccer field, sunlit and densely green. The lane, no, call it a road, led straight to the heart of the clearing. Curiouser and curiouser. Mac was becoming pretty darn sure that Jack wasn't harvesting Christmas trees. He was using the woods to screen a far more lucrative crop.

CHAPTER NINE

"I don't see any difference in the vent at all," I told Jack.

If there's a way to put this more delicately, I haven't found it. A vent is the all-purpose opening of a bird on the opposite end from its head. Sexing newborn chicks is more of an art than a science, and it involves examining the vent within twenty-four hours of hatching.

I returned the chick to Jack's hand. "I must not have your expert touch."

To my horror, I realized I was batting my eyelashes at him, a knee-jerk reaction to his rugged masculinity and the heady combination of chickens and sun-dried organic hay that wafted through the henhouse.

"This one is definitely an egg-layer." Jack put her in a box labeled "Pullet" and bent to pick up another chick. His shoulder brushed mine and a spark flew between us.

Trying to neutralize Jack's magnetism, I turned away and pretended to study his homestead. A red motorcycle leaned against one of the outbuildings. I pointed to it and asked, "Are you a biker?"

"No, belongs to my son. He's not living here right now."

"And that's his dog?" I pointed to the big black dog that had accompanied us into the henhouse. He came almost up to my waist. His coat of dense black curls shone, and he had a serious, square-cut muzzle.

"No, he's mine. His name is Teufel." As Jack spoke, the dog

butted Jack's leg with his massive head and then settled at his feet.

"He's gorgeous. What kind of a dog is he?" I asked.

"Rottler. Teufel's half Rottweiler and half poodle."

I laughed. "That's a crazy mix."

"It's perfect. He's as smart as a whip, fast, and doesn't shed. He's a great guard dog. Also, he understands German."

"Sure he does. How about French for the poodle half?"

"Naw, German is the language for military commands. French is mainly good for sissy-baby stuff like ordering omelets and buying wine."

"I speak French. Does that make me a sissy-baby, too?"

Before Jack could answer, Teufel stood, ears cocked, listening. He barked once, a deep guttural sound that rattled the windows, and streaked out the door.

"What's going on?" I asked.

"Teufel," Jack shouted, thrusting the baby chick into my hands. *"Hor auf damit."*

Whores dammit? Jack's dog was chasing whores?

Jack grabbed a shotgun from a nearby shelf. He ran after the dog and fired a burst of birdshot into the air.

I dropped the chick into the box marked Pullets (I had a fifty percent chance of being right) and raced after Jack. I heard the shotgun again as Jack disappeared down a path through a woodlot at the back of his spread. What the hell was going on?

CHAPTER TEN

Mac slowed his steps. He sniffed the air, turned around, and checked on Pete, who was kicking rocks far behind him on the track. Mac considered turning back. He'd learned on the force that "don't ask, don't tell" could be applied to more than soldiers.

A dog barked, loud and frantic, coming closer. Mac's skin crawled. Turning around was no longer an option. He couldn't outrun a dog. He grabbed a stout stick about five feet long from the leaf-covered ground, braced his legs, and faced the sound.

Not a minute too soon. The black dog, last seen rolling in a patch of sunshine, leaped out of the forest, his brilliant white teeth aimed straight at Mac's throat.

"Stop!" Mac hollered. "Stop!"

The dog paid no attention.

Mac had been responsible for the first K-9 unit at the cop shop in Prestwick. Now his training came back. Within seconds he had the mad black beast pinned against the dirt with the cudgel wedged between his jaws. Mac's nose was inches from the dog's as he crouched over it, pushing down on that muscled neck with all his might.

The dog had been eating carrion. Its breath was as sour as a jungle latrine. But otherwise, it was a fine animal with a gleaming coat and a proud face. Mac couldn't bring himself to administer the coup de grâce, and he wasn't completely sure he could kill the dog anyway. His arms were weakening, his hip was throbbing. The dog was stronger and younger in every way—faster, meaner, younger. Every couple of seconds, the black devil tried to leap up, flicking long ropy strands of saliva that clung to Mac's shirt and fell across his eyes.

It was a Mexican standoff.

Mac had seen plenty of dog maulings during his time on the force. Evidence photos danced in his mind: bloody legs, mangled faces, an eyeball dangling by a thread.

Dear God in heaven, I don't want to die like that.

Again, the dog strained to attack. Mac forced it back down. He heard an ominous crack. The stick was starting to crumble. He glanced up. Was there a tree to climb?

All he saw were firs with straight trunks and branches too thin to hold his weight.

Okay then. His only chance was to release the cudgel suddenly. At the same instant, he'd kick the dog hard. Face, underbelly, ribs? Whatever he could hit in that split second. And then run like hell.

Offering up a wordless prayer that the dog hadn't seen Pete, Mac tensed and summoned his last remaining strength to hold the beast down another minute. The dog snarled. Then a gunshot thundered through the clearing followed by a shout, "Teufel, Teufel come."

"Teufel?" German for "devil" and a fit name for the blasted animal. The dog was listening, too. He shivered, his cropped ears alert, then lunged against the stick again.

What the hell. Mac couldn't hold the fookin' dog much longer anyway.

With a crack, the cudgel broke, making Mac's decision irrelevant. He leaped back and threw himself facedown on the gravel road. He shielded his head with his arms and braced for the first rip of flesh.

CHAPTER ELEVEN

A minute later I burst through the trees into a field of emerald-green, foot-high plants, which smelled hot and disturbingly spicy. I screeched to a halt. Jack stood in a clearing six feet away, loosely cradling his shotgun under his arm. Teufel crouched next to Mac, who sprawled on the ground.

I didn't see any whores, but I did see Pete drifting toward us through the trees.

The dog quivered, as tense as a sprinter at the start line. Mac seemed to quiver, too, but his gaze was locked on Jack and Teufel.

"Are you okay?" I asked, once again master of the idiotic question.

Mac straightened his back. "Phone the sheriff, lass. Now."

"Sheriff? Why? Did the dog bite you?"

"Nae. Look around."

I glanced at Jack, who was fastening a leash on Teufel. "What happened?"

The men answered me in a ragged chorus.

"Teufel thought we had a poacher."

"Bloody dog just about ripped me to shreds."

"You were trespassing. Teufel is my guard dog. What did you expect him to do?"

"You should have warned me."

"The whole damn place is plastered with No Trespassing

signs." Jack jerked his shotgun upward. "Can't you read, fuck-head?"

"Jack." I stepped closer and touched his arm. "Put that thing away. He's an old retired guy. Leave him alone."

I should have known that calling Mac old would only make him more cantankerous than ever.

"I may be old, but I'm not blind. Look around you, lass. We're standing in the middle of a marijuana field. That's why yon chookter needs the guard dog from hell."

"Marijuana?" I felt like an idiot. Of course. The field smelled like a college dorm. The plants were thick and healthy, brimming with new growth. Buds. Oh, yeah, I got it.

"Sweet," Pete said as he came to stand next to me. He had a dreamy smile on his face.

"Call the sheriff," Mac repeated. He stood with his hands on his hips, looking as righteous as Moses come down from the mountain—if Moses had been grizzled, scratched, and covered with dog slobber.

"Don't do it," Jack said. "Nobody cares about pot." He knelt next to Teufel and began talking in a low voice while he stroked the dog's back.

"Jack's right, Mac," I said. "Let's pick up my chicks and head home."

"Marijuana is a Schedule 1 drug."

"The police don't arrest adults for possession anymore. Not in Seattle."

Pete beamed happily, and I realized I'd gone too far. I snapped my fingers to get his attention. "It's like alcohol, Pete. Grown-ups only."

He rolled his eyes and shook his head, blowing me off. Oh man, I had a lot to learn about being a mother. Five months didn't seem like nearly enough time.

"Buggeration. The point is, we're not in Seattle," Mac said.

"And this isn't a case of simple possession. Look around you. Jack's growing enough pot to supply every schoolyard in the state."

Teufel bristled, and Jack jumped to his feet. "I don't sell to kids. This is the finest local hemp available on the West Coast. Once I get a license to grow medical marijuana, I'm going to get my field certified organic by the USDA."

He glanced at me. "I told you, Sunny. A small family farmer can't make it anymore without some kind of reliable cash crop. I tried exotic poultry, mushrooms, and specialty vegetables—heirloom tomatoes, edamame beans, yellow beets, purple carrots, white eggplant, and red potatoes—but nothing's as profitable as weed."

"It's still a Schedule 1 narcotic. Yer committing a felony."

"Sunny, talk some sense into that damn Scot."

"If you don't report him, lass, yer as guilty as he."

"Why don't *you* report him?"

"I don't have my green card yet. I'm not getting mixed up with those ijits at ICE."

"This conversation is totally ridiculous," Jack said. "Sunny, I'll drop by your house tomorrow and see how the chicks are doing."

I nodded. Jack twitched Teufel's leash. "Come."

Jack and the dog marched back to the farmyard. Mac and I trailed dejectedly in their wake. Pete smiled happily. He may have skipped. I guessed adulthood was looking pretty good.

"I don't like Jack, lassie," Mac growled.

"Shhh. He'll hear you."

"He won't be hearing aught he don't already know."

I shrugged. When we got back to Mac's van, Jack and Teufel had disappeared but a shoebox of chicks sat in the shade on the passenger seat.

"Aren't they cute?" I held the chicks where Mac and Pete

84

could see them. Mac grunted and started the van. Pete grunted and picked up his iPhone.

The Rhode Islands Reds were a day old, fluffy brown and white Peeps with bright black eyes and yellow-twig legs. They cheeped noisily at every turn of the road until, exhausted, they collapsed in a heap in the corner of the box, piled on top of each other like cotton balls.

When we got back to the interstate, I set the box on the floor of the van and braced it between my shoes. The van didn't have an air conditioner. I saw enough gaps in the rusted body to provide fresh air for the chicks, but not, I hoped, blasts of carbon monoxide.

"So, what's this about Jack coming by yer house tomorrow?" Mac asked.

"He just wants to check on my brooder. I need to remember to tell George to let him through the security gate."

"George isn't working tomorrow. He's off to a revival meeting with that church of his."

"Oh, I forgot. They're pretty conservative, aren't they?"

"Yeah. Now lass, I don't want you to spend anymore time with that Jack Rabbit."

"Because of the marijuana?"

"Yeah, that. And—" Mac thumped the steering wheel.

"And what? Spit it out, Mac."

"Does he know yer a widow?" Mac glared at me.

"No, it never came up while we were examining chicken vents."

"I saw the way he was looking at you, and I dinna like it." He shook his finger at me. "Dinna like it at all. You better tell him before he gets any funny ideas."

"Now you listen to me. I'm a grown woman. I don't need you getting all hysterical if some guy looks at me sideways."

"Happen I don't agree, lass. Now search the glove box. I

think I've got some paracetamol in there."

I found a plastic bottle grimy with engine grease and checked the label. "These expired four years ago."

"Give it here."

I handed him two tablets and opened my REI water bottle. I never buy bottled water. It's a disaster for the environment. It takes more water to manufacture the bottle than the bottle contains. And then, using fossil fuel, it's shipped all over the world, even to places like Seattle, which, ironically, has about the finest tap water in the country.

Mac brushed my REI bottle aside, threw back his head, and choked down the pills.

"Give me two more."

"Okay, but you've got to drink some water, too."

"Put a sock in it, lassie."

"You're really working on that whole grumpy Scotsman thing, aren't you?" I handed him the pills and pointedly turned to stare out the window.

We were creeping northbound on I-5 when Mac cleared his throat. "Where'd ya meet up with this Jack Rabbit?"

"At Pike Place Market a couple of weeks ago. He has an upper stall selling organic, free-range chickens and eggs. I asked him if he sold chicks, too, and he said yes. I paid him, told him where I lived, and we set a date for the delivery. That's when he first said he needs a cash crop to keep his farm afloat."

"He's got more than enough to keep yon farm afloat."

"What do you mean?"

"His whole bloody field, it's got to be worth a couple of hundred thousand dollars, even with the dollar dropping as fast as an orphan down a well."

"He's also paying off some legal bills. I got the impression that his wife was long gone and their son got in with a bad crowd. It was mostly what Jack didn't say, you know?"

Another grunt. Mac scowled through the windshield without answering. End of conversation.

Although I would never admit it, I knew Mac was right. My grief counselor had warned me about jumping into a relationship before I was finished grieving for Ken. Even so, I found myself attracted to Jack. We seemed to have a lot in common and—best of all—Jack wasn't a cross-dresser. Even though it felt vaguely disloyal to Ken, I knew I would never again fall in love with a man who wore women's clothes. With that resolution, I leaned back and fell asleep.

The van bounced roughly over the speed bumps in Laurelmere and woke me up. The lurching woke my baby chicks, too, and they cheeped frantically. Mac slowed down enough for me to climb from the cab with my shoebox of agitated girls. I had planned to invite him inside for homemade scones as a thank-you, but he was acting too grumpy.

Also, I hadn't baked any scones.

As I walked to the house, I heard Nasreen screeching for Pete. I didn't hear him reply because I was astonished by the transformation of my front yard. The pieces of brick from the explosion were stacked neatly on the parking strip, ready to be hauled away. My pickup—surprise of surprises—had a new windshield. Yes! A better thank-you from Ace than flowers and candy.

The porch was swept clean of squished grapes. A wrought-iron hose caddy with a filigreed rooster in the center had been attached to the outside of my house by the front door. The hose from my rain barrel had been neatly wound around the caddy. I experimented and was delighted to discover the hose reeled off quickly and could be wound back on again with a handle concealed in the rooster's tail.

What a clever idea. A little kitschy, maybe, but still useful. More perks from having an attorney on retainer?

"You're going to like living here," I told the chicks. I didn't tell them their happy future depended on me butchering their predecessors. And the sooner, the better. With the six new chicks in my possession, I was officially a scofflaw. Like Jack.

Balancing the shoebox on one hip, I unlocked my door. I stepped inside and immediately thought I'd touched down on the wrong planet. A plasma television, as big as my dining room table, hung on the wall next to the fireplace. A tangle of electrical cords ran to an unfamiliar antique whatnot below the television. Red lights flickered behind its open-weave doors. Three remote controls, two gray and one black, perched on the whatnot and leered at me.

The air smelled weird, too, like a forest of polycarbonated pine trees. The fingerprint powder had been cleaned up, the stack of books I'd been reading had been shelved. Through the doorway, my kitchen appliances gleamed. The floor was newly waxed, and my compost bucket had been emptied, washed, and turned upside down in my sink.

After all these years of wishing, the cleaning fairies had finally arrived.

"Sunny, where have you been?"

Ace clumped down the stairway and did everything but shake his finger at me. He was clean and casual in khakis and a polo shirt—and seemed totally at home.

"I don't have to tell you where I've been."

He walked right up to me, took the shoebox of chicks, and put it on the whatnot next to the remotes.

"Don't set them so close to the TV. You'll ruin their eyes."

"Sit down," he barked. "I've got something to tell you."

"I'm not sitting down. I want you out of my house. You and all your . . ." I flung my arms wide, speechless.

"The arson squad found a body."

"Here?" I looked around bewildered, as if a dead man was hiding in the whatnot.

"No, in the basement of my house."

I picked up my box of chicks and held it close as I collapsed onto the couch. The chicks cheeped comfortingly. "Tell me what happened."

"It was Balls."

"Balls? The firemen found balls in your basement?"

"No, they found Wallace Spaulding. We called him 'Balls.' He was part of the poker club."

"What was he doing in your basement?"

"The cops think he set the bomb and it went off prematurely." Ace grimaced. "Balls always worried about that."

I giggled a little hysterically. I couldn't help myself.

"Anyway, the police found a gun next to him. They've tentatively identified it as the gun that killed Lank."

"Poor Mac."

"Mac? What's he got to do with it?"

"He'll feel terrible that he didn't find your friend in time."

"The firemen think he died instantly."

"So Balls—Mr. Spaulding—he's the killer?"

"That's what the chief of police told me."

"Why would Balls kill members of his own poker club?"

"I don't know." Ace shook his head and thumped down next to me. My baby girls protested vigorously.

"Some kind of deep self-loathing of himself and his fellow cross-dressers?"

Ace shook his head. "He didn't loathe himself. Neither do I. Neither did Ken."

I knew he was right.

Ace reached for my hand. "Anyway, the police have turned the investigations over to the FBI."

"So you weren't forced to tell the police chief about the poker club?"

Ace shook his head.

"And the killings are over."

He tightened his grip. "No, Sunny, I think they've just begun."

CHAPTER TWELVE

I believed Ace when he said the death of my husband, two more murders, and an explosion were just the beginning. I believed, too, the police had made a mistake. They shouldn't have stopped looking for the killer. These deaths had nothing to do with terrorism.

I believed Ace and I was scared.

I still had Ken's Glock, of course, locked in my gun safe, and I still had several rounds of ammunition. But unless the bad guy stood ten feet away, motionless, under bright lights with a black-and-white target on his chest, I didn't think I could kill him.

And maybe not even then. After all, I couldn't kill a Henrietta.

Suddenly I craved a visible masculine presence in my house so the killer would know I wasn't a sitting duck—or a setting hen. If I spoke German, I would have gotten a dog like Jack's Teufel, a giant male with a ferocious bark.

But it was past five o'clock and the Humane Society was closed, so I told Ace he could spend another night in my guestroom.

Despite my anxiety, I did not crave CNN. Or the hundreds of cable channels with perfect reception, outstanding production values, compelling background music, and content-free programming that Ace had dropped into my house.

"I want you to take that thing out of here." I pointed to the television, keeping my voice civilized, but firm.

"Are you sure?" Ace used the remote to turn the television on and mute the sound. He started clicking through the channels, all 546 of them. "The resolution is outstanding."

"I don't want it. Don't you know greenhouse gases are produced by the manufacture of plasma TV sets? Have you even heard of nitrogen trifluoride?"

As we talked, I set the shoebox of chicks on the floor of the guest powder room and gently eased them into the brooder so they could find food and water. They cheeped happily, their beady black eyes bright with excitement.

"Now, Sunny." Ace held up the remote like a traffic cop raising his nightstick. "Spare me the eco-geek lecture."

"Don't you 'now, Sunny' me. If you want to stay in my guest room, get rid of the television. It's the price of living here."

"But tonight Fox News is showing—"

"I don't care if they're showing the Second Coming complete with computer-enhanced graphics and the Mormon Tabernacle Choir. You aren't going to watch it in my house."

"Fine." Ace's aggrieved tone made it perfectly clear that it wasn't fine at all. "I'll call Carlos and tell him to haul the television away."

"Thank you."

"Here's what you can do if you really want to thank me."

Sigh. I was beginning to learn I would never win a negotiation with Ace. The best I could hope for was an armed truce. "What do you want?"

"Since the police have closed their investigation, we need Mac more than ever."

"Why don't you just tell Stanislaus about the poker club? Once she sees the connection among Ken, Lank, Balls, and your house, she'll have to reopen the case."

"No. I told you. I can't afford to do that."

"Well, fine. Then I will. I'm calling Detective Sergeant Stanislaus right now." I dug my cell phone out of my jeans pocket. If I kept bugging her, surely she'd have to answer. "I'll tell her everything, beginning with Ken's death."

"She won't believe you."

"Yes she will. I have evidence she doesn't know about."

"Evidence? What evidence? Where is it?"

I started to answer and choked. If I told him, would I be betraying Ken?

Then I reminded myself that Ace had seen Ken in drag. Week after week. He knew more about my husband's life—his real life—than I did. And what was the point of protecting Ken's reputation if it meant I'd end up homeless or dead?

Ace stopped pacing. I could feel his eyes studying me.

"What's your evidence?" he asked again.

"A photograph."

"A photograph? Where is it?"

Where didn't seem to matter. I gave him the what. "It's Ken in drag. With some other guy whose picture was torn away. It was taken in our bedroom."

"Yeah, yeah." Ace waved away my description. "Where is it?"

The light finally dawned. Ace cared *where* the picture was, not *what* the picture was. "You know about the photograph, don't you? You've seen it."

Like any great criminal lawyer, Ace admitted he'd lied without a trace of shame. "Lank showed it to me."

"When?"

"The morning he died, I saw Mac leave your yard while Lank and I were still talking on my front porch. He was swinging that damn bucket he uses to carry bait and heading off to the lake. So I'm sure Mac didn't have a chance to take the picture. The police didn't find it on Lank's body or I'd know by now. The chief is a buddy of mine, and Stanislaus confirmed she didn't find anything on Lank to tie him to the poker club. So that leaves you, Sunny. Where is it?"

I bit my lip. Ace was my lawyer-on-retainer, right? It would be okay to tell him I had hidden evidence in a murder investigation. He couldn't report me to the cops.

"Don't worry," I said. "I hid the picture in a safe place."

"Where? I didn't find it."

"You didn't find it?" I couldn't believe what I had just heard. I jumped up and faced him nose-to-nose. "You searched my house?"

Ace's left eyebrow twitched. That was all the answer I needed.

"I thought you were being nice when you had your cleaning lady scrub my place after the police went through it. But you weren't thinking of me, were you? You were worried about yourself. What would happen to you, Mr. Horace L. Pennington the Third, Esquire, if the denizens of your little cloistered world discovered you're a cross-dresser? That's why you've been trying to buy me off with champagne dinners and cable TV, isn't it? To cover up your secret."

"No. I mean," he choked. "Maybe it started that way, but—"

"Get out of here. Take your stuff, get out, and never come back. If you ever talk to me again, I'm going right to the cops, and I'll charge you with malicious harassment. And I've got the picture to prove that I mean business."

For a moment we stood there, face to face, without moving. I could smell his aftershave. I could hear the faint cheeps of my chicks in the guest bathroom. I could hear my heart pounding, and I was pretty sure he could hear it, too.

"No," he said. "I'm not leaving without that picture."

"Yes, you are."

I must have winced because Ace said, "Does your stomach hurt, Sunny?" He pulled out a chair from the dining room table. "Have a seat."

"What are you talking about?"

"You're holding your stomach. Does it hurt?"

I looked down. My hands were clasped over my tummy like a shield. My body wanted to stay safe.

"I'm okay," I said. "When did Lank show you the picture of Ken?"

"About twenty minutes before he was shot. He stormed into my house, waving the picture like a madman. He was sure I was trying to blackmail him." Ace snorted. "As if."

"Back up." My fingers had laced themselves across my tummy again. "Why did Lank have the picture?"

"It showed up at his house. He didn't find it until the morning he died. He was going through the mail his maid had left on his desk and found the photo in an unmarked envelope."

"So Lank was the man with Ken in the picture?"

"Right. You see, we sometimes took pictures of ourselves on poker night. You know, dressed up and goofing around." Ace finally seemed embarrassed. "After we went to all that trouble to do our hair and nails, to find the right dress and accessorize it, to stretch out our shoes and find garter belts that fit, it seemed silly not to take pictures."

I squeezed my eyes shut so I didn't have to see the images he was painting.

"We stored the pictures on my hard drive so we could have a slide show if we wanted. It was just for fun. We never thought anyone would get hurt."

"But that picture was taken in *my* bedroom." I wanted to pound something, preferably Ace's head with a shovel. Instead I tightened the protective shield around my tummy.

"Right. I pointed that out to Lank when he showed me the picture. He decided you must have taken it."

"Wait a minute. How did you know it was taken in my bedroom?"

"I helped your grandmother move furniture around a couple

of months before she died. No one would forget that wallpaper."

"So how did you get from the picture being taken in my bedroom to me taking it? And mailing it to Lank? I didn't even know that Lank . . ." I didn't know what words to use.

"Dressed up?" Ace actually sounded sympathetic. "We all knew you were broke after Ken died. We figured you were trying to blackmail Lank, or maybe you'd try to blackmail all of us. You know, to cover your property taxes or something."

"You think I'm a criminal?"

"No, of course not. Well, not now. I didn't know you very well back then."

"That was just two days ago, Ace." Although it seemed like a year.

He shrugged. He'd been doing a lot of shrugging lately. And then it hit me. "That's why you came over when you saw the police at my house. Not to help me. To find out what happened to the picture."

"Sorry." That shrug again.

"You, my friend, my fake friend, are a class-A scumbag. I want you out of here right now."

"No, Sunny, think. If you didn't send the picture to Lank and I didn't send the picture, then someone else did. That's the person trying to kill us."

"You. Trying to kill you. Not me."

"Can you spell collateral damage? Like it or not, you're part of this mess, too."

"Well, crap." Ace was right. It was getting to be a very annoying habit.

"Okay," I conceded. "So I need to show Stanislaus the picture."

Without paying attention to his agitated rebuttal, I stepped into the kitchen and pulled *Urban Homesteading* out of my bookcase. I flipped through the pages. No picture. I held the book upside down and shook it. Still no picture.

"What did you do with it, you jerk?" I slammed the book on the table. "The picture was here. You took evidence from a crime scene."

"Wrong, *you* took evidence from a crime scene. Where is it?"

"Darn, I don't know. Your cleaning lady must have found it."

"No way. Carmelita is good, but she'd never take a book off a shelf to dust it."

I sank into a chair and ran my fingers through my hair, dislodging a piece of straw from Jack's henhouse. It floated gently to my feet. I had a moment of complete and utter longing for Jack, a simple, gorgeous farmer just trying to keep his homestead intact. No lies, no cross-dressing, and no compromising pictures. As if in tune with my thoughts, a sudden flurry of cheeping erupted in the guest bathroom. Another responsibility. When Jack came to check on the chicks tomorrow, I would ask him to take them back to the farm where they would be safe.

"Sunny? Are you listening?"

Oh good, Ace was still talking. The man was tireless.

"What?"

"If you don't have the picture and the police have closed the investigation, we need Mac's help more than ever. Call him. Set up a meeting tonight."

"Set up a meeting, make coffee, and bake cookies? Is that what you want? Should I pull together a PowerPoint presentation about the murders, too?"

Turning my back on Ace, I opened the bathroom door and checked on the chicks. Despite the disasters exploding all around them, they had calmed down and fallen fast asleep under the heat lamp. Who knew what went on in their tiny little brains?

"If you want to talk to Mac, you set it up," I continued, shutting the bathroom door. "I have beans to harvest and chickens to butcher."

"Ah, Sunny. About the chickens—"

Ignoring Ace, I walked through the kitchen and stepped onto my deck, slamming the screen door behind me. "Here, chick, chick." I scooped a cup of scratch from the container in the greenhouse and walked over to the hen yard.

During the day, rain, snow, or shine, the hens stayed outside in the yard, pecking and scratching, doing their chicken thing. They always ran to me when I called "chick, chick" and tossed a handful of cracked corn into their yard.

But now, nothing. No clucks, no mad dash to the fence, no cheerful begging.

I couldn't understand why. They'd been fine when I left this morning for Jack Rabbit's house. I didn't see any holes in the fence or bloody feathers.

"Ah, Sunny?" Behind me, Ace stepped onto the deck and cleared his throat. "I have something to tell you."

"Not right now. I have to check on the girls."

"That's what I need to talk to you about."

"The girls? Why?"

"I called a friend of mine. He's retired now but he was CEO of Washington Fresh Poultry. He's still chairman of the board, of course. It's a lucrative position and they're thinking IPO— you might want to get in on the ground floor when the time comes. I'll let you know. But anyway, I called him and he was glad to help out. He got his start on his father's chicken farm in Yakima. Let's see, it must have been about thirty years ago. Time flies, doesn't it? Whether you're having fun or not."

Ace sputtered to a stop. I pitied the next jury that had to listen to his closing argument.

"What are you trying to say? Why did you call your friend?"

"He butchered your chickens."

"He did what?" I sputtered, madder than a wet hen. "How could you do that? They were *my* chickens. Where are they?"

"He killed them humanely, cleaned them, cut them into serving portions, and put them in your freezer. He said to be sure to tell you that the only way to cook hens that old is slowly, over low heat, with lots of liquid. He's got some recipes if you want. I told him he could keep the chicken fat."

"But I never got a chance to say good-bye."

Suddenly I was sobbing into the front of Ace's shirt. It wasn't just the chickens, of course. It was all the deaths: Ken, Lank, Balls. Laurelmere, the most boring place in the whole world, was falling apart just when I needed it to be safer than ever.

"There, there." Ace patted my back and offered me a clean handkerchief. Another clean, starched, and perfectly folded square of monogrammed linen.

I held it up and sniffed. Spray starch. "Where did this come from? I thought you couldn't get into your house."

"I did a load of wash here this morning. I hope that's okay. I didn't touch your clothes."

"I guess." I waved the handkerchief so the neat folds fluttered in the breeze.

"I know how to use an iron."

Okay, too much. I pushed myself away and turned back to the kitchen. "I want to see my hens." I opened the freezer compartment of my refrigerator. It was a Frigidaire my grandmother bought in a burst of extravagance in 1959. The freezer held little more than two aluminum ice cube trays and a pint of Ben & Jerry's Triple Caramel Chunk.

The Frigidaire was probably the least energy-efficient refrigerator ever made, but it held sentimental memories, and I couldn't afford to replace it.

Ace came up behind me. "Do you want to explain those dark brown ice cubes in your freezer, Sunny?"

"It's coffee. I make a big pot once a week, drink one cup, and freeze the rest in ice cube trays. When I want coffee, I just nuke a couple of cubes in the microwave. Saves time, money, and electricity."

"Ingenious. Crazy but ingenious."

"Whatever. I want to see my chickens."

"The chickens aren't there, Sunny."

"Where are they? You said your friend froze them."

"This way." Ace opened the door to my broom closet, which also is the entrance to the basement. He turned on the light and led the way downstairs. The walls of my basement are lined with metal shelves where I keep the produce I've canned: tomato juice, applesauce, asparagus, beans, and kraut. Sitting in the corner between the shelves, and humming like a nuclear power plant, stood a huge chest freezer, the largest I'd ever seen.

"What in the world?"

"Relax, it has the highest Energy Star rating of any freezer made. It runs on pennies a day, I promise."

I lifted the lid, expecting to see the corpses of my hens huddled at the bottom like pennies in a wishing well, but no, they were on a wire rack wrapped in freezer paper and labeled with the date and contents: organic, free-range, stewing hens. The rest of the freezer was filled with covered dishes.

"What are all those casseroles? Does your friend cook, too?"

"No." Ace shrugged. "They're from the good ladies of Laurelmere, who have been coming by all afternoon to hold my hand and offer comfort during my time of need."

"The good ladies of Laurelmere? Ah, you mean the cougars."

Ace was rich, single, handsome, and he knew how to use spray starch. No wonder the ladies of Laurelmere were after him, the same ladies who wouldn't give me the time of day.

"Yeah, the single, windowed, and divorced. Their concern for my well-being is one of the unanticipated benefits of having my house blown up." He smiled happily. "Like moving in here."

I snapped my fingers. "Earth to Ace. Come in, spacewalker. Come in."

He blinked. "What's wrong?"

"What's wrong? Your house blew up, idiot. I'm glad you're happy camping out here, but you can't stay forever."

"Sure, no problem. I was planning to remodel anyway. My house was functionally obsolete. Only three bathrooms, the basement rec room hadn't been updated since *The Brady Bunch*, and the closet space is totally inadequate."

"So you need his *and her* walk-in closets for both your wardrobes?"

"Give it a rest, Sunny. Someday that snarky mouth of yours is going to get you in real trouble. Anyway, the house was fully insured for the replacement value, dwelling and contents. I've been paying the damn policy for twenty years now and it's time to collect. I've already called my architect."

"I'm so happy for you."

Not.

CHAPTER THIRTEEN

Back in Kokomo, my foster mother always told me, "Don't waste your time envying people who are rich. Lead your life so they will envy you." Mom was big on character, honesty, and hard work, but I became a mortgage banker anyway.

So now with a mental salute to Mom, I decided I would not envy Ace. But darn it, I sure was irritated. What was it with rich people? His house blew up and he was delighted. It was a chance to rebuild, remodel and expand, using the insurance company's money. I, on the other hand, wasn't even sure I had home-owner's insurance. Ken said he'd take care of it. He had a buddy that would give us a good deal. I said fine—end of story.

Even if I had insurance, however, I didn't want to wait around to see if the killer would blow up my house, too. And, without the photo of Ken, there was no point in calling Stanislaus and asking her to reopen the investigation into the Cross-Dressing Poker Club Murders.

I could sell my grandmother's house and move out of Laurelmere, of course. But I didn't want to give up my dream of a safe, secure, and organic home. And I didn't want to abandon the only place in the world where I had roots.

As much as I hated to admit it, Ace was right. We needed Mac to find the killer and turn him over to the cops.

So I called Mac and invited him to dinner and a council of war.

Much to my surprise, Mac sounded relieved, almost happy

with the invitation. I think it was the offer of food that roped him in. Judging from the smells that wafted over our fence, his daughter-in-law, Nasreen, was a fabulous cook. But I imagine she made Mac wash his hands and put on a clean shirt if he wanted a seat at her table.

I was in no position to be that picky.

But Ace was. He offered to host our meeting at the Laurel-mere Golf Club, and I accepted. I'd never been in the club—membership fees were in addition to our astronomical home-owner association dues—so dinner was a chance to see how the other half lived.

I just hoped I wouldn't see how the other half died.

I showered, dressed, and checked on my chicks. They were awake again and happily pecking on the sides of their cardboard box home. Meanwhile, Ace hauled Mac from his basement apartment. When I walked outside, they were waiting for me in Ace's bright red Jaguar SL convertible, which was idling at the curb and filling the air with exhaust. He needed to find a fancy mechanic to go with his fancy wheels.

"You're planning to *drive* to the clubhouse?" I asked.

"Sure. Hop in." Ace leered at me. "I'll switch places with Mac and you can sit in my lap."

"No way. It's only five blocks. I can't believe you want to drive."

Ace and Mac exchanged glances. Someone sighed. Ace turned off the engine, and they extricated themselves from the beast's tight embrace. I had spiffed up a little with a strapless sundress, eyeliner, and lip gloss, and I had shaved my legs again—twice in two days, a record since Ken's death. Ace wore Laurelmere causal: sports coat, polo shirt, slacks, and moc-casins without socks.

Mac was resplendent in a maroon and green plaid kilt with a light green thread running through it. The kilt was pinned in front with a silver brooch in the shape of a thistle. He wore knee-high stockings and a shiny black jacket so old it was turning green at the shoulders and cuffs. Underneath the jacket was a navy-blue soccer jersey. Mac had trimmed his eyebrows and, although I couldn't confirm it, I was willing to bet he had put on a clean T-shirt. I had never speculated about Mac's underwear—boxers, briefs, or a thong—and despite the kilt I wasn't going to speculate now.

Just as long as he was wearing *something.*

Heads swiveled and conversation stopped when the three of us entered the clubhouse. I felt just like I had when I started fifth grade in the middle of the school year in Kokomo. Everyone else knew their role—the jocks, the class clown, the nerds, the popular girls. They had probably known since kindergarten. I was the only stranger, and my place was at the bottom of the totem pole.

Just like then, I set my jaw and concentrated on not tripping over my own feet.

The maître d' led us to a table conspicuously in the middle of the busy dining room. We were arranged like the centerpiece of a natural history diorama at the Burke Museum: *Homo homicidous.*

Once we were settled and the conversation around us resumed, I gawked like a tourist. The clubhouse was the oldest structure in Laurelmere, a little brick jewel used by the developer to sell homes when the community was nothing more than pretty sketches on a drawing pad. The ceiling rose two stories to an open peak, a design horribly inefficient to heat in the winter, but which kept the dining room cool and breezy in August. Behind the mullioned windows inset with leaded glass, the setting sun cast a soft golden glow across the tables. Long chandeliers with painted glass bowls, originally fitted for gas, hung from the ceiling, and an enormous fieldstone fireplace dominated the south wall. The polished wooden floor was covered with Persian carpets, lustrous with age.

The linen-covered tables were far enough apart to ensure private conversation. The china bore the coat of arms of the golf club, a griffin clutching a nine iron in each talon.

"Do you see something on the menu you'd like to try?" Ace asked. "Or do you want me to order."

That sounded good—right up until Ace told the waiter, *"Emincé de veau à la crème."*

"I refuse to eat veal," I said.

"You speak French?"

"Mai oui. But don't change the subject. I won't eat veal."

"Don't be ridiculous. The chef here does a lovely job. It's moist and tender with just a hint of *je ne sais quoi."* Ace kissed his fingertips extravagantly and grinned at me. I wasn't distracted—not even *un peu.*

"Do you know where veal comes from? It's the flesh of baby calves that are taken from their mothers, put in little cages, and force-fed milk until they're fat enough to slaughter. They aren't allowed to move around because they might develop connective tissue, which can be a little chewy. Unless the veal is certified free-raised, I won't sit here while you eat it."

I threw my napkin on my plate and pushed my chair back, bumping the waiter who looked as old as the building. He tottered and dropped his pencil.

"Sorry." I bent and retrieved the pencil for him.

"Okay, Sunny. Sit down. Calm down. We'll have line-caught Copper River salmon instead. Is that humane enough for you?"

"Yes. Thank you. At least the salmon had a chance to escape."

"We'll eat the dumb ones that didn't. That's Darwinian, right?" Ace finished giving our order. As soon as the waiter had shuffled a couple of feet away, Ace turned to me. "Do we have to experience a save-the-planet outburst every damn time? Give it a rest, will you?"

"The gal's right, Ace, about yer veal. Put a sock in it."

"Would that be an Argyle sock?" Ace pursed his lips and studied us, tapping his fingernails against the table as if we were an interesting species of alien life.

The waiter reappeared, cradling a dusty bottle in his arms as tenderly as a shoebox of newly hatched chicks and distracting Ace, who went through the whole wine-tasting ceremony with an expression of total engagement. Mac and I glanced at each other, and I hid my giggles in my napkin. Mac, of course, would have "none of ye muck" and demanded beer.

"We have all the domestics," said the waiter, "but may I recommend a draft Bass?"

"None of yer English stuff. Don't you have Belhaven?"

"Excellent choice," said the waiter and bowed.

I asked for cold water from the tap, no ice. Numb with disappointment, the waiter disappeared into the kitchen.

The important question of libations settled, Ace rapped his knuckles on the table. "Meeting called to order."

"Aye, aye." Mac saluted gravely and I bit my lip. I hadn't felt so giggly since I was caught passing notes in the fifth grade.

Ace eyed him suspiciously, but Mac, bless his heart, kept a straight face.

"Now," Ace continued in his best lecturing-to-the-junior-associates voice, "we're all agreed that the police have got this murder-slash-bombing case all wrong. Balls Spaulding is not the perp. Right?"

I nodded, but Mac harrumphed. "Yon detective, Stanislaus, seemed like a right canny gal to me, for all that she's one of them bloody Poles. If she says yer mate, Balls, done it, then she's probably got her reasons."

"But—"

I put my hand over Ace's. "You have to tell Mac about the poker club. The whole story, the unexpurgated version, or he'll never understand why you're not satisfied with the official explanation. If it helps, I'll start with the picture I found in Lank Lungstrom's hand."

Ace took a fortifying gulp of wine. "Okay."

I leaned close to Mac. "Here's what happened the day of the murder. After you left my house to go fishing—"

I felt a feather-light tap on my shoulder. "Aren't you Mamie Burnett's granddaughter?"

I turned to see an old lady hovering over my shoulder. Despite the heat, she was swaddled in a lacy white shawl over a long-sleeved lavender print dress. When she moved, she released puffs of violet-scented powder overlain with sherry, something I hadn't smelled since my grandmother's funeral. She squinted at me through her glasses and pulled a handkerchief from the alligator-skin purse hanging at her elbow.

"Yes, ma'am."

We all stood. I felt an impulse to curtsy but bobbed awkwardly instead. "I'm Sunny Burnett. And you are?"

"Elizabeth Jordan. I was your grandmother's best friend for years and years. You're the spitting image of her, my dear, as she used to be."

"Thank you very much," I stuttered, tongue-tied with pleasure.

"She was so proud of you, Sunny. I know she's resting more comfortably knowing that you're living in her home."

"So good of you to stop by, Mrs. Jordan," Ace said. "Won't you have a seat?"

"Oh, no. Must rush. I wanted to let you know, Mr. Pennington, that the homeownership association has agreed to a twenty-thousand-dollar reward for information that leads to the capture and arrest of the person who killed Lank Lungstrom. Will you please put together the paperwork?"

"Twenty thousand." Ace gulped. "That's very generous. It

will be a substantial hit to the association's bank account."

"Don't worry about that. A few of us have agreed to contribute what we can."

"Thank you, Mrs. Jordan. Let's meet tomorrow and get the details firmed up. Are you sure you don't want to have dessert with us?"

"Thank you, no. I'm having dinner with some old friends. Of course, at my age, all my friends are old friends." She waved gaily at a group of white-haired ladies at a far table, then peered at Mac. "I don't believe I've had the pleasure."

"Angus MacDougall, ma'am. Pleased to meet you."

She nodded at his jersey. "And I'm pleased to see you're a soccer fan, Mr. MacDougall. What do you think of our Seattle Sounders?"

"They're grand, mum. Just grand." To my astonishment, Mac blushed, a deep, painful red that mottled his cheeks and brought out beads of sweat on his forehead.

So that's what Mac looks like when he's telling a lie, I thought.

Elizabeth Jordan clasped her hands together, releasing more puffs of violet-scented powder. "I'm so glad you think so. I have a small stake in them, you know. Only enough to make life interesting. Escort me to a game and tell me what you think of the owners' boxes. Unless, of course, you already have season tickets, Mr. MacDougall."

"No, mum. That I do not."

"Then Sunday at three o'clock," Mrs. Jordan said with a flirty smile. "I'll pick you up at two. And let's plan on a bite to eat afterward."

"Thank you, mum."

Mrs. Jordan laid her hand on my arm. Her fingers trembled lightly against my skin. "I understand you have a splendid crop of tomatoes."

"You know about my tomatoes?"

She smiled. "Laurelmere is really just a small town. We know everything about each other. You must stop by and tell me your secret. I love homegrown tomatoes."

"Of course. Why don't I bring you some?"

"Lovely." Her fingers tightened. "Your grandmother always wondered if you had brothers or sisters, dear. Do you know?"

"What?" If Mrs. Jordan had whacked me with her walking stick, I couldn't have been more surprised. "No, there's only me. Besides, isn't that a question for Jessica?"

Mrs. Jordan tapped her lips with a finger. "Your mother has always been, ah, economical with the truth. She doesn't use a pinch more than she has to."

Despite my confusion, I had to chuckle. "That's exactly right."

With a wave and a badly suppressed hiccup, Mrs. Jordan twirled away.

"She's had a tot too much of her afternoon sherry," Mac said as we resumed our seats.

"I think she's got you lined up for husband number four," Ace replied. "Watch your step. The word around town is that she wore out the first three and it wasn't playing football."

"Watch yer tongue," Mac growled, but he straightened his shoulders in a studly way.

The waiter wheeled the serving cart to our table. The salmon was splendid, but the vegetable side dish was an undistinguished, overcooked mess of French-cut squash and green beans. No wonder rich people hate vegetables.

"Are you really going to the soccer game with her?" I asked.

"Of course. She knows all the old secrets about Laurelmere."

"And that's going to help you find the killer?"

"It's a place to start, lass."

"Okay." I moved the vegetables to the edge of my plate. "Back to the murders. Ken had a secret, Mac." I took a deep breath.

"He were a lumberjack?" Mac tapped his nose with his

forefinger and winked at me.

"A lumberjack? What in the world do you mean?"

" 'I'm a lumberjack and I'm okay.' "

I was completely floored. Mac was quoting a classic Monty Python skit about cross-dressing. So he knew Ken's secret, too. Good grief. Mrs. Jordan was right about Laurelmere. Everyone knew everyone else's business. I glanced at Ace. He sat slack-jawed, seemingly as stunned as I felt.

"You knew about Ken?"

"Aye, lass. Dinna ya know?"

"No, Mac. I didn't know. I mean, yes, I found out about Ken's lumberjack traits, but no, I didn't know that you knew about him." I took another deep breath. "Did Ken tell you about the poker club, too?"

"Nae."

Quickly I explained about the club and named the members: my husband Ken (a former alcoholic who had been dry for nine years until he supposedly died while driving drunk), Lank Lungstrom (shot to death in my yard), Balls Spaulding (killed in the explosion), Ace (house blown up), and Ollie Milliman, insurance agent, who was still alive and kicking. Ace confirmed Ollie's status.

"All in the past three months?" Mac asked.

"Yes," Ace answered.

"And you dinna tell the police a word about the poker club?" Mac brought his fist down on the table, bouncing the wineglasses and knocking a salad fork to the floor. "Good God, man. How in the world do you expect the force to find a killer with their hands tied behind their backs and wee blindfolds over their eyes?"

"An excellent question, Mr. MacDougall," a harsh voice said. "And I'm very interested in your answer, Mr. Pennington."

We looked up to see Detective Stanislaus staring at us, a

smug smile playing along her thin lips. Behind her, the waiter stood waving his hands and making the universal gesture for "don't blame me."

I suddenly remembered what happened after I got caught passing notes in the fifth grade—I was sent to detention every afternoon for a week.

It was time to 'fess up.

CHAPTER FOURTEEN

Ace and I spoke at the same moment, tripping over each other's words.

"What are you doing here, Detective?" Ace asked.

"Have a seat," I said and pulled out the empty chair.

Detective Sergeant Stanislaus fit surprisingly well with the casually swank atmosphere of the golf club. She wore a discreetly checked navy-blue jacket over a light green silk tee and khaki trousers with front pleats that strained over her massive thighs. Still no jewelry, no makeup, no hair stylist, but on the other hand, no coffee stains or cigarette burns. I was pretty sure wearing a jacket in this heat implied she carried a gun in a shoulder holster, but I didn't ask.

Stanislaus ignored Ace and me. Looming over our table, she glared at Mac. "What are they hiding?"

Mac harrumphed, but he didn't spill the beans. Possible he didn't know which beans to spill first.

"Please sit down." Ace rose and pointed to the empty seat. "We're about to order coffee and dessert. Won't you join us?"

"Thanks, I've eaten." She jerked her head at a table in the corner, where a man in slacks and a polo shirt hunched over a cup of coffee. I recognized the police chief from his picture in the paper that morning. The chief was short and barrel-chested, a thick, concentrated man, like potato soup left too long on the stove. A bottle blonde with too many bangle bracelets on her thin wrists whispered furiously in his ear. The chief saw us staring and gave a preoccupied wave.

"The chief wants me to set you straight," Stanislaus said.

"Set us straight?" Ace repeated with a bland smile. "I wasn't aware we were in danger of being crooked."

Suspicion washed over Stanislaus's face as if she thought she was being played. Before she could answer, I glanced around. "I want to talk to you," I said, "but not here."

Seattle may have many great locations for informing a police detective you've been withholding evidence in a high-profile murder investigation, but the Laurelmere Golf Club is not one of them. I saw too many rheumy eyes turned our way, too many hands cupped behind hairy, geriatric ears. If I was going to convince Detective Stanislaus that Ken's death was tied to the Cross-Dressing Poker Club Murders, if I was going to persuade her to pull the investigation back from the FBI, I needed to find a more private spot to make my case.

Also, I needed time to figure out what to do if Ace denied the whole feather-boa thing.

I motioned to our audience and said, "Let's go somewhere else."

"Are you inviting the chief and his wife, too?" Ace asked.

"No." Stanislaus and I answered simultaneously. We stopped and studied each other, suspicious of our sudden agreement. For my part, I trusted Stanislaus to handle the information about the poker club responsibly. But the chief was an unknown and as for his wife—well, Mom always said, "Never trust people without a bit of meat on them."

Next to her stylishly thin body, I was sure I'd bob like a water balloon.

Ace signaled for the check. After scrawling his name on the tab and putting the cork back in the wine bottle, he walked quickly out of the clubhouse, the bottle tucked under his arm. I hurried after him. Detective Stanislaus and Mac trailed behind us, arguing in furious whispers like an old married couple.

I caught up with Ace at the entrance to the parking lot. "You can't take an open wine bottle out of a restaurant. It's against the law."

"This is not a restaurant, it's a private club. And this bottle isn't just wine, it's a two thousand and six Trittenheimer Apotheke Spatlese. I'm not leaving it for the busboy to swig down with his Whopper and fries." Ace glanced around the parking lot. "Where's my car?"

"We decided not to drive, remember?"

"Oh, yeah, save the planet." He grinned at me. "For a second, the thought of a killer on the loose in my neighborhood drove baby polar bears out of my mind. We can't talk to Stanislaus standing here on the sidewalk." He raised his eyebrows. "What do you want to talk to her about anyway?"

"I want to know how much trouble we're in."

"Trouble? For what?"

"For withholding evidence in a murder investigation."

Ace snorted. "We didn't withhold evidence. We withheld guesswork, speculation, and questions about possible connections among the victims. Connections, I might add, the police should have been able to uncover without any assistance from us civilians."

"I want to tell her about Ken's photograph."

"You don't have the photograph."

"I still want to tell her. And I'm going to tell her about the poker club, too."

"I'll deny every word."

"You admitted it to Mac."

"No I didn't. If you think back, *you* told Mac that Ken was a cross-dresser. I didn't say a word."

"But—"

"We're going to stick to the original plan, Sunny. You call

Mrs. Jordan and arrange to chat with the old Laurelmere hens, the gossipy ones, not the egg layers. Mac will tell you what questions to ask. If you turn up something useful, we'll go to the police. Otherwise, we'll let it ride."

"Until someone else is killed?"

"You mean a person, not a baby polar bear?" Ace tightened his mouth and shrugged. "Could be my theory is wrong."

I didn't know what to say. I believed the picture of Ken in drag was tied to the murders; otherwise why would Lank Lungstrom have been carrying it when he was shot?

On the other hand, despite Ace's assertion, I was pretty darn sure Detective Stanislaus would be pissed because I hid the photograph, maybe even pissed enough to throw me in jail for interfering with a crime scene. So that was a reason to keep on keeping quiet.

On the other hand (the third hand?), if the police were going to understand the connections among Ken's death, Lank's murder, Balls's death, and the explosion in Ace's basement, they needed to know about the feather-boa aspect of the poker club, which meant outing Ace. And Ace's reputation with his fellow lawyers, judges, and other assorted rich people in Laurelmere wouldn't survive exposure as a cross-dresser. A reason to keep my mouth shut.

On the other hand (I was up to four hands by now), from a purely selfish point of view I was beginning to realize that my grief counselor was right. I needed to move on with my life. But my feet were stuck in emotional Qwikcrete as long as I didn't know the truth about my husband.

Ken had fooled me about cross-dressing and the poker club. What other secrets had he hidden from me?

Had he gone back to drinking? Did he use drugs? Had he been partying the night he died? Partying with someone like Balls Spaulding? Or with the person in the photograph? Was she, or he—I couldn't tell from the fingernails alone—a transvestite, a drag queen, a prostitute?

Or had the Cross-Dressing Poker Club Killer murdered Ken and managed to get away with it by somehow making his death appear to be drunk driving?

Horrible as it seemed, murder was the least odious option.

If Ken had been murdered, I could hang on to my belief that our marriage—my happiness—had been as real as it felt.

So what to do about the police and the picture? I was still debating, and Ace was still watching me speculatively, when Stanislaus and Mac caught up with us.

"Let's go to my house to talk," I said to Stanislaus, hoping inspiration would strike if I had a little more time to think. And an infusion of chocolate. "I'll make coffee and see if one of those casseroles in the freezer is really a plate of brownies."

"Sounds good." Stanislaus paused by the door of a Crown Victoria. "Meet you there?"

"How about giving us a lift?" Mac countered. "We walked all the way over here."

He made it sound as if we had trekked across the Olympic Mountains barefoot in the dead of winter, shooting bears and drinking their rendered fat to stay alive.

"Okay. But you've got to lose the skirt," Stanislaus said with a smirk.

"Don't be daft, Detective. I ain't driving around with my bloody arse hanging out." Mac's Scottish burr grew thicker as he spoke. "Besides, it's no skirt, it's a kilt and a fine 'un, too. This here's the MacDougall tartan, and it's got a long and proud history, starting in 1284 with—"

Stanislaus rolled her eyes and unlocked the car doors. "Tell me about it while we drive." She glanced at Ace and me. "Coming?"

"We're going to walk our wine bottle home." Ace assumed

116

his lawyer voice. "That way we won't put you in a compromising position vis-à-vis the State Liquor Control Board, Detective Sergeant."

"You are so considerate, Counselor." Stanislaus may have slammed her car door a little harder than necessary, a natural civil-service-employee response to being patronized by a richer-than-God attorney.

When Stanislaus arrived at my front door after dropping Mac at his apartment, I put her to work setting up a table and chairs on my back deck. The coffeepot burbled, and Ace chipped apart a stack of frozen chocolate chip cookies. I filled a colander with tender young green beans and Bambino cherry tomatoes. I'd raised the tomatoes in wire cages. This late in the season, I had to stand on tiptoe to reach the highest globes. I rinsed the vegetables and put the colander on the table next to my seat. Folic acid and a little organic roughage would do me a lot more good than chocolate.

I checked on my baby chicks, who slept, fat and fluffy, in the middle of their dish of crumbles. I turned off the overhead light and gently shut the bathroom door. When I returned to the deck, the scent of coriander, cumin, and turmeric floated in the air, which meant two things: Mac's daughter-in-law was grinding spices for curry and her kitchen window was open so she could spy on me again.

"Here's what we didn't tell you, Detective," Ace began when we were settled on the deck with mugs of strong coffee.

"Keep your voice down," I said, nodding at Nasreen's window.

"Okay." Ace regained control of the conversation as effortlessly as he produced that unending stream of neatly folded handkerchiefs. "The dead men, Lank Lungstrom and Wallace Spaulding, were members of a weekly poker group that met in my media room. The bomb was planted in the exact spot where we held the game."

Ace sat back expectantly waiting, I guess, for her jaw to drop.

"I know that," Stanislaus said.

"You do?" Keeping his eyes focused on her face, Ace fumbled for a cookie.

"Sure. Mr. Spaulding's ex-wife told us all about the poker club."

"*All* about it?" The cookie crumbled in Ace's white-knuckled hand.

"I'm not sure what you mean by 'all,' Mr. Pennington," Stanislaus replied, dusting a few crumbs from her jacket. "Mrs. Angstrom told me her ex-husband played poker in a house game here in Laurelmere. She also said he had been seeing a psychiatrist for the past two years. I can't share his diagnosis, of course, but his wife said she believed he was depressed. Do you have anything to add?"

Ace shook his head.

"Who's left in the poker club?" Stanislaus asked. "Besides yourself, I mean."

"Oliver Milliman. It's just him and me."

"Have you been in contact with Mr. Milliman?"

"In contact? You'd better believe I'm in contact. Ollie's my insurance agent. I'm expecting him to show up with a fat check any minute now."

Stanislaus sighed. "I mean, have you talked to him about the deaths of Mr. Lungstrom and Mr. Spaulding?"

"Yeah, Ollie is scared shitless. But I warned him. He can't leave town until he settles my claim."

This conversation wasn't getting us anywhere. Ignoring Nasreen's open window, I shoved my face between them and said, "If Wallace Spaulding planted the bomb, did he kill my husband, too?"

"Your husband, Ms. Burnett? Why would you ask that?"

"Ken was part of the poker club. And he died under mysterious circumstances."

"Your husband had a blood alcohol level well above the legal limit when he drove into a telephone pole and flipped his car, Ms. Burnett. I read the accident report from the Washington State Patrol. I'm sorry for your loss, but there was nothing mysterious about it."

"Don't believe the accident report. Ken wasn't a drinker. I told them that. He'd been in AA for over nine years."

"No longer a drinker but always an alcoholic." The detective's face softened marginally. I wondered if she was speaking from experience.

"That's true," I said. "But Ken would never drink and drive. Especially not that night."

"What do you mean, Ms. Burnett?" Stanislaus asked. "Why not *that* night?"

I sat back. Self-consciously I smoothed my dress over my stomach, revealing my baby bump. "I'm pregnant. Just over four months along."

Detective Stanislaus pushed her chair away from the table. She leaned back and folded her arms across her chest. She nodded to me. "And your husband knew?"

"We suspected. I had a doctor's appointment the afternoon Ken died to confirm the results of my home pregnancy test. Ken told me to call him as soon as I talked to the doc." I gulped. "But Ken's cell phone was turned off. Finally, hours later an officer from the state patrol came to the house and gave me the news."

"I'm sorry, Ms. Burnett. It sounds like a very difficult situation. Maybe that's why your husband was drinking that night. To celebrate."

"Don't say that. Don't blame my baby."

Tears pooled in my eyes. I brushed them away. "Someone killed Ken. Someone smart enough to fool you and fool the state patrol, too. I'm going to prove you're wrong about my husband. I don't know how, but I'm going to do it."

"Ms. Burnett, I'm warning you. Don't try to prove anything. If you should happen to come across any facts related to the murders, real facts and not just speculation, you need to contact me immediately. If your ideas have merit, I'll pass them along to the FBI. Otherwise, you have to accept that we actually do know what we're doing."

I hated the tone of Stanislaus's voice. So calm. So self assured. That voice had haunted my childhood—smug, well-fed adults offering stupid advice to a homeless kid. I wanted to pull the picture of Ken wearing his red boa from its hiding place and rub her nose in it. I wanted to say, "See? You don't know everything. Here's one really important fact your so-called murder investigation failed to uncover."

But I didn't have the picture anymore.

I don't know when Ace had taken my hand, but now he squeezed it and said, "You're expecting? That's wonderful, Sunny. I'll do whatever I can to help."

Like a gas main exploding, a shriek erupted from Nasreen's kitchen. "Expecting?"

I knew that voice. Oh, crap.

Seconds later, a blur of slithery silk and French perfume dashed through the gate that connects our backyards.

My mother, Jessica, rushed up the steps to the deck and latched onto my arm. "You're expecting?"

"What are you doing here?" I cried, trying to pull away from her embrace.

She clutched me harder. "Nasreen's showing me how to make fesenjan. It's chicken with pomegranate syrup and—"

"Ma'am, how the hell did you get past the security guards?" Detective Stanislaus asked, her deep voice halting the tug o' war.

Jessica dropped my arm. "And who the hell are you?"

I grabbed a handful of green beans from the colander and snapped them like firecrackers.

CHAPTER FIFTEEN

Jessica pulled herself up to her full five-foot-three, thrust out her 36DD chest, straightened the handkerchief hem of her flowered dress, and planted her silver sandals inches from Stanislaus's sensible pumps. She ran her eyes up and down the detective's clothing. "I *belong* in Laurelmere. And you do not."

"Jessica, stop it." I wanted to crawl under the picnic table. "You can't talk to her like that, she's a police detective."

"I will not be intimidated by the police state."

"Oh, good grief." I turned to Stanislaus. "I'm sorry. I can't control her. She's an ex-hippy and she's my mother. Sort of."

"Sort of?" Jessica squealed. "I'll have you know—"

I turned away, clenching my fists. *This time, I'm not going to let her get to me. No matter what she says.*

Meanwhile, Stanislaus had opened her cell phone. Making no attempt at secrecy she said, "Wilson, I want you to talk to the guard at the security gate at Laurelmere. Find out if—" She covered the receiver and glanced at me. "What's your mother's name?"

"Jessica Burnett Lee."

"If the guard has a record of Jessica Burnett Lee entering Laurelmere today. Call me back as soon as you know." She snapped the phone shut.

"Why are you checking with George at the security gate?" I asked Stanislaus. "You can't believe Jessica shot anyone."

"We're concerned about whether the guard's log is accurate.

I wanted to know if he writes down the names of people he knows, like former residents of Laurelmere, as well as strangers."

"I'm sure he does."

"We'll see."

"May I change the subject?" Ace asked. "That's why you've been such a nutcase about all this environmental stuff, isn't it? Because of the baby."

"Baby, baby," Jessica echoed softly like a mourning dove.

We all pretended not to hear her.

"Yes. I want my daughter to have birds and trees and flowers in her world." I smiled at Ace. "And, of course, baby polar bears."

"Her. Her." Jessica actually nudged Detective Stanislaus, who teetered stiffly at the edge of my deck like a granite headstone in an earthquake. "It's a baby girl. I'm going to have a granddaughter. Pink. I love pink!"

"But no killers." Ignoring Jessica, I glared at Stanislaus. "And no guilt. I don't want anyone—especially not you—to even hint Ken got drunk because of my baby girl."

Stanislaus sighed. "Ms. Burnett—" Her phone rang. She listened, nodded, and said, "Okay. She's on the guard's log. Got it."

"Of course. Ken would never drive and drink," Ace said. "We'll rule out suicide." He turned to Stanislaus. "So if Ken was murdered, do you think the perp was the same guy who got Lank and Balls?"

"Balls?"

"Wallace Spaulding. We called him Balls."

"No, I don't think the 'same guy' killed Mr. Burnett."

"Dahl," I interjected. "My husband's name was Ken Dahl."

Stanislaus grimaced. "Right. I forgot in all the confusion. Well, I'll tell you what I can. It'll all be public in a day or so anyway. Based on the evidence, the FBI has determined that Mr. Spaulding shot Mr. Lungstrom and then planted the bomb in Mr. Pennington's house. So far they haven't found a link to any known terrorist groups."

"Don't talk about that nasty stuff where the baby can hear you." Jessica put a death grip on my shoulder. She turned me away from Ace and the detective and talked directly into my ear, as if I were deaf, not pregnant.

"Have you thought about names, sweetie?" she said. "It's your decision, of course, but if you wanted to name her for her grandmother, I'd be thrilled. Jessica Ann Burnett, the Second."

"You can't call a girl 'the Second,' " Ace said. "That's only for men. Like me, I'm Horace L. Pennington the Third."

"Are you sure?" Jessica frowned. I could tell she was mentally thumbing through Emily Post.

"Yes, I'm sure. Although those idiots at the newspaper don't get it, either. Nowhere in any of the articles about my house exploding did they use my full name, including 'the Third.' They kept referring to me as Horace Pennington, which is my grandfather's name. He died fifty years ago. Never believe anything you read in the newspaper."

"Can you postpone this discussion?" Stanislaus asked. "I need to get back to my office before I hit retirement age."

"Okay." I covered my mother's hand with mine and braced myself. I was about to leap into an emotional quagmire. "Jessica, I need you to decorate the baby's nursery. I don't have your good taste and besides, I can't manage all the heavy lifting by myself. Do you have time to help me?"

When her squeals died down, I said, "There's a tape measure in the scissors drawer in the kitchen. Would you measure the windows in the nursery so we can shop the thrift stores for curtains tomorrow? And maybe a changing table?"

"Thrift stores? For my granddaughter?"

Something snapped. "Don't argue with me, Jessica."

She actually took a step back. For the first time in my life I had absolute power over my mother. If she wanted to see her granddaughter, it would be on my terms. Oh, I'd be a reasonable and righteous despot, but a despot all the same.

Jessica must have seen the glint of steel in my eyes because she nodded. "Oh, sweetie, of course. Whatever you say." She darted into the kitchen and started banging cupboard drawers.

"I can't find any paper," she called.

"There's some by the phone," I said.

"But it's all used. I need some clean paper to write down the window measurements."

"The paper is used on only one side. Turn it over. There's no point in chopping down a tree for scrap paper when I get a ton of junk mail everyday."

"I guess that's okay." A moment later we heard a sharp gasp followed by the castanet clatter of her high heels on the wooden stairs.

"Okay, we've got about fifteen minutes of peace and quiet," I said. "She moves pretty darn quick. Detective, you were going to tell us why the FBI closed the murder investigation."

Stanislaus glanced upward toward the rumble of Jessica shifting furniture in the guestroom-soon-to-be-nursery and cleared her throat. "First, the autopsy evidence is indisputable: Mr. Spaulding died from injuries he suffered in the explosion. A piece of shrapnel severed the artery in his neck and he bled to death within seconds."

"So Mac couldn't have saved him." I felt a spurt of relief. "Does Mac know?"

"I'll stop by his apartment and tell him when I leave here. Also, the ME did not find any evidence of injuries sustained prior to the explosion, no gunshot wounds, for example, or other trauma."

"But—" Ace stopped and glanced at me. "Do you mind if I ask a question about Balls's body, Sunny? I don't want to gross you out."

"Go ahead. You can't say anything worse than what I've already imagined." But I folded my hands over my stomach. Jessica was right. This discussion wasn't something I wanted the baby to hear.

"Okay." Ace stood and began pacing my small deck. Four steps, turn, four steps, turn. The detective was in the witness stand and I was in the jury box. The jury of one reached for another handful of cherry tomatoes.

"Detective, there must have been bruises on his body, from the explosion if nothing else. How does the pathologist know that Balls wasn't knocked unconscious before the blast?"

"Do you mean, did an unknown individual render Mr. Spaulding unconscious, set the explosive, and leave?"

"Yeah. Maybe detonated it with a cell phone. That's what terrorists do."

Stanislaus shook her head. "That's exactly the kind of bullshit a criminal defense lawyer might propose, Mr. Pennington: An unknown person with an unknown motive who, unseen, infiltrates a secure, gated community. Sorry, that kind of hypothetical might distract a jury but it flies in the face of the evidence. We concur with the FBI. Mr. Spaulding was acting alone when he blew himself up."

Ace stopped pacing. "And the weapon that killed Lank Lungstrom?"

"It was a Phoenix Arms HP25A. It's a single-action, semiautomatic, .25 caliber pistol, small and light-weight, easy to conceal. The state firearms expert determined that the weapon found next to Mr. Spaulding's body in your basement was the same one used to kill Mr. Lungstrom. The pistol was not registered. It was what is commonly called a Saturday night special and untraceable."

"Why didn't I hear a gunshot?" I asked. "Do you think he used a silencer?"

"Probably," Stanislaus answered. "We haven't found it yet."

"It usually takes weeks, if not months, to get that information about a gun from the state crime lab," Ace said.

"Not when the weapon is found in Laurelmere, one block from the chief's house."

"Okay." Ace shrugged. "Fingerprints?"

"No. The interior of the gun appeared to have been wiped clean. Any prints on the exterior were destroyed by the heat of the explosion. Get zinc hot enough and it burns."

Ace began pacing again. "But Balls Spaulding was a dentist, for God's sake. He specialized in fitting braces on spotty teenagers. I suppose everyone learns about fingerprints from TV, but what would an orthodontist know about explosives? Did he Google bombbuildingforwackos.com?"

"Mr. Spaulding was a munitions expert during the Vietnam War."

"Oh, I didn't realize that." Ace leaned against the wall, apparently to consider the detective's statement. Jessica's voice filtered into the quiet air, singing a nursery song off-key.

A shiver ran down my spine. Jessica was going to be a grandmother. Oh, dear Lord. What was I in for? Only five months of hell or a full eighteen years?

"Getting back to Lank Lungstrom." Ace's voice jumped a register. I glanced at him, surprised. "Did the police find anything on Lank's body or in Sunny's garden that would tie him to Balls or to any of the other members of the poker club?"

Oh, that's why Ace's voice had jumped. He was worried about the poker club.

"No." Stanislaus shook her head.

"Okay." Ace cleared his throat. "What about the fifth guy? Is Ollie Milliman in danger?"

"Like you, Mr. Milliman is one lucky man. If Mr. Spaulding hadn't died in the explosion, my guess is that he would have tried to kill you or Mr. Milliman or possibly both."

"So the investigation is closed."

"Yes, Mr. Pennington. Considered in its totality, the chief found the FBI's evidence persuasive and decided to close the case."

"I've never heard of the SPD closing a murder investigation that fast. There must have been political pressure from somewhere."

Stanislaus stiffened like someone had prodded her with a cornstalk. "I can't comment on the chief's decision. But all the pieces fit together, if you'll pardon the expression."

I had a horrible vision of poor Balls Spaulding. His pieces would never fit together again. Even if he had been responsible for the bomb, it was a terrible way to die.

"I see." Ace turned to me, the makeshift jury, and frowned magnificently. "I guess we're forced to accept the official disposition of the case, Sunny."

I bit into another cherry tomato. My deck was too small to hold *une paire d'* dueling attorneys cross-examining the witness, but I wondered if Stanislaus had even considered the possibility that Ollie Milliman was the killer.

"I'm not satisfied," I said. "If the case is closed, Detective, why did you follow us to the clubhouse? Why did you sneak up on us and eavesdrop on a private conversation?"

"Interesting point," Ace said, but he squeezed my shoulder like he wanted me to stop arguing.

"It was strictly a courtesy," Stanislaus growled. "Mrs. Elizabeth Jordan, your grandmother's friend, told the chief that the three of you were hatching conspiracy theories. The chief told me to make sure you understand the investigation is wrapped up. He doesn't want you to do anything foolish."

Stanislaus had the grace to look uncomfortable. We both knew that was a load of chicken poop. The police chief wasn't concerned about my welfare. He lived in Laurelmere, and it was the gilt-edged sanctity of Laurelmere he wanted to protect. But Elizabeth Jordan, that nice old lady in the shawl who smelled of violet bath salts, my grandmother's best friend. Why did she rat us out?

"What about motive?" I persisted. "In the official story, what's the explanation for Balls Spaulding suddenly going berserk? Why was there such a long time between him killing my husband and killing Lank Lungstrom?"

The detective sighed heavily, like an old dog curling up to sleep. "Ms. Burnett, a homicide investigator focuses on means and opportunity. Motive is something juries care about, a nice story that ties everything together. But in this case, the forensic evidence is so persuasive re intent that we really don't need to establish motive. And, to repeat, there is no evidence that Mr. Spaulding had any involvement in your husband's accident."

"So, if motive doesn't count, what we know about the killer is that he lives in Laurelmere or he can pass through the security gate without the guard seeing him. If we eliminate ghosts, we know he had access to a Saturday night special and he's an expert shot. And, of course, he could be a she." I scowled at Stanislaus. "Detective, it could be you. I assume you're an expert shot. You could have pulled a gun from the evidence room, and the security guard would let you through the gate without question."

"I resent the implication that I would tamper with evidence, Ms. Burnett." Stanislaus's voice could have refrozen the ice floes in the Arctic. Her eyes could have cut a new hole in the ozone layer. "You've been watching too much television."

"I never watch television. I don't even own a television."

"I don't care where you get your ideas from. You're wrong. I came to tell you the case was closed as a courtesy. I need to get back to work."

"So you refuse to reopen the investigation into Ken's death?"

"That's correct. I read the letters and email you sent to the State Patrol demanding they investigate the accident further. I could see that you were—" She swallowed and substituted "distressed" for whatever she had started to say. "I'm sorry for your loss, Ms. Burnett, but there really is nothing more to investigate." She stood. "Don't bother to see me out."

Ken's picture danced before my eyes. This was my last chance to tell her about it, my last chance to tell her the poker players were all cross-dressers, my last chance to change her mind.

I reached out and touched her sleeve. She turned and stared down at me.

I saw pity, but also stolid determination. I knew that look, I had seen it all my life from good-hearted, well-intended people busy following the rules and regulations, so busy with the rules that they couldn't hear me, couldn't see me.

In that instant I had a glimmer of understanding. I knew Ken didn't give a darn about the rules, never had. That's what I loved about him, still loved in spite of everything. And when Ken listened to me, he didn't worry about what I *should* say or what I *ought* to say, he listened to what I *did* say. He really heard me.

If only I could learn to listen that well to my daughter.

I stood. I had decided what to do. "Goodnight, Detective," I said and shook her hand. "I know you've helped all you can. Thank you for your time."

I watched Stanislaus's broad back as she walked through the kitchen in time to Jessica's delirious rendition of "Rock-a-Bye Baby." In a minute I heard the front door slam behind the detective.

I turned to Ace. "Call Mac. And Ollie Milliman. We're going to play poker."

"What about Jessica?"

"I suppose shooting her is out of the question."

Chapter Sixteen

After Detective Stanislaus dropped Mac at his basement apartment, he kicked off his shoes and poured himself a Belhaven. He sucked down a mouthful, then hung up his kilt and jacket, carefully smoothing out the wrinkles before he shut the closet door. He padded back to the kitchen, wearing only his football jersey and knee-high socks. He wasn't in any hurry to paw through the pile of dirty laundry on the bedroom floor for a pair of knickers.

When he'd first moved in, he'd had a few inadvertently intimate encounters with his daughter-in-law, Nasreen, which quickly led to an ironclad rule enforced on both sides: No one entered Mac's domain without knocking first.

With no fear of interruption, he took another swallow of beer, scratched his groin thoughtfully, and considered Stanislaus's position in the murder investigation.

When Mac had been part of the Strathclyde Constabulary, there'd been a couple of times when politics interfered with good police work. Not in a murder case, but he'd seen a couple of rapes and some drug busts that had been dismissed as naught but high-spirited pranks because Daddy, or in one case Mummy, was well connected. Cases like that left a burn in yer gut that took a shite load of pints to quench.

Today Stanislaus had exhibited all the symptoms of gut burn, including a fist-in-yer-face bellicosity that hadn't been present the night Ace's house blew up.

Stanislaus was too much of a professional to do more than tip him a nod and a wink during the drive from the clubhouse, but Mac knew she wasn't satisfied with the outcome of what that daft wanker, Ace Pennington, insisted on calling the poker-club murders.

But if he was right, and the chief had ordered the investigation closed for political reasons, so fookin' what? Stanislaus hadn't asked him to interfere—couldn't ask him to interfere. If Stanislaus had told the chief what she thought of his decision, her position on the job would be delicate enough without her inviting an outsider like himself to come tromping through the rye. Besides, she probably sensed his loyalty wasn't to the Seattle Police Department, but to that cheerful young woman, the aptly named Sunny Day.

And there was the rub. Mac believed—*knew,* fook it—the poor bastard found in Ace's basement wasn't the killer. If Mac was right, then Sunny was still at risk. Another gut burn calling for another swallow of Belhaven.

In the end, Mac's problem boiled down to one question: how to unearth a killer everyone else believed was dead.

That one problem spawned a whole host of smaller problems as dark and unknown as a badger sett. He needed to think on it.

Mac flipped on his telly and started his *Braveheart* DVD from where he and Pete had last left off. When his grandson dropped by, they automatically turned the movie on, part as background noise, part in defiance since Pete's mother, Nasreen, had banned violent movies for her thirteen-year-old son, and part as sheer male bonding. For a Bible-thumper, yon Gibson had a right deft hand with the muck and the gore.

Mac knocked back another couple of pints of Belhaven and was well on his way to Highlander heaven when someone banged on his outside door.

"I'm coming, I'm coming. Hold yer knickers."

Under his bed, he found a pair of boxer shorts, bright scarlet with black and white Scotties prancing across them, a gift from his daughter-in-law, which he so despised that, consequently, they were the only clean drawers left.

After pulling the boxers on and over them a pair of sweat-pants, Mac peered through the peephole and saw Detective Stanislaus standing under the security light. The frown lines on her forehead looked like they'd been etched with a dull blade. Despite her grim appearance, Mac felt a tickle of excitement. Mebbe her visit signaled the opening of a wee badger hole.

"I'll have tha' pint o' ale now," she said with a credible Scottish burr as he held the door wide. She fell onto his sofa like she lived there, picked up the remote control, and muted Mel Gibson's death agony.

Mac didn't bother to ask questions. He poured a Belhaven for each of them and set the brimming glasses on the coffee table.

Stanislaus looked at her glass. "That's pretty dark. Haven't you got something lighter?"

"I'd rather drink my own piss than light beer."

"That's not your piss in there, then? Good." She swallowed before he could answer.

"Now, luv." He shoved an open tin of salted peanuts across the coffee table in her direction. "Wha' fettle?"

She took another swallow and wiped her mouth with the back of her hand. "Speak English, for God's sake. How long have you lived in this country?"

"You can drink my beer or you can insult me. You can't do both." He emptied his glass and set it down with a thump. Stanislaus glared at him. She half rose, signed, sat back down.

"Sorry. That was rude."

"Ah, Detective. I'm sorry, too. I think yon killer is still out there. Don't you?"

CHAPTER SEVENTEEN

After Detective Stanislaus left, I begged Ace to help me convince Jessica that she did not have naming rights for my baby. "Jessica Junior. That's worse than Sunny Day. I don't want my daughter to be a joke in kindergarten."

"Sorry, Sunny. The first rule I learned in law school was never argue with a woman who changed your diapers."

"So far, I don't see much point in having an attorney."

"You've gotten everything a five-dollar retainer will buy you." He leered and waggled his eyebrows. "Now if you want to reopen negotiations on payment options, I'm ready to consider anything. And I do mean anything."

"Go away. Go back to work and gouge somebody rich."

"So I can afford to keep my indigent clients happy? Of course."

"You always have to have the last word, don't you?"

"Yep." With a smile and a nod, Ace left.

I walked upstairs to confront Jessica. I wasn't tiptoeing exactly, but I didn't make any effort to let her know I was on my way. And a good thing, too, because I caught her rummaging in my closet. I stopped in the hallway, appalled. Half an hour ago, I thought I had her over a barrel. But she must have guessed my threat was meaningless. I wouldn't really keep her away from her granddaughter.

But I would keep her out of my closet.

Jessica caught a glimpse of me in the full-length mirror and whipped around, dropping something white and frilly on the rug.

"Why, Sunny. I didn't expect to see you here."

"This is my house. Remember? And my bedroom. What are you looking for? The nursery will be in the guestroom across the hall."

Jessica shrugged her shoulders and plastered a coy smile on her face. "Your guestroom seems to be occupied. By a man. I thought I should leave his stuff alone. I didn't want to cause you any problems."

"And I'm supposed to believe that?"

"Sunny."

"Sorry, Jessica. I'm a little frazzled. Ace has been camping out in my guestroom while he decides what to do about his house."

"He's been sleeping there?"

"He hasn't been sleeping with me, if that's what you're asking."

"Good. A man will never buy a cow if he can get the milk for free."

"That's wrong on so many levels. First of all, I'm not a cow."

"And you're not a spring chicken either, honey. You're thirty years old, unmarried, pregnant, and unemployed."

"But I have plenty of food. Tons of homegrown vegetables and a freezer full of casseroles and organic chickens."

Jessica continued talking right over me. "You're living in a house you can't afford, and to top it off, you've got yourself mixed up with something pretty creepy. I think you should move out of here. For your sake and for my granddaughter's. Lawrence and I can help you find a nice little apartment somewhere and take this house off your hands."

Back in Kokomo, when I complained the other kids were picking on me, Mom would quote Eleanor Roosevelt: "No one can make you feel inferior without your consent."

Well, this time I was withholding my consent.

"No apartment, Jessica. I'm fully capable of managing my own life. By myself. In my own house."

"But, Sunny." She actually took a step closer and put her hand on my stomach.

I felt a jolt and then realized what it was.

"Oh my God," I cried. "I felt the baby move. It's the first time."

"She likes her grandma's touch." Jessica's eyes misted over. She patted my stomach and sighed wistfully. "There's nothing as wonderful as a baby. She's a gift from God."

Any normal person would have starting sobbing at this point, would have hugged her mother and forgiven her. But I wasn't a normal person. I was Jessica's daughter. Sensing she might be vulnerable, I asked the question Mrs. Jordan had raised at the Laurelmere Golf Club. "Do I have any siblings?"

"Siblings?" Jessica paled and turned aside.

"Yeah, you know. Do I have a brother or sister?" A gift from God that you gave away.

"Who put that idea in your head?"

"It doesn't matter. What's the answer?"

"I really don't think it's any of your business, Sunny."

"If you don't tell me, I'll ask Lawrence." My stepfather might have as much dramatic flair as a November drizzle, but he'd always been a straight shooter. I knew he'd tell me the truth.

Jessica stared at her hands and twisted her rings. Her engagement ring could have been a Cracker Jack prize. Her wedding ring, although less ornate, could have paid for a decade's worth of premium organic chicken feed.

"Don't ask Lawrence. I'll tell you the whole story." She slumped down in the chair at my dressing table like that sack of chicken feed and took a deep breath. "But don't interrupt me."

"Okay." I sat on the floor, my back against the closet mirror. The carpet tickled the undersides of my knees, and I smelled Ken's aftershave, which lingered on his clothes. I hated having Jessica in my bedroom. It held so many intimate memories of my too-short marriage, like that little white nightgown she'd found. I didn't want her destroying the last good vibes left in this place.

Of course, I was sitting on the exact spot where Ken and his "friend" stood to have their picture taken. That killed more good vibes than anything Jessica could do.

"You have a brother thirteen months younger than you," Jessica said slowly, as if the words hurt her mouth. "He was born in Chicago at Cook County General Hospital. In the charity ward. We named him Robert for your father. We gave him up for adoption." Her face crinkled, became the face of an old woman. "I never held him, never even saw him."

"What—"

"Don't interrupt." With her fingertips, Jessica patted her eyes dry. Those mink-fur eyelashes had to be preserved at all cost. "After Lawrence and I were married, we hired a private investigator to find Robbie."

I nodded. She didn't see me.

"Robbie had a difficult childhood, not like you."

Not like me? Homeless. Foster mother. Nits in my hair. That wasn't difficult?

"After high school he joined the army and supposedly became a member of Special Forces. He was scheduled to be discharged a couple of months ago. The investigator told Lawrence we shouldn't contact him. I don't know why. Lawrence wouldn't tell me."

She straightened up. "That's it. That's all I know about your brother."

Again, a different daughter might have hugged her mother at

this moment, offering reassurance and love. But I couldn't do it. I couldn't bring myself to look at her. Studying the carpet between my outstretched legs, I said, "Jessica, I am going to choose my daughter's name. Not you. Do you understand?"

"But Sunny, tradition—"

"Yes or no, Jessica."

"Okay. I understand." With a heavy sigh, she pushed herself upright. She checked her reflection in the mirror and fluffed her hair. The old woman was gone and Jessica was back, perky and brittle. "I'd better go now. Lawrence's invited some colleagues over for drinks, and I need to find a bartender and order munchies. It's too bad we don't have the Laurelmere clubhouse for entertaining."

"Yep. Too bad."

I stood in the bedroom doorway and watched her walk down the stairs. I listened to her open and close the front door. I swore I would be a different kind of mother. I wouldn't abandon my child, no matter what. Oh, I could understand why Jessica thought adoption might offer her son—my brother!—a better chance of happiness than living in our old station wagon. But it sounded like she had been wrong. Robbie had not lived happily ever after.

Maybe it was pregnancy hormones messing with my head, but I suddenly felt the need to find Robbie, to talk to him, to let him know he always had a home with me and as many chicken eggs as he could eat. But how could I find him? I couldn't afford a private investigator.

But I did have an attorney on retainer.

CHAPTER EIGHTEEN

After finishing high school in Kokomo, I attended Purdue University on a state scholarship that covered tuition but nothing else. Even though my foster mother helped all she could, I still ended up working the dinner shift at a steakhouse about twenty miles from home. Usually I'd climb into bed around midnight, completely exhausted, with no memory of anything that had happened in the previous eight hours.

The day after dinner at the clubhouse passed in a blur, just like that. I must have done something, because every once in a while I'd come out of my stupor and find myself staring at a stack of clean plates or a pile of freshly folded laundry. I do remember worrying about my garden. I had put off so many chores since Ace moved in: weeding, watering, harvesting green beans, and cleaning out the chicken coop. Which one first?

After I cleaned the bathroom, I stepped to my bedroom window and studied the garden below. Overnight, morning glories had snuck up on my corn plants determined to strangle them. Their white flowers waved to me from the corn tassels like defiant flags. The best way to get rid of morning glories is to pull them up by hand, making sure to get every last bit of the long stems that snake underground like fat white worms. It's also the most tedious way possible to spend an afternoon.

The thought of all that work was exhausting. The baby and I decided to take a nap instead. I awoke after nine P.M. when I heard footsteps in the hallway. Half-awake, I called out, "Ken?"

"Naw, it's me."

Ace, of course. How many more times would I wake up expecting to see my husband? For an instant the pain was just as sharp as the moment I learned he was dead. I wiped my eyes and realized I was starving—and I needed to talk to Ace about finding my brother Robbie.

"Dinner on the porch in five?" I called to him.

"Great. I'll take a shower."

After I dressed, I put a bottle of wine, a pitcher of tap water, two glasses, and a plate of my world-famous chilled pasta salad with pesto dressing on a tray. I carried the tray to the front porch and set it on the table next to the swing. Ace was right behind me.

"I'm starving," he said. "What is this stuff?"

"Delicious."

He poked the pasta with his fork. "I see something green."

"Basil, garlic, tomatoes, red peppers, green beans, and kale," I said. "All from the garden. And I made the noodles with my eggs, organic flour, and sea salt."

"And the vegetables were fertilized with the chicken manure tea in your water barrels? Did you wash them first?"

"Of course. And the thing about chicken manure is that you can wash it off, unlike toxic chemical fertilizers that accumulate inside lettuce leaves and you don't even know it."

"I suppose it's too much to hope for a meal without a lecture."

"I'm just trying to be informative."

Ace took a small bite of my salad and swallowed, but he didn't ask for the recipe.

We sat down in the swing, which faces Nasreen's house, but I couldn't take my gaze away from the ruined hulk across the street. The patrol car that had idled in front of Ace's home since yesterday was gone, but yellow police tape hung from the rhododendron bushes, and I smelled the acrid odor of explosive.

What would it take to make Ace's house livable again? How soon could he move back home? He had to be gone before the baby moved into the guestroom.

"The insurance adjuster is arriving tomorrow," Ace said, reading my thoughts. "I've already told him I want to scrap the whole damn thing and rebuild it from scratch. Maybe set the house back from the street another ten or twelve feet."

"Hmmm."

When Laurelmere was built in the Roaring Twenties, the developer created wedge-shaped lots to maximize the number of houses that could be squeezed around the golf course. Most homes had only token front yards so the back was big enough for a swimming pool or tennis court or both. Over time the servants' quarters at the rear of each house had been converted into garages for the third or fourth car—or in my case, a chicken coop and tool shed.

"Rebuilding from scratch sounds like a big project," I said.

"Three or four months. I can be home in time for Christmas if I start right away."

"And I'll be eight-and-a-half months pregnant by Christmas. It seems impossible."

"Why don't you try to push her out before the end of the year? Or get your doc to schedule a C-section. It'd be a huge tax break, especially in your bracket."

"Ace, I'm not going to manipulate my daughter for financial gain. She'll come out when she's ripe and ready."

He shrugged and poured himself another glass of wine.

I started the swing moving. The night was gently illuminated by bluish beams from the theater-sized television screens in my neighbors' living rooms.

"If it weren't for all this light pollution, we could see the stars," I said. "That'd be nice."

"It'd be even nicer if we could watch the Seahawks' preseason football game with Kansas City," Ace countered.

I tensed, ready to leap into battle about cable television again, but Ace took my hand. "Don't ruffle your feathers, Sunny. I'm only kidding."

"Sorry. My sense of humor has evaporated. Jessica has that effect on me."

"I noticed. Do you want to talk about it?"

"You know my family's story. I'm sure it's a legend in Laurelmere. Jessica was a terrible mother. Pregnant at sixteen, not married to my dad, doing hashish, abandoning me in a foster home. All that stuff. And if she wants to make amends by becoming Super Grandma, that's cool. Good for her. The problem is, I'm not sure she knows how to be a grandmother anymore than she knew how to be a mother. And I'm positive I don't want her experimenting with my baby while she figures it out."

"If you don't want Jessica hanging around after your daughter is born, you may have to shave your head, glue a beard on the baby, and leave the country."

"I know." I took a deep breath. "Speaking of Jessica, I've another favor to ask you. Nothing to do with the murders."

"What is it now?"

"It turns out I have a brother. I want to find him." Rapidly, I repeated what Jessica had told me about Robbie. When I finished, Ace snorted.

"Great, that's all you need now," he said. "A long-lost relative looking for a handout."

"He's not looking for a handout."

"How do you know? If he finds out you live in a place like Laurelmere, he'll figure you can mortgage your house and bail him out of whatever trouble he's in."

"Don't condemn Robbie when you don't even know him."

"Look, Sunny. Anybody who meets you immediately figures

out you're a soft touch. You want everyone to be happy and eat their green and yellow vegetables. But the world's not like that. When this is all over, when your baby is born and things have settled down, if you still want to find Robbie, I'll help you. I promise. But not now."

"Okay. I guess I don't have a choice."

"That's a good girl."

I hate being called a good girl. It makes me want to smash something.

Nothing on my porch was worth smashing, so we sat quietly a little longer, swinging back and forth while the air slowly cooled.

Mac's son and his wife had remodeled their carriage house into a semiprivate apartment for Pete. The bottom story was a soundproof music studio, and the top floor was a bedroom suite with mullioned windows in the gables. The display on his oversized computer monitor was visible from my front porch.

Tall, skinny, and tongue-tied, Pete was the neighborhood go-to guy for technology problems. He had installed my wireless network, putting the router in my bedroom where it was protected from the bugs and dirt that accompany an urban farm. He fixed my computer so everything I did was backed up in the cloud, and he cleaned out a really nasty virus that had clawed its way through my system. The neighbors all agreed Pete was an off-the-scale genius, but who knew whether he'd use his magical powers for good or evil.

I'd bet Pete could find Robbie for me. And Ace would never have to know. Neither would Jessica. I smiled to myself and glanced at Pete's window.

The display on Pete's monitor changed from lines of print to soft-core porn. Pneumatic breasts filled the screen, expanding like pink balloons. Oh man, what would I do if Pete were my kid? I didn't have a clue.

Maybe I wasn't any more prepared to be a mother than Jessica was to be a grandmother.

"I have a proposal . . ." Ace's voice trailed off in the darkness. He squeezed my hand. It was the most intimate physical contact I'd had with a man since Ken died. My whole body felt warmed by the gesture.

"Yes?"

"Would you consider going out to dinner with me? A real dinner—candlelight, lots of steamed vegetables, and nonalcoholic champagne substitute with a milk chaser?"

I chuckled. "And no Scotsmen?"

"Nary a one. I promise."

I squeezed back, then pulled my hand free. "That's awfully sweet, Ace. I appreciate the offer. You've been really supportive the last couple of days. But after Ken, I don't think I want to get involved with someone who . . ." Now *my* voice trailed off. It was a night full of loose ends.

"Who's a cross-dresser?"

"That's right."

"I thought you loved Ken." Ace shifted his weight, rocking the swing. "I thought you understood men like him. Like me."

"I *did* love him, but I still don't want to do that again. Sorry."

Until this moment, I hadn't realized how strongly I felt. Ken had been wonderful, but once was enough. If I ever got back into the dating scene, the only person wearing a dress would be me. Suddenly, Jack Rabbit popped into my mind—denim shirt, tight jeans, cowboy boots. No way was he a cross-dresser.

"Okay, so be it." I heard Ace take a deep breath. "New topic. About the poker game you proposed having with Ollie Milliman and me."

"Yes?"

"What's the point?"

"I want to question Ollie," I explained, trying to remain

patient. How many times would I have to repeat myself? "He's the only member of the poker club who hasn't been attacked. The police think Balls died in the explosion before he had a chance to kill Ollie, but what if they're wrong? What if Ollie is the murderer? Or, if he's not the killer, maybe he knows something the police tabled when the FBI took over the investigation."

"So you're going to interrogate Ollie?"

The skepticism in Ace's voice was totally justified. I was no more prepared to be a murder investigator than I was to be a mother.

"I wouldn't call it an interrogation," I said, leaning back and setting the swing in motion again. "Maybe I can be a charming hostess and warm Ollie up, and then Mac can come in with the hardball questions. He's experienced at that kind of stuff."

"Always assuming Ollie can understand what Mac is saying. Have you noticed? His Scots burr gets deeper when he's pissed off."

"There's always that. Maybe you should question him, Ace. It's your line of work."

"No, I don't want to get involved. I want to leave it up to the FBI to nail the killer. I want to rebuild my house, move in, and move on. You should, too."

"I can't move on. Not until I get this thing settled. Not until I know why Ken died."

Okay, so I didn't need to wear my bunny slippers to sound like a whiney twit. But I felt like we were going around and around in circles. I needed to do something to break the cycle or twenty years from now I'd still be wondering what happened to my husband.

"If you're determined to play poker with Ollie," Ace said, "I think it's time we spread our cards out on the table face up. So to speak."

"What do you mean?"

Ace stood and braced his forearms against the porch railing, his back to me, like he was trying to get a closer look at the breasts hanging above the neighboring yard. They'd changed from pink balloons to tawny brown cones with nipples the size of half dollars. Did pubescent boys like Pete think real women had breasts like that? If so, adulthood was going to be pretty darn disappointing.

"Do you know why Lank Lungstrom was in your yard?" Ace asked abruptly. Maybe he hadn't been studying the breasts after all.

I thought about the torn picture of Ken I'd taken from Lank's hand. Lying in a firm voice, I answered, "No. I don't have any idea."

"I started to tell you about Lank and the photograph yesterday, but we were interrupted."

"By Stanislaus."

"Right. Anyway, the day before he died, Lank got an envelope in the mail, anonymous, hand delivered. When he got home from work and opened it he found a snapshot of himself and Ken dressed up, like they dressed up for the poker club. He spent all night stewing about it then called me at six o'clock the next morning. He demanded to know what was going on."

My heart sank. I could sympathize with Lank. What was going on?

Ken had kept so many secrets from me. Before he died, I thought we had a completely open and honest marriage, but he hadn't told me about dressing up at the poker club, hadn't told me about taking pictures. What else was I going to find out about my husband?

While I worried, Ace began to pace again, like his brain couldn't work unless his feet were in motion. I had a quick image of him on a treadmill in his office, interviewing clients as he trotted up a virtual mountain trail.

148

Ace must have mistaken my silence for understanding because he continued. "Lank thought I had mailed the picture to him. He was furious. He accused me of trying to blackmail him, which was total nonsense. First of all, there was no note demanding a payoff. And second, maybe a couple of years ago when his real estate business was booming, someone might have tried to put the squeeze on him. But not now. His net worth has tanked. Everybody knew that. I mean, consider what he drove: a three-year-old Caddy. What kind of serious real estate agent drives a car like that?"

"Three years old? Horrors."

Ace didn't hear my comment or he didn't care. "So even if I were the kind of person who would stoop to blackmail—and I'm not—Lank wouldn't have been my first choice."

"Who *did* send him the picture?"

"I don't know. It didn't come from me. The picture file on my computer is password protected, so I was pretty sure no one else could have viewed them. But when Lank came over on his way to work that morning, we went through the thumbnails anyway. We couldn't find that exact picture."

Ace turned to face me. He leaned against the railing and folded his arms across his chest. "The whole thing was baffling. Finally Lank admitted that he and Ken had been trying on clothes at your house, but he swore no one else was there taking pictures."

Each sentence felt like Ace had grabbed a hoe and was hacking away at my heart. The truth hurt, but lies would hurt even more. I bit my lip and said, "Then what?"

"Then Lank decided to come over and talk to you. He thought maybe Ken had somehow taken the picture and stored it on his own computer. Then, after Ken died, you printed it out and sent it to Lank. We all knew you are . . ." Ace sputtered to a stop.

"Poor. You can say it. Being poor isn't a crime, even in Laurelmere."

"Right. Anyway, the more Lank talked, the more agitated he got. If I hadn't taken the picture and Ken hadn't taken the picture, then someone outside our little group knew Lank was a cross-dresser. He was terrified about being exposed. It would have ended what's left of his real-estate business."

"So Lank left your house, walked into my yard, and then someone just happened to come along and shoot him?" I frowned, trying to imagine the sequence of events. "How could that be? Wouldn't you have heard something?"

"I shut my door when he left and went upstairs to take a shower. I wouldn't have heard a shot, especially if the weapon had a silencer."

All I had heard was a thud, and I was only ten feet from Lank when he died. I'd been around the corner of my house, but still I should have heard gunfire. I guess he was right about the silencer.

"But why would Lank and Ken get dressed up and take a picture at my house when all the clothes and makeup were in your basement? And who tore the picture? Who has the piece with Lank on it?"

"Good questions, Sunny. I don't know any of the answers. And it's too late to ask Ken and Lank."

I stood and paced alongside him. "Maybe Ollie will know. We've got to talk to him. Can't you call him right away?"

"Calm down, Sunny. I never met anyone who jumps into things like you do. Ollie's supposed to bring my insurance check over tomorrow. We can ask him then."

"I'm not going to calm down. Why didn't you tell me all this when Lank was shot? Why did you lie to me?"

"It wasn't a lie exactly. I just didn't tell you things I thought you didn't really want to know."

"You're fired. I don't want you to be my attorney anymore."

A flashlight beam swept across the yard and blinded me. I blinked. A black shape moved toward my porch. Then Mac shouted, "Guess what, Sunny? I told Detective Stanislaus about yer nancy boy. She's going to reopen the investigation."

CHAPTER NINETEEN

The next morning I wedged myself on the floor of my guest bathroom between the toilet and the wall and watched my baby chicks chase each other around the brooder box. The cool porcelain fixture was a pleasant contrast to the rising heat outside, but I noticed a fuzz ball of yellow pinfeathers clinging to the baseboard. Someone—that would be me—hadn't scrubbed the bathroom floor lately.

With Mac's appearance last night, Ace had finally realized he couldn't hide his cross-dressing from the police any longer. He walked back to his bombed-out house, moving as slowly as a shell-shocked soldier. I let him go, still trying to come to terms with his duplicity—and my own naïveté.

I'd always prided myself on my hard-won street smarts. Before I moved to Laurelmere, I never would have let myself be taken in by a smooth-talking lawyer in a three-piece suit, even a really cute lawyer in an Armani suit. Maybe the haze of deception that permeated my marriage to a cross-dresser had blunted my bullshit detector.

Ace had never cared about me. All that charm, the hand squeezes, the concern for my baby—it had been part of his plan to neutralize me and keep his secret hidden.

At least I was smart enough to turn Ace down when he asked me for a date. I didn't need my grief counselor to tell me it was too soon after Ken's death to even think about a romantic relationship. And when I *was* ready—in a decade or so—I wasn't going to get involved with another cross-dresser.

But refusing to get caught up in the whole dating scene wasn't the only thing I had to do. If I was going to create a calm, stable, and ecologically responsible environment to raise my daughter in, I needed to uncover all of Ken's lies and root them out. I had accepted him without question because I loved him, and because he'd been sexy as hell. Now I realized his passion for cross-dressing was like the morning glory vines that threatened to take over my corn patch: pretty, insidious, and perfectly capable of choking out everything in their path.

Ken would always be part of my life. My garden, my chicken yard, and my worm box each held a thousand memories of Ken. If nothing else, Jessica Junior—and I sensed a horrid inevitability about that name—would be here to remind me of him. Maybe her eyes would be like his, maybe her smile. Maybe JayJay—was that really any better than Jessica Junior?—would have her father's sense of the ridiculous. I hoped so.

But during the night I had decided to stop shielding Ken's memory. At seven A.M., after feeding my baby chicks, I called Detective Stanislaus and reminded her answering machine that I had phoned three times the previous day to say I had helpful new information about the murders. This time I said I had a photograph.

My sudden urge to be honest would have been more commendable if I had made the decision before Mac spilled his guts to Stanislaus about Ken, my "nancy boy." But once I gave her the picture, my involvement in the murders would be over and, best of all, I would never need to see my ex-attorney again.

I didn't trust Ace anymore. I trusted him less and less with every passing minute.

He had dismissed the whole idea of blackmail pretty darn quickly, and now that I thought about it, his presence on my deck when his house blew up smelled of alibi as much as of explosives.

Atomizing your home to cover up a Cross-Dressing Poker Club doesn't make much sense, but doing it to derail a potentially career-ruining murder investigation isn't beyond the realm of possibility. Ace was fully insured and, like he said, he had always wanted to move his house another few feet back from the street.

Pinning the murder on Balls Spaulding seemed too easy a solution, especially since Balls wasn't alive to defend himself. If Balls had been a munitions expert in Vietnam, wouldn't he have been smart enough to avoid being killed in the explosion? Once the cops had the picture of Ken and started looking in the right places, I was sure they could figure out why Balls Spaulding had been in Ace's basement when the bomb went off.

And why my husband had been murdered?

I couldn't quite decide why the police chief seemed willing to go along with Ace's explanation of events, but I sensed something moving under the placid surface of Laurelmere, something dark and murky that undulated like the worms in Mac's bait bucket.

While I waited for Stanislaus to call back, I checked the Twitter-bitch network (nothing new) and emailed Pete, asking him to help me find Robbie.

When my cell phone rang, I jerked up, bumping the lid of the toilet and scaring my baby chicks. They cheeped frantically and raced around their brooder box, knocking crumbles into their water dish. The food instantly dissolved into a thick, unpeckable paste.

I hushed my girls and answered the phone without checking caller ID, expecting Detective Stanislaus. Much to my amazement, Jack Rabbit said, "How are those Rhode Island Reds doing?"

"Thriving."

"Great. And what about you?" Jack had an odd tone in his

voice. He sounded younger, and nervous, like he was trying to think of things to say.

I rubbed my bruised hip. "Surviving. Nothing more."

Of course, surviving in Laurelmere was becoming a job in itself.

"I'm delivering produce to a couple of restaurants in Seattle. One of them has been a pretty slow payer, and he offered me a complimentary dinner for two to make amends. Want to join me?"

"Tonight?"

"No, tomorrow."

Now I recognized that uncertain tone in Jack's voice. He was asking me out on a date. Our first date. I smiled to myself. It was completely inappropriate. I was four months pregnant. I must still look pretty good, not a total water balloon after all, but a date? Not a good idea. I should turn him down.

"That sounds like fun," I heard myself say. "What time?"

"How about if I pick you up around six?"

"Great. I'll let the security guard at the gate know you're coming. Is it a casual kind of place or should I dress up?"

Now that I'd accepted, Jack voice flowed as smooth and yummy as sun-warmed honey. "It's pretty casual, but I would like it very much if you dressed up."

Of course you would, I thought as I closed my phone. *You won't wear a dress cuter than mine, and you won't lean across the table and whisper that your bra straps are killing you.*

Jack might be nothing more than a small-time farmer, scraping by on organic lettuce and a field of illegal marijuana, but at least he appeared to be honest about what he wanted. Nervous but honest. And who was I to be holier-than-thou about growing pot? My own father was still doing time in a federal penitentiary for a drug bust.

I was really looking forward to getting to know Jack better.

Maybe after dinner, we could come back here, split a bottle of sparkling water and wander through my garden. I liked to show off how much I could grow in such a small space, and Jack might have ideas for improvements. My Flat-of-Egypt beets, which I hoped to grow over the winter and eat until spring, had developed rust spots on the leaves. Maybe Jack would have a remedy I hadn't thought of yet.

Maybe he had a lot of remedies I hadn't thought of yet.

A clanging bell broke into my fantasy.

CHAPTER TWENTY

I opened my door to Detective Sergeant Stanislaus. The muscles of her square jaw were knotted, her eyes narrowed to suspicious slits. Detective Wilson flanked her right shoulder, his face equally grim. They seemed bigger than I remembered, fluffed up with righteous indignation like a flock of hens staring down a rat.

That rat would be me.

Behind the detectives, a blue-and-white patrol car idled in front of my home. Another cop car waited in front of Ace's. I watched Ace walk out the front door of his ruined house. Ash puffed around his feet with every step. He was escorted by a pair of uniformed officers and followed by a third officer who cradled a laptop computer.

Ace looked miserable, as only a soot-smeared attorney in wrinkled golf shorts and a day-old beard can look. Had he actually spent the night in his wrecked bedroom instead of a downtown hotel? As Ace ducked into the backseat of the patrol car, he shot me an imploring stare.

What did he want me to do?

This morning I had almost convinced myself that Ace had blown up his house so the police wouldn't find out about the Cross-Dressing Poker Club. Now I realized I must have been completely crazy. I couldn't imagine anyone choosing to be homeless, even temporarily. Especially someone who lived in a multi-million-dollar Tudor palace.

"What's happening?" I asked Detective Stanislaus. "You can't arrest Ace."

"You called me, Ms. Burnett. You said you have a photograph you took from Mr. Lungstrom's hand after he was murdered."

"I know I called you. But what about Ace?"

"Mr. Pennington will be helping us with our investigation."

I knew what that meant. Like me, they suspected my attorney of being the killer. Together we were sliding deeper and deeper into a pile of chicken poop.

"What about the FBI? I thought they were in charge of the case."

"Nope. It's been tossed back to us."

"So, not terrorism after all?"

"No comment."

"Come in, both of you," I said, stepping back from the doorway.

Stanislaus and Wilson squeezed their massive bodies into my narrow vestibule. My house seemed to shrink until it felt no bigger than a prison cell.

I hurried into the living room and motioned them to follow. "Coffee anyone?"

"No, ma'am. The picture, please."

"Well, there's a slight problem."

"Problem?" Detective Wilson rocked toward me. I took an involuntary step back.

I pulled *Urban Homesteading* from my bookcase and fanned the pages. "I put the picture here after you confiscated my clothing. But it's gone. It disappeared."

Stanislaus handed me a piece of paper. "I have a warrant that allows us to search these premises for a photograph. You'd better hope we find it. The penalty for destroying evidence in a murder case is quite severe."

"But I didn't destroy anything!"

Stanislaus tightened her lips.

I squinted at the paper, which was filled with lines of small type and signed at the bottom with a judicial flourish. "It says you are going to examine my computer, too. What's going on?"

I glanced at Detective Wilson, who stood behind Stanislaus, shoulders square, hands crossed loosely in front of his shiny brass belt buckle. *Ex-military,* his posture said. Also, *Go ahead, make my day.*

"During the previous search of your home, we discovered you own a computer and an InkJet printer capable of printing color photographs. We believe the picture you took from Mr. Lungstrom could have been a digital image stored on a computer and printed at home." Detective Wilson's voice quivered with majestic rage. "It may be too late to find the image, but we are checking the computers, printers, and cameras of everyone associated with Mr. Lungstrom's death."

"I didn't print the picture. I found it, just like I told you."

"You've told us a number of things, Ms. Burnett. Some of them appear to be true. Others are demonstrably false." Stanislaus wrinkled her nose as if she smelled a stinky pile of chicken manure.

"But my desktop computer's as old as dirt," I protested. "The lithium battery's dead, so if you unplug it to move it, you'll have to reset all the drive information and date stuff before you can do anything."

I was blathering again, filling air time while I tried to get my brain to work. It was a nervous habit I couldn't kick. Verbal diarrhea, my foster mom called it, which is totally gross, but, like so much she said, completely true.

Stanislaus stepped aside and nodded to Wilson. "Detective Wilson is the department's IT expert. I am sure he can solve any access issues."

"Okay. But you should know Pete—that's the neighborhood

computer geek—fixed up two login accounts, one for me and one for Ken. Ken used Quicken to balance his checkbook on the computer. He bought some bookkeeping software so he could manage his business accounts at home, but with building the chicken coop and all, he never got around to setting it up."

Oh man, like Mom always said, I needed Pepto-Bismol for my mouth.

Detective Wilson produced a small, black, leather-covered notebook and a matching mechanical pencil, both polished to a high sheen. "What's your password, Ms. Burnett?"

"Wormbin. No spaces, no caps. Ken didn't have a password."

Four months ago, after I saw Ken's checkbook showed a positive balance, $128.76, I'd put his computer files out of my mind. Like cleaning out his side of the closet, closing Ken's bank account was one more part of my husband's life that I hadn't gotten around to dealing with and, thank God, I didn't need to.

Two days after the funeral, his partner in the shoe boutique brought me a certified check and an offer to buy Ken's share of the business. He offered me almost three times what Ken had invested in the shop a couple of years ago, so I thanked him profusely and signed the bill of sale. If I pinched every penny until it whimpered, the money was enough to last me until Jay-Jay went to kindergarten and I went back to work.

Assuming the Great Recession was over by then and there were banking jobs to be had—other than robbing them.

"The computer's upstairs?" Wilson broke into my thoughts.

"Yes. In my bedroom."

Ninja-quiet, Wilson glided past us and climbed the steps. I didn't try to stop him. My bedroom was as clean and tidy as a nun's cell. Except for Jessica's invasion last night, nothing interesting had happened there in the last four months. I was beginning to believe nothing interesting would happen there ever again.

At the thought of sex, a wave of guilt surged over me. Ken's car crash was all my fault. If only I'd forced him to go to the doctor's office with me when I learned I was pregnant. Then he wouldn't have been driving around by himself that night. None of this would have happened. Ken would still be alive and—

"Ms. Burnett," Stanislaus rapped her knuckles against the bookcase to get my attention. "Are you completely positive you don't have the picture?"

"I'm sure. But when you find it, you know, you'll discover my fingerprints are all over it. I mean, I found it and everything."

"Found it on a murder victim and hid it. Thank you, Ms. Burnett. I'll take that into consideration. Do you mind telling me where the picture's been? The lab tech might need to know."

"I hid it in my kitchen compost bin."

"Compost?" Stanislaus winced. "So it might be stained?"

"Not might be. Is. Tomato. One-hundred-percent organic, if that makes a difference, forensically speaking. Any chemicals the technician finds have to be residue from the gunshot. Unless, of course, Lank used some kind of lotion on his hands. Ken did, but I'm pretty sure Bag Balm doesn't contain any artificial colors or preservatives."

"Bag Balm?"

"Yeah, it's meant for cow udders, but it's great for people, too, especially if your hands are dry or cracked from working outdoors. I can get you a sample if you want. I have a tin in the guest bathroom."

Drat. I was babbling again.

Stanislaus scowled. "Don't bother. I'll tell Forensics about the tomato stains."

I nodded.

"Anything else you care to add to your statement? Any other lies you want to confess?"

"No, I don't think so."

I still had a bunch of lies all right, but none I wanted to confess.

"Ms. Burnett, I am conducting a murder investigation. You are a witness in that investigation. Let me remind you that every statement you make must be complete and accurate. Failure to do so—"

"Quit threatening me. I get it. So I didn't want the whole world to know my husband wore a dress. Big deal. Don't make a federal case out of it. The FBI didn't." I grabbed the doorknob. "Good-bye." I needed to get back to brushing away the yellow pinfeathers behind my toilet.

"Not so fast, Ms. Burnett. I want you to accompany me downtown."

Detective Wilson chose this moment to come down my stairs. He carried my computer, the cord trailing behind him dejectedly. He walked out my front door without even acknowledging me. I snarled at Stanislaus and said, "Downtown? Now? But I told you about the picture. What more do you want?"

"I want to try something unusual. We're going to put you, Mr. Pennington, and Mr. MacDougall together in a small room and let you simmer until you all decide to tell us the truth."

"But I've told you the truth."

The totally humiliating, completely embarrassing truth, not the least of which was that my husband looked better in a peignoir and feathered mules than I did. Also—according to Ace—he owned a lot more peignoirs and mules than I did. Except for the chicks and Ken, my life was pretty much feather-free.

Stanislaus's shoulders rose and dipped, an "I-don't-give-a-darn" shrug. Ace had mastered that shrug. I was still working on it.

"But Ace is my lawyer. Don't we have attorney-client privileges?"

"Mr. Pennington said you fired him last night." Stanislaus set her jaw and stared at me.

"I'm going out for dinner tomorrow. At six. I've got a million things to do to get ready."

"You have a date?"

I knew what she was thinking. Pregnant, newly widowed, and already dating?

"No, Detective. It's not a date. A friend of mine, another farmer, is going to help me deal with some kind of blight on my Flat-of-Egypt beets. I can visit your office the day after tomorrow."

Stanislaus sighed. She was big on heavy sighs that invoked the full weight of the law. "Ms. Burnett, as it stands I could arrest you under RCW 9A.72.150, tampering with physical evidence, which is a gross misdemeanor under the laws of Washington State. If found guilty, you would be subject to incarceration in the King County jail for a term of not more than one year or a fine of not more than five thousand dollars, or both. Either penalty would seriously blight your social life not to mention your beets."

"Did you make a joke?"

"No, I did not. It is your choice, of course, but I strongly recommend that you accompany me to headquarters, answer my questions to the best of your ability, and hope that we conclude the interrogation expeditiously."

I decided to comply with Stanislaus's request. It seemed like my civic duty.

Also, I didn't want to give birth to JayJay behind bars.

"Let's go, Ms. Burnett." Detective Stanislaus swung my front door wide and gestured to the policeman sitting in the patrol car. "Officer Vanderhorn will drive you."

"Just one more minute. My girls need fresh water." I opened the door of the guest bathroom. The chicks greeted me with joyful peeps. Stanislaus peered over my shoulder.

"Exactly how many chicks do you have in that box, Ms. Burnett?"

"Didn't they teach you to count at the police academy?" I said. It came out a little more snarky than I intended.

"I see six. According to Title 23 of the city's Land Use Code, each household in Seattle is allowed three hens. Not six. Three."

"Those three belong to Mac." I pointed to the chicks preening themselves under the heat lamp. "They're over on a play date. Chickens are sociable animals."

"Play date? So tonight they'll be—"

"Back home at Mac's. Sleeping in their very own brooder." Or they would be as soon as I built one for them.

If Stanislaus had rolled her eyes any harder, they would have bounced off the ceiling.

CHAPTER TWENTY-ONE

Thirty minutes later, I stepped through the full-body metal detector at SPD headquarters. Stanislaus met me on the other side and escorted me to an interrogation room on the third floor.

The interrogation room was as bland as if it had been decorated by a dead person—beige walls, darker beige carpet on the floor, lighter beige paint on the ceiling. Fluorescent lights. Plastic chairs. Formica-topped table. Institutional pine air-freshener.

The only break in the blandness was an aperture in one wall, which anyone who had ever watched *CSI Miami* knew concealed a two-way mirror. Or did I mean a one-way mirror? Whatever it was, they could see me and I couldn't see them. I checked my hair in the mirror and shot the watchers a middle-finger salute.

I suppose I should have been intimidated. Maybe if I hadn't been a farmer. But police interrogation held no terror compared to the horrors I wrestled with every day: tomato worms, powdery mildew, and the gray garden slug.

What the room did hold was Mac, looking like an alert terrier in his blue and white Scots soccer shirt, and Ace, looking like a pathetic, middle-aged, homeless guy.

Which he was.

The two men stood as I entered, and Ace pulled out a chair for me. I couldn't help it, my heart beat a little faster when his shoulder brushed mine. So totally inappropriate.

Stanislaus's cell phone rang. Holding it to her ear, she left the room, shutting us in. The door lock clicked loudly. I turned to my former lawyer and said, "I want my retainer back."

Mac flashed his yellow-toothed grin, and Ace said, "Of course you do." He opened his wallet and pulled out five one-dollar bills. Wrinkled and stained, they were the exact same bills I had given him the morning Lank died.

That piece of business concluded, I really didn't have much else to say. I turned on my cell phone to call Detective Stanislaus and ask her to release us when she opened the door. Behind her in the beige hallway stood Detective Wilson, as inscrutable as ever. Stanislaus held a piece of paper in her hand.

"Detective Wilson found this document under your husband's login on your computer. It is date-stamped May thirteenth, which I believe was the day of your husband's accident. The file was in a folder of documents and was password protected. The password was not 'wormbin.' "

There was something portentous about Stanislaus's tone.

"What was the password?" I asked, although I was pretty sure I didn't want to know.

"Sunni." She spelled it out.

"You mean my name, Sunny."

"No, Sunni, like Sunni and Shi'a, like Iraq and fundamental Muslim terrorists. Wilson has turned your computer over to Homeland Security. Do you wish to make a formal statement about the contents of your hard drive?"

"Homeland Security? Because of a computer password? You've got to be kidding."

"Shut up, Sunny," Ace muttered, nudging me with his elbow.

Mac slammed his fist on the table. "So that explosion *was* a terrorist bombing. I knew it. I knew I smelled TATP."

Stanislaus silenced Mac with a cold glare. She stepped closer to me and said, "No, ma'am, I am not kidding. We are required to surrender your computer to the feds under protocols established by Title II of the USA Patriot Act of 2001."

Without dropping my gaze, I pulled the wrinkled dollar bills out of my pocket and slid them back across the table to Ace.

Still holding my gaze, Stanislaus walked over to my chair. She dropped a paper on the table in front of me, face up. "This is the document that Detective Wilson found under your husband's username. It appears to be relevant to your questions about your husband's death."

Stanislaus may have said something more. I don't know. My attention was completely fixed on the words that danced and wavered in front of my eyes.

Dear Sunny. I'm sorry, but I don't think I can handle being a parent. It wouldn't be fair to you or to the baby. So,

The rest of the page was blank. I pushed back my chair, jumped up, and faced Detective Wilson. "You bastard. I've never seen this paper before in my life. You made it up. You're trying to trick me."

The pity on his face was more than I could bear. The floor buckled under me.

I returned to consciousness sobbing into Mac's soccer shirt, which smelled like stale beer and fish bait. He was patting me on the back, holding me awkwardly so none of our intimate body parts brushed against each other. "There, there, lassie."

I thought of the half-finished letter on Ken's computer. If Ken really had written that letter, what had he planned to write after "so"?

So what?

So you'll have to get an abortion if you want me to hang around?

So long, sucker?

Or maybe: *So sorry, Sunny. It's over.*

Somewhere in front of me, a man's voice said, "Ms. Burnett, Ms. Burnett?" It was Detective Wilson. He shoved a box of tissue across the table. It seemed like a pretty empty gesture from the man who was meticulously destroying my life. Homeland Security? Good grief. The only security threat Ken had posed was to the pheasants and peacocks that donated feathers for his more extravagant outfits.

Stanislaus cleared her throat noisily. "We have additional questions for you, Ms. Burnett. Some of the pictures Wilson found on your computer may be relevant to our investigation of Mr. Lungstrom's murder. I'm going to ask Mr. Pennington and Mr. MacDougall to leave the room while I question you."

"No, don't do that." I clutched Mac's shirt so hard the top button popped off. It landed softly and invisibly on the beige carpet. "I'm not answering anymore questions. I'm going home."

"Are you sure, Ms. Burnett? We may be able to clear up this murder investigation right now."

"I have nothing to say. If you have questions about pictures of my husband, ask Mr. Pennington."

"Is he back to being your attorney?"

"Yes. No." I buried my head in Mac's shoulder.

I had clung to Mac after Ken died, just like I was clinging to him now. And the thought of clinging to him, or maybe it was the smell of fish bait, brought back a memory. A middle-aged woman—the insurance adjuster? the state patrol?—had delivered a cardboard box to my house a couple of days after Ken's accident. The bag contained the things they'd found in my husband's car.

Mac had been with me that morning. I was transplanting lettuce seedlings, seedlings Ken and I had started in the greenhouse, trying to convince myself that I could go on without him. I was crying so hard that I kept mashing the fragile stems between my fingers.

When the woman—short, squat, blonde, too many teeth—handed the box to me, I'd taken a cursory glance at it before I shoved it at Mac. I don't know what he had done with Ken's effects, but something told me I needed to find out.

CHAPTER TWENTY-TWO

Despite being trapped in an interview room too small to swing a dead cat, Mac was feeling bloody chuffed. When Ace's house blew up, Mac had informed Stanislaus the bombsite smelled like TATP, the explosive terrorists had used in the underground in London. But had she believed him? Hell, no. She'd treated him like last month's rubbish, fit to be swept up and tipped into the bin. But today the detective was humming a different tune. He couldn't resist shooting her a smug smile over the top of Sunny's head.

The smile wasn't reciprocated.

"Take me home." Sunny lifted her face from Mac's snot-soaked jersey and snuffled like a lost baby pig.

"Nae, luv." Mac peeled her away from his shirt, but she continued to cling to his arm like he were a bleedin' Mae West life vest. "We should hang around. If you've gotten yerself mixed up in terrorism, you'll be wanting the detective and me to sort it out."

"We don't need your help, Mr. MacDougall," Stanislaus said.

At the same moment, Sunny said, "But the FBI said it wasn't terrorism."

"And now the SPD has changed its tiny little mind," Ace interjected.

Stanislaus harrumphed but Mac agreed with Ace. He'd tried and tried to get on the same page as the detective and been rebuffed every time. But injured feelings were no reason to put

170

Sunny's freedom in jeopardy.

"I'd advise you to cooperate with the police as best you can," Mac said.

"He's right, Ms. Burnett." Stanislaus nodded ponderously. "I need to examine your husband's bank records and his cell phone log. Also, I'll need the names and addresses of his friends and business acquaintances, and—"

"Don't try to intimidate my client with an unwarranted fishing expedition."

That friggin' wanker Ace pushed back his chair and stood, releasing a puff of soot that grayed the fake wood-grain tabletop. He fanned five wrinkled dollar bills, proof of his standing as Sunny's attorney, before folding them into the pocket of his golf shorts. Then he crossed his arms across his grimy chest.

"This whole idea of terrorism in Laurelmere is ridiculous," Ace said. "What message would a terrorist send by bombing my house? 'Down with gated communities?' 'Stamp out faux Tudor siding?' 'Free the world from three-car garages?' "

He glanced at Sunny. "Don't say another word."

Sunny, exhibiting the good sense that Mac so admired, paid no attention to Ace. Neither did Stanislaus or Wilson. The detectives stood on either side of the door, not exactly blocking the exit, but managing to suggest that only a greased forward could make it through the scrum line. Mac recognized the technique. The Glasgow Celtics had used it effectively against Manchester United last season, but as a containment strategy it was overkill for a wee lass like Sunny.

Of course, Ace had fixed Stanislaus between a rock and a hard place. She couldn't detain Sunny without arresting her, and no American judge would sign an arrest warrant based on a suspicious password on the computer of an otherwise blameless chicken farmer. Not even a post-9/11 judge elected by the far right.

Meanwhile Sunny had begun to hiss like a teakettle on the boil.

She spat out, "Ken was not a terrorist. End of story." She clenched her jaw and headed for the door, dragging Mac behind her by the sleeve of his jersey. It was as compelling as a vise lock on his scrotum. His old dad had been wearing that shirt when the Celtics reached the finals of the European Cup in 1970. Next to his kilt—and his balls—the jersey was his most cherished possession.

At the last possible second, the detectives shifted clear of the doorway to let Sunny and Mac pass through. As they burst into the hall, Mac heard Stanislaus say, "Okay, Mr. Pennington. Sit back down. We're going to discuss the pictures on your client's computer."

Great idea, grill the bastard. If anyone was responsible for the explosion of crime in this world, it was the bloody defense lawyers.

Sunny paused and glanced over her shoulder at Stanislaus. "You can't—"

"Don't worry, I'll protect your interests. You just go on home." Ace waved his hand, lawyer-imperious despite his tramp appearance. "We'll talk as soon as I'm done."

"But—"

"Mac, get her out of here."

It was the first sensible thing Ace had ever said.

A few minutes later, Mac and Sunny stood outside police headquarters. Mac had reclaimed his shirt—and his balls. He surveyed the crowded intersection of Fifth and Cherry while Sunny caught her breath. After two weeks without rain and temperatures in the nineties, Seattle was beginning to look a little shopworn. A brown rim of smog hovered over Puget Sound, and Mount Rainier was hidden in a chocolate haze. Cruise boat tourists climbed up Cherry Street from the waterfront, all smiles and blather, but the natives exchanged edgy glances and wiped sweat from their necks.

Not Mac. He loved a spell of uninterrupted heat. August in Scotland was oft a fickle mix of rain and wind interspersed with bits of sunshine bright enough to make your heart ache. Global warming, no matter what Sunny might say, would be as welcome in Prestwick as Kate and William on a royal visit.

"I'm not waiting around for Ace," Sunny said. "Where's your van? I need to get to your apartment."

"My apartment?" Mac pictured his living room, strewn with dirty underwear, garnished with foam-streaked beer glasses. Had he remembered to throw out the bucket of fish guts? "You don't want to go there, lass."

"Yes, I do."

"What for? Are you looking for a hidey-hole? Don't be daft. If she's needing you, Stanislaus will get an extraction order or whatever the fook it's called in the States."

"No, that's not what I want. Do you remember a couple of days after Ken died? Some woman came by to drop off the stuff they found in his car. She had it all in a big cardboard box. Remember? I was a basket case, so you took the box and put it in your apartment."

"Yeah, I think I still have it."

"I need to go through that stuff."

"Are you sure? Yer bound to rake up some painful memories."

"Maybe so. Or maybe I'll finally figure out why Ken didn't call me that night. Maybe I can put this whole business to rest." She touched his arm. "The police haven't searched your place, right? So they haven't seen it?"

Mac nodded reluctantly. He knew where this plan of action was heading. Straight to a pig pile on the fifty-yard line.

Sunny tugged on his shoulder. "So, where's your van?"

"Officer Vanderhorn drove me here." Mac stepped to the

curb. "I'll flag down a cab."

"No. Let's take a bus. It's almost as fast and doesn't create as much pollution."

Mac felt his pockets. "I don't have anything smaller than a twenty."

"I think I do." Sunny turned out her pockets. "Rats. I gave those dollar bills to Ace."

That bloody wanker. Only Ace could screw up Mac's life by remote control.

A green panel truck stopped in the lane of traffic in front of them. Painted on the side of the truck was a six-foot-tall pink rabbit with white ears and a toothy grin. Circling the rabbit's head in gilt letters like a bleedin' halo were the words "Jack Rabbit Farms." Below the rabbit: "Fresh Organic Produce." Stomach-churning cute.

"Jack." With a happy shriek, Sunny ran to the curb and waved.

The cars backed up behind the green panel truck began to honk, un-Seattle behavior induced by the spell of nerve-shredding dry weather. The panel truck pulled into the three-minute loading zone in front of the police station, two steps away.

Sunny yanked open the passenger door of the truck and jumped in. A monstrously big black, curly-haired dog squeezed past her and leaped out—Teufel. He bounded through the crowd of startled pedestrians and leaped up to thump his front paws on Mac's shoulders. His long pink tongue flicked drool into Mac's face.

"He likes you," Sunny called from the front seat of the truck, her voice full of joy.

"Aye, lass." Mac wiped a long wet strand from his chin while he studied Teufel's black eyes. "Sure the bastard likes me. He'd like me baked, broiled, or fried."

Or maybe just plain raw.

Sunny leaned through the open door. "Jack can give us a ride home. Hop in."

Apparently Teufel understood the Queen's English. He turned around and leaped next to Sunny, who scooted closer to Jack. The dog settled down on the bench seat, completely absorbing all the available space.

Mac paused by the truck. Jack's arrival at the exact moment when they needed a ride was too bloody convenient. "Let's stick with the plan. I'll change my twenty and get money for the bus."

"Don't be silly. This will be a lot faster." Sunny grabbed Teufel's hindquarters and pushed him to the floor. Mac shuddered. He had always admired the wee lass, but never before had he noticed her resemblance to Queen Boudicca.

Which didn't mean she could handle Jack.

With a repressed sigh, Mac hauled himself into the truck and shut the door. Teufel settled on the floor between his legs, his breath hot against Mac's knees. Now, more than ever, Mac was glad he had not worn his kilt.

"Hey-ya, Mac," Jack said, his attention focused on his side mirror as he waited for a break in the traffic. "Next stop, the fortified gates of Laurelmere."

Despite the pleasantry, Mac had the distinct impression that he was cramping Jack's style. He smiled happily to himself.

The interior of the truck was blessedly cool and humid, even with the windows rolled down. Mac craned his neck and saw the back was packed with crates of fresh vegetables, all bearing Jack Rabbit Farms' pink bunny logo. Bags of ice flanked the boxes and dripped water onto the floor. Mac drew in a deep breath and thought he detected a faint hint of marijuana under the prevailing smell of organic greens. If Mac owned a truck packed with Schedule 1 drugs, he didn't think he'd be cruising police headquarters, not even in liberal Seattle.

Not unless he had a compelling reason.

"Making deliveries?" Mac probed, deliberately vague. "How does that work?"

One thing Mac knew: Farmer Jack liked to complain. All he needed was an opening.

"It's okay. I prefer to make my rounds before sunup, if I can. Traffic's a hassle this time of day, and if the governor keeps piling taxes on the price of gas so she can rescue the homeless, she's going to shut me down."

As he talked, Jack reached between Sunny's knees for the stick shift. With a groan, the old truck pulled into traffic, a maneuver that made Sunny flush and Mac hold his breath.

"So, what about you guys? What were you doing at the police station?" Jack continued. "Did they find the guy who blew up that house near you?"

"No." Mac felt no need to elaborate.

"What about the guy who lived there? Is he dead, too?"

"No," Sunny said. "Actually, Ace is staying with me until he can rebuild."

"Lucky guy." Jack chuckled grimly while he waited for the light to change. "I wouldn't mind losing my house if it meant moving in with you."

Sunny laughed. "Nothing like that. I'm just being neighborly."

Like so much of this encounter, Jack's clumsy attempt at flirtation made Mac's left foot tingle. He'd injured the foot during his first week in uniform thirty-odd years ago. He'd stumbled into a fight between two drunken louts in a back alley of Glasgow after last call at the neighborhood pub. As soon as he tried to separate the combatants, both men jumped him. Mac had given a good account of himself, pounding them with his truncheon until backup arrived. At some point during the melee, one of the buggers had stomped Mac's left foot and broken his toe. By the time his toe healed, it'd entered into the folklore of the station as a bugger detector as reliable as the desk sergeant's weather-forecasting knee.

When Mac retired, the toe had seemed to go into hibernation, too, but maybe this little dustup was what he needed to get it calibrated to American soil.

Jack changed lanes and headed north on I-5. He glanced over at Sunny. "What's the status of the police investigation? According to the Orting newspaper, the FBI is off the case. Do you think the cops know who the killer is or are they making it up as they go along?"

Sunny opened her mouth, ready Mac was sure, to babble like a Highland stream. For some reason he couldn't quite articulate, he didn't want her telling Jack anything they knew or guessed. With that spirit of self-sacrifice for which the Dumfries and Galloway Constabulary was renowned throughout Scotland, Mac aimed the toe of his boot at the soft underbelly next to Teufel's balls and kicked.

Chapter Twenty-Three

From the vicinity of my sandals, I heard a noise like a garden tiller slowly grinding cornstalks into dust. Instinctively my toes curled under. I looked down at Teufel. His growl deepened. He bared his fangs. Red lights flickered in his eyes.

With a roar, he leaped from the floor of the truck and tried to bury his teeth in Mac's neck.

I screamed, "Watch out!" and reached for the dog's ruff. It was like trying to grab a hurricane.

Mac threw a forearm in front of his face and thrust it between Teufel's jaws. He pushed the dog's massive head against the dashboard and pinned it with his other hand. His biceps quivered under the strain. I slid along the bench seat toward Jack, as far from Mac and the dog as I could get. Mac couldn't hold Teufel forever.

"Jack, do something," I squawked, clutching my tummy. I couldn't seem to breathe.

Jack was already yanking the truck across three lanes of traffic into the darkness of the tunnel under the convention center. Horns blared from every side, but he managed to dive into a clear spot on the shoulder of the freeway. He hit the brakes. I slammed forward. My seatbelt caught me right before I smashed into the windshield.

With a loud thunk, Teufel's head smacked against the dashboard. His jaws flew open. He slumped to the floor. Mac jerked his arm free, but shreds of his jersey hung from Teufel's teeth.

"Ye fookin' monster," Mac muttered under his breath, his growl as fierce and as full of spit as the dog's had been.

Teufel pawed cloth fragments from his mouth. He shook his head, snorted, and began to slurp noisily at his privates.

"What the hell happened?" Jack killed the engine. He unsnapped his seatbelt and turned toward me. His jaw knotted. A sheen of sweat covered his forehead.

Mac held his shredded sleeve in front of my nose. "Cast yer eyes on that. Yer fookin' monster liked to take my arm off. And my jersey."

I couldn't think about Mac's shirt. My heart was pounding. I still couldn't draw air into my panic-constricted lungs. If Jack wasn't such a good driver—and such a lucky one—my baby could have been killed.

Jack put his arm around my shoulders and wedged me tightly against his body. His chest felt as solid and secure as a sun-warmed rock. My heart rate thought about returning to normal.

"Mac, what did you do to Teufel?" Jack asked.

I was astonished at the mild tone in Jack's voice. If I could have untangled my tongue from my tonsils, I would have been shrieking like a banshee.

"It weren't me," Mac said. "It were tha' beast of yers. You ought to have tha' bloody thing put down."

I knew Mac was lying. I'd caught a glimpse of his boot poised next to Teufel's balls just before the dog attacked.

Mac shifted in his seat. Teufel raised his head and glared at him. I'd been right. There *were* red flickers in the dog's eyes.

"Mebbe you'd better take yon black devil for a walk and see if you can calm it down," Mac said to Jack, returning the dog's stare, flicker for flicker.

"Here?"

We all glanced at the side mirrors and studied our position. We were parked on the right-hand shoulder of I-5. Behind us, the freeway curved so sharply to the left that we couldn't see oncoming traffic. Ahead of us, the shoulder led in a straight line to sunlight and the Olive Street exit about a hundred yards away. Brave scatterings of Scotch broom were rooted in the cracks between the shoulder and the retaining wall. Their yellow flowers trembled with each passing vehicle. My insides sympathized.

"Yeah. Walking the dog is probably a good idea," Jack said.

"Not here." I stroked Teufel's head. "It's too close to the traffic."

"I'll keep him next to the wall. He's trained to heel."

It took Jack a couple of minutes to leash Teufel and get him out of the truck without stepping in front of the oncoming cars. Being Seattle, being August, all four lanes of the freeway were as congested as a smoker's lungs. How had Jack managed to cut across the freeway without killing us? I could only shake my head and press protective hands over my baby bump.

Mac and I watched Jack lead Teufel north along the shoulder. The dog stopped to pee on every piece of litter they passed. Too bad he couldn't pee on the idiots who'd thrown the garbage out in the first place.

I wrenched my attention back to Mac and glared at him. "What's going on? I saw you kick that poor animal."

"Tha' beast almost destroyed my shirt." Mac touched the torn sleeve of his jersey. His cheeks puffed in and out. He waggled his finger at me. "It were yer fault, lassie."

"My fault? You go completely wacko and it's my fault? I don't think so."

"I couldn't think of any other way to stop yer gums from flapping."

"What are you talking about?"

"You were going to blab everything about the murder investigation to Jack. I could see it coming. I had to stop you, lass. Kickin' the bloody dog was my only choice."

"You old goat. I can talk to anyone I want to, Jack included."

"But not about the murders, luv. Didn't Ace tell you to keep yer mouth shut? Isn't he yer bloody lawyer?"

"He meant I shouldn't talk to the cops. And I didn't."

"Naw." Mac put a heavy hand on my shoulder. A faint odor enveloped us. Fish guts? "You shouldn't talk to anyone. Not until this whole thing is settled. I was a policeman since before you were born, luv, so trust me. I know yer sweet on tha' farmer bloke, but you never know who's a snout and who isn't."

As usual, I understood only about a third of what Mac was saying, but he seemed sincere, and he'd sacrificed his beloved soccer jersey to keep me quiet.

I raised my hand in the Girl Scout salute I'd learned from my foster mom in Kokomo. "I promise I won't blab to Jack, not even if he puts burning splinters under my fingernails."

Mac frowned. "I'm serious, luv."

"Okay, okay. I understand. I won't talk to Jack about anything except farming. And chickens."

"Brilliant."

We waited in the cab while vehicles of all sizes roared past us, shaking Jack's truck and forcing carbon monoxide into our lungs. I didn't like sitting here, not one little bit. It wasn't good for me and it was probably terrible for poor baby JayJay.

And I had run out of things to say to Mac. In full-blown Scottish cop mode, he was truly irritating, and a little bit frightening. His high-handed action had almost gotten us killed. But I remembered what Mom had told me: "Keep your beeswax to yourself." I was sure she would agree with Mac. The uproar in Laurelmere, whether terrorism or not, wasn't any of Jack's beeswax.

Except Mom wouldn't have tried to kill me, just to make her point.

A cell phone rang. I dived for my purse and Mac pulled a phone from his pocket.

"You have a cell phone?" I couldn't believe it. Mac with an electronic gadget was as unlikely as fresh corn in January. He checked a text message and opened the truck door. "I've got to go, luv. Don't forget yer promise."

"Where are you going? Wait for Jack. He'll drop you off."

"Can't wait. And I'm not riding anywhere with tha' fookin' dog. Sorry." Mac slammed the door. He took a step away from the truck, turned, and looked back at me, opened the door again. He leaned in and shook a finger in my face. "Mind. Don't forget yer promise. Keep yer trap closed tight."

I nodded. He shut the door again and started trotting south along the shoulder of the freeway back toward downtown, in the opposite direction from Jack and Teufel.

Five long minutes later, Jack returned to the truck, leading the dog. Both of them seemed to have mellowed considerably, as if they had ingested some of Jack's homegrown weed.

"Where's Mac?" Jack asked, opening the passenger door for Teufel.

"He took off. Someone called him, but he wouldn't tell me what's going on."

Jack shrugged and sat behind the wheel. Teufel settled onto the seat in Mac's spot. Crowding me against Jack, the dog went back to licking his balls. He seemed to be enjoying himself.

Jack turned on the engine. "There's a tavern at the next exit. Want to stop for a pint and a burger? I can drive there on the shoulder without trying to squeeze back into traffic."

"No, thanks. I've got to get home."

I knew Jack would have accepted a counteroffer of lunch on my deck, maybe a fresh herb omelet, a glass of Chardonnay for him, water for me, and a consultation about my blighted beets. But I wasn't quite ready to invite Jack into my world. The mere fact that my body had been so happy to snuggle against his was a warning sign. *Calm down, take it slowly,* I thought. Keep some daylight between his thighs and mine.

He started the engine. "But dinner is still on for tomorrow?"

"Of course." I nudged Teufel with my hip, first subtly, then forcefully, trying to get him to move over, but he wasn't going to be dislodged from Mac's seat. He seemed to have grown bigger since he attacked Mac, puffed up with the doggy testosterone.

Jack flashed a grin. He reached past me and pushed Teufel back down on the floor. "He likes sitting next to you. Can't say I blame him."

I smiled back a little desperately as Jack shifted into first gear and crept along the shoulder to the exit. Before things went much further, I was going to have to tell Jack I was a widow. But how? I hate the "W" word. Why wasn't there something else that didn't sound so—well, so old, so grim, so desperate?

Fifteen minutes later I was still debating what to say as Jack pulled the truck up to the security gate at Laurelmere. He leaned out the window and called, "Hey."

The guard nodded at him through the window and pushed the button to open the gate. "How's it hanging, Captain?"

"Fine."

"Who you got with you?" The guard leaned sideways, and I waved. George was in his fifties, a retired military man who was very proud of his army career. Right after we bought our hens, his wife had fallen ill, and I had made her crème caramel from my organic eggs. George claimed my custard had brought her back to life. An exaggeration, but very sweet. As soon as I had a minute, I was going to ask George if he had any contacts in Special Forces who could help me track down my brother Robbie.

"Mrs. Burnett? Is that you?" From the tone of George's voice, you would have thought I had morphed into a drunken slut roaring home at three A.M. I'd forgotten about his conservative outlook on life. I guessed we were done exchanging recipes.

"Hi," I called back, aware that Jack's body had stiffened. From the corner of his eye, he glanced at my ring-less left hand but didn't say anything until he'd driven through the gate and stopped next to the golf course.

"*Mrs.* Burnett?" Jack said, with a deep emphasis on my honorific.

"Yeah. I guess."

"You guess?" Jack frowned. "Either you are married or you aren't."

"I'm a widow." There it was—the W word.

Jack leaned away from me until he was tight against the door.

"I'm not contagious," I said.

"Yeah, but." Jack swallowed. His hands whitened where he clutched the steering wheel. "The man who died in your yard. Was he your husband?"

"No. He was a neighbor. I didn't really know him at all. My husband died three months ago in a traffic accident."

It was a sentence I had worked hard to perfect. Right after Ken's death, I'd poured out the whole story to anyone who seemed remotely interested: the clerk at the grocery store, the gas station attendant, the guy who came to read my water meter. Then I'd gone through a period when I couldn't mention Ken without sobbing. But now I had that sentence, "My husband died three months ago in a traffic accident." I had practiced in the mirror until it was almost perfect. Nine words I could say without crying, without stammering, and without embarrassing my listener.

Now all I had to learn was to say, "I'm pregnant."

CHAPTER TWENTY-FOUR

Jack had tried to deliver my chicks the morning that Lank was shot, but he hadn't been able to penetrate the police barricade. Now I directed him through the winding morass of culs-de-sac and blind intersections that make Laurelmere's streets a trap for the uninitiated. When he pulled to a stop in front of my house, I saw curtains twitching in my neighbors' windows. The Jack Rabbit Farms logo, a pink bunny with a golden halo, was so not tasteful.

I didn't see any trace of Mac. The Mini Cooper belonging to his daughter-in-law stood next to where Mac parked his van. The splatter of oil that marked Mac's spot bore an uncanny resemblance to road kill, skunk maybe, or a fat old possum.

Or maybe a giant pink rabbit.

Mac's daughter-in-law, the Twitter-bitch Nasreen, had been the first person in Laurelmere to discover our assistant grounds-keeper was having a torrid affair with the nanny at 1775 Rainier Drive, and the only person to broadcast it in a series of salacious tweets. I was so far out of the gossip loop I didn't even know Laurelmere had an assistant groundskeeper. I couldn't make sense of the tweets until Mac filled me in on the whole story.

I prepared myself to read the tweet about Jack driving me home. Something like: WHAT PREGNANT WIDOW IS DATING A GIANT PINK BUNNY? TBC.

I wasn't worried about getting into Mac's apartment to search for the box of Ken's belongings. After my husband died, Mac insisted that we exchange house keys in case of an emergency. But I didn't want to deal with Nasreen. If she knew what I was after, she'd never let me leave without pawing through the box herself. I might have to stage a fit of hysterical sobbing to escape unmolested.

Right now, coming up with a fit of hysterical sobbing didn't seem that much of a stretch.

"I didn't know this was where you live," Jack said. "You've made nice use of limited space."

"Thanks."

He parked the truck in front of my house and scrutinized my yard. I had planted Shuksan strawberries in shallow raised beds that terrace up the slope from the street to the front porch. I also had put dwarf Rainier cherry trees in the parking strip. Both crops were finished for the year and the fruit trees drooped dejectedly. A thick mat of dried leaves circled the trunk of each tree. I hoped they could survive another six weeks until the rains came.

"You should have treated those cherries with dormant oil spray and lime sulfur before they budded out in the spring," Jack said. "They're covered with scale. I can see it from here."

"Yeah." Last spring I had been burying my husband, not worrying about the darn cherry trees.

Teufel had followed us out of the truck. Now he lifted his leg on the nearest strawberry plants. I made a mental note to put in a dog-proof fence before they blossomed in the spring.

"Who's that guy on your porch?"

I glanced up. "I don't know. I'm not expecting anyone."

A stranger leaned against the wall next to my rooster-festooned hose caddy. His body was hunched in the cramped and focused position of someone texting on his phone. I didn't recognize his lanky silhouette, and the grapevines on the arbor over my porch created lacy shadows that hid his face.

A week ago when my faith in Laurelmere's security system was intact, I would have been curious about a stranger on my front porch, but not worried. I would have assumed he was a neighbor I'd never met or a deliveryman, someone George had vetted before letting him through the gates. Now I felt a twinge of anxiety.

Make that more than a twinge. As Ace said—either the killer lived inside the security gates or the security gates had failed to keep him out. Either way, strangers meant trouble. And even if he was harmless, I didn't want to deal with him right now. I needed to search Mac's apartment for the box of Ken's stuff.

"Oh, crap. Whoever it is, I wish he'd go away."

"Want me to handle it?" Jack asked.

"No, thanks. I'll talk to him."

I hopped down from the truck and walked up the path. Heat rose in waves from the concrete sidewalk, making my eyeballs feel like eggs in a skillet and my inner thighs itch. The sweet, foxy smell of ripening grapes hung like a curtain over the path, and I heard honeybees buzzing overhead as they fed on oozing grape juice.

I called, "Hello? Can I help you?" and mounted the steps to the porch. Behind me, Teufel barked, one fearsome bark.

The man straightened abruptly, but his thumbs finished hammering out his text message. The pattern of his silk suit, brown stripes shot with flecks of red, reminded me uncomfortably of Teufel's eyes. The collar of his white shirt drooped around his narrow neck, and his tie (a tie? in this heat?) dangled limply. His eyes darted nervously from my face to something over my shoulder and back again. His mouth twitched and his eyebrows jumped.

"Is Mr. Pennington home?" the man asked. "He's not answering his phone."

His voice sounded anxious, high-pitched and shrill, as if he suspected the Laurelmere killer was hiding in my scale-covered cherry trees.

Behind me, the door of Jack's truck slammed. Teufel barked again. The stranger glanced over my shoulder. His eyes widened. Maybe this guy was scared of organic farmers. Or maybe dogs. I wanted to tell him that Teufel, like most American males, was perfectly amiable until you kicked him in the balls.

But before I could question him, the stranger thrust a business card in my hand, a card as sweat-stained and wilted as his tie. It read: OLIVER "OLLIE" MILLIMAN, CLAIMS ADJUSTER, STATELY HOMES INSURANCE. FIRE, THEFT, CASUALTY, LIFE. "SUPERIOR PROTECTION FOR SUPERIOR PEOPLE."

"Tell Ace his insurance claim has been denied," Milliman said. "Also, headquarters canceled his policy. I'm sorry, but that's the breaks. I gotta go."

"Denied? Canceled? Why? I thought you were his friend."

I was still protesting when Oliver Milliman vaulted over the side of my porch, landed neatly on his loafer-clad feet, and disappeared into my backyard.

"Hey, come back here!" I shouted and ran to the railing. "You're trespassing."

"Hold up a minute," Jack called out at the same time. "Listen to the lady."

I turned around. Teufel and Jack were galloping toward me. Sometimes Jack was in the lead, sometimes the dog was. They crossed the finish line simultaneously and stood panting in front of me.

"Do you want us to get him?" Jack asked. "Maybe he's the guy the police are looking for." Teufel strained at the leash, white teeth flashing, waiting to hear Jack yell "sic 'em."

Or "kill."

I weighed the consequences of all three of them tearing

through my vegetable patch and shook my head. "That guy's probably in Tacoma by now."

I lied. My yard is completely fenced. Ollie Milliman was trapped back there with my chickens. But I could deal with Ace's insurance adjuster. I didn't need Jack's help and I really, really didn't want Teufel's.

Jack signaled Teufel to sit. The massive dog grunted as he obeyed. Teufel was not happy. Clearly his mission in life was to find, capture, kill. Sort of a canine version of *veni, vidi, vici.*

"Who was that guy anyway?" Jack asked.

"Oliver Milliman, insurance adjuster. He's looking for Ace Pennington."

"Here? I thought this was your house."

"It is. I told you, Ace moved in two days ago."

"Oh right. I forgot." Jack's face fell. He could have been George, the security guard, disappointed I wasn't acting like a grieving widow, capital G, capital W.

"It's nothing romantic," I said, twisting Milliman's card. My sweaty fingers smeared the ink. Not the highest-quality print job for a superior insurance company. "Ace needed to keep an eye on his house while it's being fixed. Although I guess that isn't going to happen any time soon."

We both turned to study the ruins across the street. They, too, seemed to have wilted in the heat. Ace's gardeners were mowing the lawn—green patches interspersed with blackened sinkholes—and they had trimmed back the rhododendrons broken by the firemen. Someone had washed the empty window panes and polished the brass knocker on the front door, which still hung by one hinge. Their work made as much sense as giving King Kong a pedicure.

Ace's lawn sprinklers came on. I gritted my teeth as I remembered the policeman draining the rainwater from my barrels, water my poor scaly cherry trees needed right now.

Jack turned to me. "I see you collect rainwater. Is this where it comes out?" He pointed to the wrought-iron hose caddy fastened to the wall.

"Yeah, I apologize for the chintzy hose reel. Once you start owning chickens, everybody wants to give you something with a chicken on it."

He stared at the hose reel. "What kind of rooster is that supposed to be?"

"I think a Buff Orpington. Deep orange feathers, big red wattle."

"But the legs and feet are black."

"Poetic license?"

"I'd say ignorance." He followed the line of the hose up to the tower. "So how are those rain barrels working out for you?"

"Splendid until the police thought I had tossed a gun up there. They drained away about half my water."

"Cops." Jack shook his head. "No idea of how the real world works."

I didn't know what to say. Stanislaus seemed to have a pretty good grip on the real world, but while we were talking, Jack had somehow captured my hand and was gently massaging the pad of my thumb.

I hoped if I pretended not to notice, Jack would keep on doing it, at least until my insides melted and I collapsed on the porch. So I said, "Ace drives me crazy. Wasting all that water to keep his grass alive. If he wants to water something, he should be raising vegetables. Tomatoes. Any fool can grow tomatoes. Even a lawyer."

Jack frowned. His eyes were my favorite color, golden hazel with flecks of green. His lips were rough, but full. Below the neck, his lean, hard body strained inches from mine. Sweat prickled in my armpits, and I wondered how bad I smelled.

"Don't worry about Ace. Worry about yourself."

"What do you mean?"

Jack's mouth tightened. "You should think about moving, Sunny. This neighborhood seems to be turning into a war zone. I don't want you caught in the crossfire."

He stared into my eyes with painful anxiety and squeezed my hand. My inner thighs had started to itch again. I was getting some kind of heat rash down there.

I pulled free and shook my head. "I'm not moving. This is my home."

"But Sunny, that Ollie Milliman guy could be the killer."

"No way." As soon as Jack expressed my fear, I realized how completely crazy it sounded. Ollie was nervous, sure. He had to tell a big-time, hotshot attorney that his multi-million-dollar insurance claim had been denied. I'd be nervous, too. But my gut said the Laurelmere killer was anything but nervous. According to Detective Sergeant Stanislaus, the killer was an excellent marksman, knew how to build bombs from household chemicals, and had evaded Laurelmere's security system like smoke in the wind. None of that pointed to a guy like Ollie Milliman.

But not being a homicidal insurance adjuster wasn't reason enough to explain why Ollie had run into my backyard.

I wanted to know what he was doing back there and I wanted him gone. And I didn't want Jack hanging around, either. I needed to think. I couldn't let my attraction to Jack go any further until I understood what had happened to my marriage. I had believed Ken was my soul mate, the man who wanted to be the father of my children. If I had been wrong, if Ken had been a liar and a cheat, I needed to get my act together before I fell in love again. Or fell into bed again. Which was seeming more and more likely by the second.

"Say good-bye to George for me when you leave," I said with my hand on the front doorknob.

The time to be subtle had passed.

"Sure thing." Jack grabbed Teufel's leash. "Are you positive you're going to be okay? I know I've seen that Milliman guy before. He had a different name or maybe his hair was longer. Something was different."

Teufel growled, a low menacing sound, as if he already had poor Ollie trapped between his paws.

"I think Milliman's still back there. Let's get 'em, boy." Jack started to unhook Teufel's leash. I grabbed his arm.

"Stop." Holding Teufel's collar, I danced around until I was between the dog and the walkway to my backyard. "Go home. Water your dog, weed your vegetables. I'll see you tomorrow."

"Okay. If it'll make you happy."

I dropped Teufel's collar, and Jack dropped the leash. He took my chin in his hands and planted a feathery kiss on my lips. "I want you to be happy, Sunny. Very happy." He sauntered back to his truck, Teufel strutting beside him.

All that confident, muscular masculinity made my stomach lurch and my knees wobble.

I took in a deep breath of hot air and blew out steam. I knew one thing for sure about dinner tomorrow. If I was going to have any chance of getting my act together around Jack, the restaurant would have to be air-conditioned.

CHAPTER TWENTY-FIVE

I slipped off my sandals and put on my green gardening boots. Then I grabbed the pitchfork leaning against my woodpile, hoisted it over my shoulder and marched into my backyard.

"Oliver Milliman. Where are you?"

"Over here." A hand waved from the other side of the raspberry bushes. Oliver had wedged his body behind the compost bin in the northwest corner of the fence, the farthest possible spot from Jack's truck and Teufel's teeth.

"I'm not coming out until you put your weapon down," he said. "Is Jack Rabbit gone?"

I congratulated myself on my gut instincts. That quavering tenor was not the voice of a homicidal maniac, not that I had spent a lot of time with homicidal maniacs. Honeybees drunk on fermenting grapes are the most out-of-control creatures you find on an urban farm.

"Why are you so worried about Jack?" I asked, shoving the pitchfork into the ground next to my asparagus bed. "And how do you know his name?"

"Jack? I'm not worried about Jack," Oliver blustered. He slowly emerged, brushing raspberry pollen from his shoulders like dandruff. He sneezed and wiped his red-rimmed eyes on the sleeve of his silk suit. Where had Stately Homes found this guy? Anyone else, including Teufel, would have been more stately than he.

"That contraption is a fire hazard." Oliver pointed to my

rotating compost bin, a green metal cylinder about three feet long and two feet in diameter. It stands four feet off the ground on metal legs and cost as much as a flat-screen TV.

"A fire hazard? Good grief, it's a compost bin. You put in kitchen scraps, turn it once a day, water it occasionally, and in a couple of weeks you have black gold."

"The metal is hot. It's a potential fire hazard. It could touch off a brush fire. Or start your fence smoldering. You need to get rid of it."

"Nonsense. A compost bin doesn't get much above eighty degrees, even in direct sunlight. It's full of worms, live red worms. They make the compost. They'd fry if it got too hot. I'll open it and show you. They're all healthy and alive."

"Get away. I don't want to see any worms, living or dead." Oliver stepped to my chicken yard and fingered the wire fence. Without the Henriettas, the chicken yard was a barren stretch of dirt dotted with green and white clumps.

Ollie pointed to a clump. "What's this stuff, toxic sludge?"

"No. It's chicken manure, a natural organic fertilizer, full of nitrogen, phosphate, and—"

"Chicken manure doesn't belong in Laurelmere. It looks funny, smells bad, and—"

"Doesn't cost me a dime. No wonder you don't like it."

"Your whole place is a disaster. It's a good thing your husband turned me down."

"What do you mean Ken turned you down? For what? Why?"

Oliver straightened his wrinkled suit and felt for his business cards. He handed me one.

"You already gave me a card."

"Then you know who I am, Oliver Milliman. You can call me Ollie. I represent Stately Homes Insurance Company. I tried to convince Ken to buy a homeowner's policy from us, but he refused. Good thing, too. We don't insure hazardous waste sites."

"Hazardous waste? Give me a break. Everything here is organic. No heavy metals, no petrochemicals, no pollutants."

Ollie shook his head. "It's not grass. A backyard should be grass. Maybe a nice little flowerbed, a pool or a tennis court, a barbeque, but mostly grass. And flowers. You need flowers."

I went back to the main issue. "You tried to sell Ken homeowner's insurance?"

"Yeah. He turned me down. He said it was all he could do to keep up payments on his life insurance. I figured anyone living in Laurelmere would meet our requirements, but I didn't realize how much mess you made here. Your grandmother would be spinning in her grave if she saw this yard."

"Wait a minute. Back up. You sold Ken life insurance?"

"Yes. About ten years ago when I first joined Stately Homes. His wife—uh, that would be his second wife, I think her name was Ellen. Yes, Ellen. She insisted. They had purchased a big house in Leschi, four bedroom suites, two more baths, and Ellen was worried about making the mortgage payments if something happened to Ken."

"Ken owned a house in Leschi? You're kidding."

Leschi, one of Seattle's more classy neighborhoods, sits on the western shore of Lake Washington. It's a great place to spend a hundred dollars on a steak dinner. When I met Ken, he'd been living in an apartment above his shoe store on Capitol Hill. Quaint, charming, historic, but definitely not upscale. I did know about Ellen, the second wife, as much as anyone knows about a previous spouse, which is to say essentially nothing except that she existed and "didn't really understand him."

But as intriguing as this glimpse of my husband's former life was, I brushed it aside for my immediate concern. "If you sold Ken that life insurance policy, you can explain why Stately Homes won't pay me. I've filled out about a million forms, I've had my signature notarized twenty times, I sent a certified copy of our marriage license by registered mail, and still no check. I need that money, Ollie."

"Ken's life insurance? Uh, I looked into that. The home office called me. They had a lot of questions."

"What questions? Ken carried life insurance, he died, I'm the beneficiary, send me the check. How hard can it be?"

"You don't understand. First of all, he had a suicide exclusion clause. It reduced the cost of the policy and Ken was always looking to, well, not cut corners exactly, but get the best deal possible."

"So what? The accident report from the State Patrol insists he was drunk. That's not suicide, right?"

"I had to check it out. You know, take an independent look-see. We never assume what the cops say is God's truth." He pointed an accusing finger at me. "Neither did you. I saw all the letters you wrote to the State Patrol. And the email you sent. I mean, Ken was in AA. He'd been sober for nine years, ever since he ditched Ellen. You said he wouldn't drive and drink. I believe you. And there was no evidence of another car being involved in the accident. So if it wasn't drunk driving or an accident, suicide had to be the only option. Right?"

What could I say? That I knew Ken wasn't going to commit suicide because he planned to leave me instead? It sounded like a classic setup for murder—with me as the perp. Even if Ollie couldn't prove I killed Ken, Stately Homes might use the murder investigation as another reason to put off paying me.

"What about bad luck?" I asked. "You insure against that, right?"

"It's all moot, anyway," Ollie replied with a wave of his hand.

"Moot? What does that mean?"

" 'Moot' is an interesting word. It originated in Middle English as a meeting of the freemen in a shire. Now it means something of no practical importance, and—"

"Oh, for God's sake, shut up, you pedantic twit. I know all about moot and I don't care. What I want to know is, why did you say paying off Ken's life insurance is a moot point?"

"Ken cashed in his policy. A couple of days before he died. Headquarters thinks he got the money, gave it to you, and then committed suicide. Actually, they're thinking of instigating an action for fraud, so I wouldn't cash that check if I were you. You know, just in case we prevail in court."

"Check? What check, what money? Where did it go? Ken's bank account had less than five hundred dollars in it when he died."

"Not my problem, Sunny. Just trying to give you a friendly warning, that's all."

It didn't feel very friendly.

"How did you meet Ken in the first place?" I asked. Maybe the clue to Ken's death was in his previous life or lives.

Ollie tilted his head to the side and stared at me as if I were too stupid to live.

"Oh." Mental head slap. "You're a member of Ace's poker club, which means you 'dress up.' " I made air quotes. "So you bought shoes from Ken. Funny thing, except for Ace, you're the last cross-dressing poker player left alive in Laurelmere. And the only live one with an intact house."

Ollie winced. "Don't put it like that. I'm almost positive those events are an unfortunate coincidence."

" 'Unfortunate coincidence?' Two guys murdered, one house exploded, and you think it's an unfortunate coincidence?"

Ollie hunched his shoulders and tucked his long neck into his collar. He glanced next door. "For God's sake, keep your voice down. I think Nasreen's home."

"How do you know Nasreen?"

"She's the Twitter-bitch. Everyone in Laurelmere knows her.

She's got spies everywhere. She knows more about my life than I do."

"Whatever. I'm glad Ken didn't buy homeowner's insurance from you. Especially since your company refuses to pay any claims."

"What do you mean? We pay all legitimate claims, promptly and in full." He sounded remarkably like the former CEO of a worldwide oil company—full of shit.

"All claims except Ace's." I jerked my head in the direction of Ace's bombed-out house. "Are you trying to tell me he didn't have a fire?"

"Of course there was a fire. But the official police report says the destruction was the result of terrorism. That means an act of war. No insurance company covers an act of war."

"But the FBI concluded it wasn't terrorism."

"Be that as it may. So far we think terrorism is the only reasonable explanation."

"Stately Homes thinks Muslim fundamentalists decided to bomb Ace's house? What kind of message were they trying to send? Down with fake-Tudor exterior siding? Destroy all three-car garages?"

As I spoke, I realized I was quoting Ace. He had said almost exactly the same thing at the police station this morning, when he made an impassioned plea for Stanislaus to reopen the investigation into Ken's death. Right after Wilson confiscated my computer and announced Ken was planning to leave me when he died.

"As long as the police say Ace's house was destroyed because of terrorism, Stately Homes Insurance can't pay his claim," Ollie continued. "Ace knows that."

"He knows that? Ace knows you won't pay?"

"Of course. I left him a message yesterday. After he got it, he shot off a threatening email to the home office. It freaked

everyone out, and they canceled his policy. I came by to tell
him in person. As a courtesy to a neighbor and a friend."

Stupid, credulous me. I had thought Ace was on my side. But
now I understood his speech at the police station. It was inspired
by the sight of his multimillion-dollar insurance claim flying out
the window, not by Ken's death—or by my need to know what
happened.

Rats. How had I let myself be fooled by Ace again?

Jack's face popped into my mind. I remembered the scrape of
his rough lips against mine. Maybe in his own way, Jack was as
self-centered as Ace, but, like Teufel, Jack didn't pretend to be
anything else than one-hundred-percent male.

I felt a smile tug at my lips. That was one piece of mail I'd
like to open.

"Sunny? Sunny?" Ollie snapped his fingers, and I realized it
wasn't the first time he had called my name. "Return to earth,
Sunny."

"What do you want?"

"If you got rid of the chickens, the worms, and the compost
thingy, I could make you a pretty competitive offer on insurance
for this fine home. Have you replaced the knob-and-tube wiring
in the attic?"

"Get out!" I flew at Ollie Milliman, squawking and flapping
like an enraged hen. "Leave me alone, you little blood-sucking
louse."

He jumped straight up and came down on a cluster of ripe
tomatoes. They exploded like a bomb, spraying his polished
loafers with shrapnel-sized chunks of pulp and seeds.

"You're one crazy lady!" Ollie screamed, hopping on one leg
and then the other trying to shake off bits of tomato. He shook
too hard and one shoe flew off his foot. It flipped and landed
with a splat in the chicken manure I had raked into a neat pile
against my tool shed.

Ollie's sock—brown silk with a faint pink thread—had a hole in the heel. I guess the insurance biz wasn't going too well.

He sat down abruptly on the railroad tie that made the wall of a raised bed for my cabbages. He put his head between his hands and rocked back and forth muttering, "Crazy lady, crazy lady."

I patted Ollie awkwardly on the shoulder and rescued his shoe from the chicken poop. The damage wasn't too bad: a few brown splats and a really large white one.

I sighed. The dress I was wearing was getting too tight anyway. I spit on the hem and used it to rub the worst of the manure off Ollie's shoe. I handed the shoe back to him.

He put it on and started walking away from me. Apparently he wasn't aware of the patch of squashed tomato stuck to the seat of his pants. Then he turned around. "Ken said you were hot. He didn't warn me that you're crazy, too."

"Ken told you I was hot?"

"Yes, I think he loved you very much."

"Then why?" I stopped.

Oliver Milliman wouldn't know if Ken had really decided to leave me, or if the cops had faked that farewell note to pressure me into spilling my guts. I needed to find the box of stuff my husband had with him the night he died.

And I needed to find it before my date with Jack tonight. I checked my watch. Yikes. I only had two hours left.

CHAPTER TWENTY-SIX

After his close encounter with chicken manure, Ollie Milliman quit trying to sell me insurance and departed for the downtown offices of Stately Homes Insurance. Ollie didn't thank me for cleaning off his shoe, but I wasn't surprised. One thing I'd learned from hawking Girl Scout cookies in Kokomo: *If you don't make the sale, there's no percentage in being nice afterward.*

I followed Ollie out of the backyard and dropped my pitchfork on the woodpile. With the insurance guy out of my hair, I no longer needed a weapon of ass destruction.

I was heading across my front yard to Mac's basement to retrieve the box of Ken's things when Ace's Jaguar convertible screeched to a stop at the curb. He jumped out of the car and bounded over to me, brushing more leaves from my desiccated cherry trees.

The last hour at the police station had not improved Ace's appearance. Soot and ashes still clung to his shorts and shirt, his five-o'clock shadow was hours past midnight, and his hair bristled at odd angles. Despite his wretched exterior, Ace seemed strangely happy, as if a weight had dropped from his shoulders.

"Sunny, I have to talk to you."

"Later."

I knew I sounded rude, but I was in a hurry. I wanted to examine Ken's stuff before my dinner engagement with Jack Rabbit. I needed to decide whether I was going out on a real, i.e., romantic, date. If the police were right and I found evidence in the box that Ken was planning to leave me, then I could stop feeling like a slut and have a good time with Jack. On the other hand, if the police had forged the letter on Ken's computer as part of some stupid entrapment scheme, then my marriage hadn't been a sham and treating Jack with anything more than polite interest—one organic farmer to another—was out of the question.

Ace ignored my response. He grabbed my arm. "I've got really great news. I did it."

I pulled away. "You murdered Lank and Balls?"

"No, don't be ridiculous. I convinced Stanislaus to take the investigation into Ken's death seriously."

"How did you do that?"

"I told her about the Cross-Dressing Poker Club."

"But Mac already told her that Ken wore a dress. He convinced her to reopen the investigation."

"Yes, but I told her everything about the club."

"Everything?"

He smiled broadly. I put my hands on my hips and stared at him. The sidewalk under my feet may have rocked a little.

"Let me get this straight," I said. "You told Detective Sergeant Stanislaus you are a cross-dresser, my husband was a cross-dresser, the two dead guys were cross-dressers, and the killer is trying to murder all the members of the Cross-Dressing Poker Club?"

"That's exactly what I said."

"Does Oliver Milliman know you ratted on him?"

"Oliver Milliman? You know Ollie?"

"I know a lot more than you give me credit for. I know Ollie Milliman is a member of the poker club. I know he works for Stately Homes Insurance. I know Stately Homes refused to pay your claim when the FBI decided the bombing was an act of terrorism. I know if they change their minds and conclude the bombing was simply a murder attempt, you will have all the money you need to rebuild your mansion. I realize once again you are trying to screw me over."

"Screw you over? What do you mean?"

"I mean you are trying to use me. At the beginning of this whole mess, you volunteered to be my attorney so you could throw a smoke screen over the homicide investigation, not because you care about what happens to me."

"But—"

"And I fired your ass. Then at the police station, you wanted to be my attorney again so you could persuade Stanislaus to take the case away from the FBI and reopen it as a murder investigation."

"But—"

"And then you told Stanislaus about the poker club, a secret I hid for the two worst days of my life, just so you could get your insurance money."

"But—"

"And finally, I know you are moving out of my house. Today!"

By now I was shouting at Ace. Out of the corner of my eye, I saw Nasreen open the window of her office so she could hear me more clearly. Great. Once again I was going to make the six P.M. Twitter-bitchcast: FYA SUNI & ACE NO MORE H&KS. WHY? IHNI, BUT A STUDLY GUY BROUGHT HER HOME. WHERE IS THIS LADY SPENDING HER NIGHTS? TBC.

"Wait a minute." Ace grabbed my wrist again. He glanced at my face, saw murder in my eyes, and let go. "Most of what you said is simply not true."

"Stately Homes?"

"That part *is* true. They don't want to pay my claim."

"FBI? Terrorism?"

203

"That part is true, also."

"Money to rebuild?"

"Of course I need the insurance payment to rebuild. But I'm not trying to screw you over. Not like that."

"How then?"

"I really don't like to use the word 'screw,' but I thought I'd get cleaned up, take you someplace nice for a dinner of organic vegetables over brown rice, and then—"

"And then not use the word 'screw,' but do it anyway."

"Something like that."

"Not going to happen. I have a date tonight and when I get home, *if* I get home, you and all of your stuff better be gone. Or else."

With a fierce scowl, I turned on my heel and stomped away. It would have been a little more impressive if I hadn't been wearing my green rubber duck boots.

Chapter Twenty-Seven

Mac passed through the gates of Laurelmere with only a nod for George, the security guard. Mac had done the unthinkable, spent good folding money on a cab from downtown. Apparently George realized the taxi signaled a true emergency, because he lifted the gate and ducked back into his little hut without waving hello. The cabbie, who was shouting into a mobile phone headset, didn't even slow down.

At the police station thirty minutes ago, Detective Wilson had described the wireless webcam he found in Sunny's bedroom. As soon as Wilson started speaking, Mac knew he had to get home and sort things out. Sunny's husband might have been God's gift to the world of automatic doors for chicken coops, but he was hopeless when it came to technology more sophisticated than point and click. No matter what Wilson thought, Ken hadn't installed the webcam.

Ken couldn't have, but what about Pete?

That little shite. What kind of a mess has he gotten himself into now?

Like a kid with oversized feet, Pete came equipped with more gray matter than he could handle. He cruised porn sites freely—parental controls had been laughably easy to circumvent—and hacked into corporate computer files to ferret out hidden secrets.

That same family inclination had led Mac to becoming a detective. But Pete's instincts had to be controlled, shaped and channeled until the moral circuits of his brain grew as powerful as the logical ones.

Mac knew he was the best person to keep Pete out of trouble until he matured. Not because Mac understood hacking or encryption or webcams, but because he understood Pete's compulsion to solve puzzles.

And because he'd dealt with little fookers like Pete for more than thirty years.

Really, all Pete needed was time.

Which was different from *doing* time.

And doing time, in juvie hall if nowhere else, would be Pete's future unless Mac untangled the muddle the blasted bairn had gotten himself into before Detectives Stanislaus and Wilson did.

Mac figured he had twenty minutes tops.

Mac had sent Pete an urgent text from the police station: Meet me. When Pete responded, "yr place," Mac headed right back to Laurelmere.

Even while he was stewing about Pete, Mac automatically scanned the neighborhood for signs of the killer. The taxi bounced over speed bumps, which infested Laurelmere's twisted streets like boils, and swerved around beaters belonging to the maids and gardeners. Ace's convertible was angled awkwardly at the curb in front of Sunny's house, doors open, the backseat piled high with clothes on hangers. Nasreen's Mini Cooper was parked by the side of his son's house, and Pete's bike leaned against the fence.

The cab stopped, the driver still arguing with someone in Somali. From his wild gesticulations, Mac figured he was describing some obscure method of preparing pasta with bananas. Mac checked the meter and opened his wallet. The fare was outrageous for a fifteen-minute ride, but he had no time to quibble. He could feel Stanislaus and Wilson closing in on Pete.

Mac dug into his pocket for quarters and added his usual ten-percent tip. "Here you go. Ta." He dropped the money into the cabbie's palm and opened the door.

"Wait, sir." Tucking the phone in his armpit, the cabdriver thrust his hand over the front seat and clanked the quarters together. "You've made a mistake."

Mac stuck a gnarled forefinger in the man's palm. He made a show of laboriously counting the coins and comparing the total with the amount on the fare box. "Yer right, laddie. I made a mistake. I gave you too much." He picked up a quarter and stared into the driver's eyes.

The cabbie cursed and threw up his hands. He tossed the remaining coins through the open door and into the street. Without making sure Mac was out of his cab, he cranked the engine and roared away. Seconds later, the taxi slammed into the speed bump at the corner. Bits of muffler scattered across the road like rabbit turds.

Pleased, Mac hitched up his pants. Quite an excellent bit of entertainment for only twenty-five cents. He lumbered down the steps to his front door ready for a come-to-Jesus meeting with his grandson. Turning the key in the lock, he hollered, "Pete!"

Chapter Twenty-Eight

Mac pushed open the door of his basement apartment. For one confused moment he thought Pete had set up *Braveheart* to run on a continuous loop. He stopped, shook his head, and sorted out the screeching voices.

Sunny knelt on the floor in front of Mac's closet, sobbing as she cradled an open cardboard box. Nasreen clutched Sunny's shoulder with one hand and with the other pointed to a steaming hot cup of tea and a plate of sweets on Mac's coffee table.

"Come and sit over here. Have a nice cup of tea." As she spoke, Nasreen's voice became louder and more shrill. "You cannot sit on this floor."

Nasreen had met her match in Sunny. Despite the tears streaming down Sunny's face, her jaw was thrust out in that familiar angle of stubbornness. Mac was delighted he hadn't been appointed to shift her.

On the other side of the small apartment, Ace stood at the kitchen sink, a stained towel tucked into his belt, scrubbing dishes and whistling, not that Mac could make out the tune over Sunny's sobs. Why wasn't he comforting the lass? And where had he found the towel?

Mac's mam had given his wife that particular towel to commemorate the wedding of Charles and Diana. It came with stern instructions. It was not to be used to wipe dishes and certainly not for an apron. Worse yet, someone (please, sweet Jesus, not Ace) had tossed a couple of pillows and a sheet on Mac's couch. Surely that bloody wanker didn't think he could doss down here. No amount of dishwashing would earn him that privilege. Mac would rather eat bangers off the bathroom floor than be saddled with a defense attorney as a roommate.

And Pete? No sign of the little shite.

Mac drew in a deep breath and bellowed, "Shut yer bloody traps and get out of my house! Now!"

The duty sergeant hadn't dubbed Mac "Laird of the Last Call" for naught. Instantly the room stilled, bloody traps shut, bodies froze, and hands hovered in midair. Sunny wiped her eyes, picked up the cardboard box, and scooted through the front door. With a sweep of his arm, Mac pushed Ace out after her.

Nasreen, however, stood her ground, hands on hips, black eyes flashing. Her burgundy silk blouse slithered around her shoulders. Mac was a guest in her house, pure and simple. And a guest didn't order the hostess to leave. She wouldn't be satisfied with thrashing Mac. His son was in for a bollocking tonight, too. *Them's the breaks, mate,* Mac thought. *You married her, you get to tame her.*

"You have the manners of a pig," Nasreen said. "That poor girl, you scared her to death. You had no right to come barging in like that."

"It's my apartment."

"It's my house."

"Where's Pete?"

"Why do you want him?"

"None of yer business." Mac would no more give up Pete to his mother when she was in this mood than he would pull fur from a baby rabbit.

She swept past him with an exasperated sniff, leaving a trail of turmeric and sulfur hanging in the hot air. Mac closed the door behind her, pulled out his cell phone, and dialed Pete's number again.

You can run, buddy boy, but you can't hide. Not from the long arm of Grumps.

CHAPTER TWENTY-NINE

I stood in the shower of my upstairs bathroom, scrubbing furiously as tears ran down my face. I hadn't stopped crying since I opened the box of Ken's effects.

Or should I say Kendra's?

A fresh gush of tears.

In Mac's apartment, Nasreen treated me as if I were newly bereaved, and maybe I was. She'd patted my shoulder and brought me comfort food: a mug of steaming hot tea and a plate of artfully arranged rectangles of gaz and wedges of halvah. As she tried to maneuver me onto Mac's couch, I saw her nose twitch and her glance slide toward the box. I refused to yield. No one was going to paw Ken's things but me.

And I did.

So was I crying because my husband was dead?

Hell, no. I was crying because I was furious.

At least now I knew where the money from Ken's insurance policy had gone—to a clinic in Bangkok that promised the utmost in discrete penis loppers. Everything had been paid up front: airfare, pre-op counseling, hormone therapy, surgery, and a month of recovery at a seaside resort with pool boys and bar girls.

No wonder Ken wanted out of our marriage.

Right now, I did too.

I had nothing against same-sex couples. Some of my best friends blah, blah, blah. But I felt pretty strongly that all those "what's my gender today?" questions should be resolved before a guy gets married and fathers a child.

Right?

I turned off the shower and reached for a towel. I wiped the steam from the mirror and stared at the face that stared back at me.

The glass seemed to waver. Through a blur of tears, I was looking at my blotchy eight-year-old reflection in the window of our old station wagon. After ordering me to keep the car doors locked and the dome light off, my parents disappeared into a seemingly abandoned building. I knew the drill. They'd be back before dawn, giggly, poking each other and then slowly mellowing out until they slumped in their seats, staring at nothing.

I should have been smarter about Ken. After growing up with liars, I should have pegged him immediately. But, for some reason—love or something darn near like it—I'd let myself be fooled.

"I'm not going to be that kind of parent," I promised the face in the mirror. "No secrets, no lies. Never, never, never."

The mirror wisely withheld comment.

Another thing changed when I went through Ken's box. The all-but-empty bottle of bourbon tucked away in the corner convinced me. He *had* started drinking again. Maybe it was the pressure of deciding to have the sex-change operation. Maybe it was guilt about leaving me and our baby. Maybe the booze just tasted good.

Whatever. The state patrol was right. Ken wasn't killed because he was a member of Ace's Cross-Dressing Poker Club. He died because he was a fool.

One thing about discovering Ken's secrets. I sure as hell didn't feel any remorse about going out with Jack. As for helping Ace find the killer? No way. Ken wasn't involved, I wasn't involved, and the police knew what they were doing. As Mom would say, it was time to go back to minding my own beeswax.

I glanced at the clock. Jack Rabbit was due to pick me up for our dinner date at any minute. I toweled off and found my good bra, which had been languishing for months at the back of my undies drawer. I carefully brushed on makeup and clipped my hair up, leaving a few tendrils to twine down my neck. I decided on a loose fitting, V-necked print dress with a flouncy skirt. I'd bought it a couple of years ago for the bank's annual picnic, but I didn't think Jack would notice it was out of date. Besides clinging to my cleavage, and I was definitely developing cleavage thanks to JayJay, the dress couldn't be wrinkled by a one-hundred-fifty-pound dog who thought the front seat of Jack's truck belonged to him.

I found my pink strappy heels. Despite my baby bump, my feet and ankles hadn't swollen at all. The shoes fit perfectly, the week-old polish on my toenails was still intact, and I slipped silver rings on several toes. A final check in the mirror. Except for my crooked teeth, I looked good enough to eat.

From our wedding picture on the bureau, Ken's eyes seemed to be watching my every move. I picked up the photograph, held it for a second, and stared him down. Then I slammed it into the wall, frame and all.

The glass shattered. The doorbell rang.

With a determined smile, I tripped downstairs to start my new life.

We did the whole hello-how-are-you thing and then Jack said, "Where's Ace?" at the same moment I asked, "Where's Teufel?"

Jack smiled. "You first."

"I expected to see Teufel."

"I left him home to guard the farm. Didn't think I needed a security force around you." Jack treated me to a wolfish grin.

"But I wore this dress especially for him."

"You dressed up for my dog?"

"Long story. What were you going to ask?"

"Where's Ace? You said he lives here, right?"

Jack had missed his cue to tell me how incredibly great I looked. Was he blind? Or had I blimped out with retained water in the last few minutes?

"Ace used to live here. I told him to move out. He's gone."

"To a hotel downtown?"

I shrugged. "Don't know, don't care."

"I suppose you could call him if you need to get in touch."

"Call him? Sure, I know his cell number. But why would I want to?"

Jack rubbed his jaw. "In case he left something behind?"

Jack had veered way off course. I pouted, cutely I hoped, and said, "Forget Ace. You promised me free-range, grass-fed steak." I took Jack's arm and herded him onto my porch.

"It may not be steak," Jack said. "It's not that kind of place."

"No problem." I locked the front door and glanced around. No giant pink rabbit anywhere. "Where's your truck?"

"I brought the BMW. Thought you deserved something more classy than a veggie van."

"Thanks." I flashed him a quick smile as he opened the door. The immaculate, cream-colored BMW had leather seats and glossy trim. It fit smoothly into the Laurelmere ambiance like butter on lima beans.

Jack slid behind the steering wheel and started the car. He glanced at me. "It may be old, but it's been well maintained. It starts right up and goes the distance."

"Like you?"

"Yes ma'am. Just like me."

There was that wolf smile again, those shiny wolf teeth. I was going to have to figure out how to tell Jack I was pregnant before he bit me.

CHAPTER THIRTY

Mac paced his living room while he dialed Pete's number again. Pete, of course, did not pick up. Mac ground his teeth. The lad was taking the piss. Any number of times he'd watched his grandson check caller ID, then mute his iPhone instead of answering. Mostly his parents got the non-response response. Pete was too busy with his virtual life to have time for the real world of homework, chores, and family dinners. Now Mac dreaded going upstairs to search for him and risk arousing the sleeping lioness that was Nasreen.

Bollocks. Mac had to talk to Pete about the webcam now. Once the cops barged in, it would be too late. He wouldn't be able to save the kid from his own idiocy. But how in the bloody hell could he get Pete's attention if the little jerk wouldn't answer his phone?

Mac heard a scuffle outside. He opened his front door to find Ace holding Pete. One hand clutched the neck of Pete's T-shirt, the other made the mother of all wedgies with the seat of Pete's jeans.

Brilliant.

Ace shoved Pete inside, solving Mac's most pressing problem. He had Pete cornered. And now for the second problem—getting the bloody bairn's attention. Ace had usurped the role of Bad Cop, so Mac would play Good Cop. No sweat.

"Take yer hands off the lad," Mac roared. He shut the door so all three stood nose-to-nose inside his living room, which

215

was not much larger than a billiards table. "That's my grandson, and I'll not have you banging him around."

For a second, Mac wondered if he'd gone too far, if Pete heard the chuckle under the bellow. Apparently not. But Ace caught it. He dropped the boy with the faintest hint of a wink in Mac's direction. Great, they were on the same page.

But what page would that be?

"Look at this." Ace reached into his pants pocket and pulled out a small black cylinder with several thin wires dangling from it. The wires ended in frayed bits of copper, like they'd been yanked from the wall. "I found it mounted in Sunny's bedroom."

"What were you doing in her room?" Pete demanded, a commendable attempt to steer the conversation into less perilous waters.

"I was searching for something exactly like this." Ace thrust the cylinder into Pete's face like he was going to shove it up his nose. "You put this spy camera there."

"Wait a minute. This thing is a camera?" Mac grabbed the cylinder from Ace and bounced it in his palm. Strange to think an object so small could create such a shiteload of problems.

"Tell him about it, Pete," Ace said.

"Well." Pete took the object from Mac and studied it carefully, pursing his mouth and blinking rapidly as if staring through an electron microscope.

"Quit stalling."

"I can't say what it is exactly." Pete glanced at Ace, a faint grin curving his cheeks. The kid was having way too much fun badgering his technology-impaired elders. "Some of the pieces appear to be missing, but it looks like an E-Ray 2000."

"That's a camera?"

"Yeah, a five-point-eight gigahertz pinhole spy camera. About the size of a quarter. Motion activated. Night vision. Color, of course. Digital output."

"Wait a minute." Mac was drowning in details. "Explain yerself. Queen's English."

Ace took over. "Let me make an educated guess. Pete installed this camera above the full-length mirror in Sunny's bedroom. He disabled the red light which normally warns people that a video cam is operating. Any motion in the bedroom, and the camera started shooting pictures, which were streamed to Pete's computer through a wireless connection." He glanced at Pete. "Does that sound about right?"

Pete shrugged. "Yeah, close enough. The details are a little more complicated, but so what? What's the big deal?"

"In Washington State that's voyeurism, a Class C felony. You're looking at five years in prison, ten-thousand-dollar fine."

"You're fucking me."

Ace snorted. "No, kid, I'm not. I've made a career of defending budding juvenile delinquents like you."

Time for the Good Cop.

"Sit down," Mac said. "Let's figure this thing out. Pete, when did you install the camera?"

"I'm not sitting. I'm not talking. I want a lawyer."

Mac groaned. "Yer a minor, jerkbutt. Hiring a lawyer means yer mom finds out what you've been up to. Do you really want Nasreen to be part of this discussion?"

Pete's face paled.

Finally a threat with some real teeth. Mac smiled.

"Nah, we don't need to talk to Mom," Pete said. "Here's the deal. About four months ago, Ken—"

"Mr. Dahl to you," Ace interjected.

"Yeah, whatever. Mr. Dahl picked up a really nasty virus on his computer and asked me to clean it out. At the same time, Sunny—Ms. Burnett—wanted a wireless network installed. The PC was in their bedroom. I figured as long as I was working in there anyway . . ." He shrugged. "I way undercharged them."

"This was before Ken was killed?" Mac asked.

"Well, duh. He hired me. I don't work for dead people."

"And the picture of Ken and Lank Lungstrom in dresses?"

"Yeah." Pete's face lit up. "Totally awesome. I didn't expect to get anything that off the wall."

"What *did* you expect to see?"

"Uh, well, you know. Ms. Burnett's got a great body. Even though she's kinda old."

Mac growled. Pete looked at him and said, "Mature. I mean, like you know, mature."

Ace took over the interrogation. "And when you saw the guys in dresses, you printed out a picture. And mailed it to Lank Lungstrom."

"Yeah, for a laugh, but not until months later. Lungstrom was always so full of himself. Big real estate mogul. Last week he got on my case because I was skateboarding in front of the clubhouse. So I decided to prick his balloon. So what?"

Pete swiveled his head back and forth, looking from Ace to Mac. "Again, what's the big deal?"

"What's the big deal?" Ace roared. His face turned red. Beneath the silver bristles, his scalp glowed like a Christmas tree light. "I'll tell you what the big deal is."

"Just a second." Mac stepped between Ace and the boy, facing the outraged lawyer. He lowered his voice and said, just loudly enough for Pete to overhear, "He's trying to be a tough guy, but he's naught but a kid. Let's figure out where we're going before we drop the bomb. Okay?"

Ace blew out a long, exasperated hiss between clenched teeth. "But Lank is dead, dammit. And so is Balls. Pete's gotta take responsibility for his actions."

Pete shuffled his feet. Mac lowered his voice another notch to keep Pete's attention.

"Right. Couldn't agree with you more. But this picture yer

yammering about? Let's figure exactly what Pete did before we string him up, okay? Maybe we can set things right without getting the police involved."

Ace raised his hands, palms outward, and took a step back. "Okay, we'll talk for exactly ten minutes and then I'm calling Detective Stanislaus."

"Fair enough. Let's step outside." Mac half-turned and said to Pete, "Wait here. Watch the telly or something. Don't go anywhere."

Pete nodded, his hand already snaking toward the remote control.

"Keep outta the porn!"

"No worries."

The front door to Mac's apartment opened into a concrete pad about six feet square and five feet below ground level. A short flight of cement stairs connected the pad with the yard above it. Before Mac moved in, Nasreen had planted orange and purple impatiens around the perimeter of the stairs to soften and beautify what was basically a hole in the ground. Under Mac's care, the plants had died in the fierce August heat, leaving him and Ace with an unobstructed slug's eye view of the street and Sunny's walkway.

"Tell me about the picture," Mac said as he closed the door.

"It was a picture of Lank Lungstrom and Ken Burnett dressed up in—" Ace swallowed and his Adam's apple bobbed like a teenager's. "In fancy dresses, feathers, shoes, wigs. Do you know what I mean?"

"Yeah. Yer were lumberjacks. Don't spell it out. *Please* don't spell it out. But why does the photograph matter?"

"You heard what Pete said. He mailed it to Lank. The morning Lank was shot, he was on his way to work when he opened his mail. Lank found the picture and stormed into my house. He thought I took it at a poker game. He thought I was trying to blackmail him."

"Which seems a little crazy. Yer a lumberjack, too, right?"

"You can call me a cross-dresser."

"You don't want to hear what I'd like to call you, mate."

"Yeah, well, Lank wasn't thinking at all. He was hysterical, there's no other word for it."

"And then?"

"I told him I had nothing to do with the picture. If you looked closely, you could see bits of wallpaper behind Lank and Ken, garlands of pink roses. Obviously, I had nothing like that in my media room. Lank finally calmed down enough to realize that the picture had been taken in Ken's bedroom—Ken and Sunny's—so he stormed across the street to confront Sunny. He decided she was the blackmailer, which made more sense, actually. We all know she's been broke ever since Ken died."

"And that's when Lank was shot?"

"Yeah. As soon as he stepped into her yard."

"Did you hear anything?"

"Nope. After he left, I went upstairs to take a shower. I didn't hear a thing."

"What happened to the picture?"

"Sunny found it. She hid it from the cops for a while, but finally decided to give it to Detective Stanislaus. It's evidence."

"Of what?"

"I don't know. But I'm sure that's why Lank died. Because of Pete's damned photograph."

"What did Stanislaus say?"

"That didn't pan out. By the time Sunny decided to turn the picture over to the cops, it had disappeared. She thought I destroyed it, but I didn't."

"So now that you've removed the camera from the bedroom, there's no evidence Pete was spying on Sunny except what's on his computer. We could erase those files."

"Fine, as long as the picture Sunny took from Lank doesn't

reappear. Otherwise, we're looking at evidence tampering, also a crime in Washington State."

Mac leaned against the front door while he thought out the implications. He wanted to protect his grandson, but Ace was right. The kid had to learn a lesson.

Mac heard laughter and glanced up to see Sunny and Jack getting into a Beemer parked in front of Sunny's house. She looked terrific, all sparkly and promising, like a birthday present the moment before it's unwrapped.

Too old? Nae, that daft Pete had a lot of growing up to do.

Ace nudged Mac's arm as the car slowly pulled away from the curb. "Who's that?"

"Sunny."

"I'm not blind. I meant the man. Who's she leaving with?"

"The farmer who sold her the six wee chicks living in her bathroom."

"I don't care about the damn chicks. What's that guy's name?" Ace's hand gripped Mac's bicep like a vise.

"Lemme go, you bloody fool. She's out with Farmer Jack, of Jack Rabbit Farms, organic marijuana and free-range hens."

"Damn. Come on. I want to get a good look at him."

Ace tried to pull Mac up the steps, but Mac wedged his fourteen stone in the cement stairwell and refused to move. "Nae. I know yer jealous of anyone dating the wee lass, but we're dealing with Pete's problems now. Let Sunny be. She deserves a night on the town."

Ace opened his mouth to argue, but a tremendous boom rocked the inside of Mac's flat. Mac tossed Ace aside and threw open the door, releasing billows of black, acrid smoke.

Dear Mother of God, what had Pete done now?

CHAPTER THIRTY-ONE

I'm not sure where I expected to go on my first date with Jack Rabbit, but certainly not to a joint with black painted windows and iron bars on the door. The Hammered Man didn't look like the kind of place where you whispered about the joys of pregnancy. It looked like the kind of place where you got knocked up in the back alley.

Jack snagged a spot in front of the restaurant. He smiled at me as he turned off the Beemer. "How about that?"

"Rock star."

A brick behemoth once a factory stood across the street. In my grandmother's time, heavy industry had been the heart and soul of Georgetown, a neighborhood in southwest Seattle bounded by I-5, Boeing Field, and a wasteland of closed machine shops. According to a faded sign leaning against the entrance, the factory was being converted into four stories of condos and live-work lofts as real estate developers tried to drag another blue-collar community into yuppiedom.

In my previous life as a mortgage banker, I had funded a lot of deals like the factory conversion. They had all gone tits-up (a technical term we mortgage bankers use) in the Great Recession. Maybe this developer had found a conduit to Chinese money. Anything less would ensure the factory stood empty for another decade.

Jack noticed I was studying the building. "What do you think?" he asked.

"I love the whole idea of restoring and reusing old structures. My church bought a movie theater in the north end and converted it into a sanctuary. They laid linoleum tiles in the lobby in the shape of a quilt pattern."

"That's nice. Anything's better than paving over decent farmland to build a mega-church with a parking lot the size of Safeco Field." Jack opened the restaurant door as he spoke. "One of those big-box churches offered to buy me out. I don't have anything against religion, but I told them to keep their goddamn grubby hands off my property."

I'd forgotten Jack could rant with the best of them.

The bar was dark, especially after the bright sunshine outside, and crowded with guys in sweat-stained T-shirts. Hip-hop played in the background, but not loud enough to induce brain swelling. We appeared to be the only customers who might need a menu with actual food on it.

The bartender, a shadowy figure in black, waved us toward a door that led to an outdoor terrace enclosed by bamboo mats that hung from a structure of two-by-fours. The roof of loosely woven rattan let shafts of sunlight through at unexpected places. A hodgepodge of tables and chairs was scattered across the brick floor and interspersed with massive sculptures of found material. The nearest piece of art was a rebar fence holding back a torrent of broken Mexican pottery.

"This is great," I said to Jack as we picked a path to a table in the corner.

"If they can't afford decent tables and chairs, no wonder they can't pay me. I'll get my money up front next time."

"I think the fixtures are making a statement. It's like recycling the old factory into apartments. Tables and chairs don't need to match to be functional."

"But they need to work." Jack sat across from me on a chair that squealed under his weight. He stood, kicked the offending chair away and sat down to my left, effectively boxing me into the corner.

"This is better." He sighed and leaned back, a smile playing over his lips.

While it was closer, I wasn't sure it was better.

I liked Jack, but I didn't want things to move too fast. I still had to figure out how to tell him about baby JayJay.

Our waitress appeared, young, skinny, poured into black leather pants and a sleeveless leather vest. From shoulder to wrist her arms were covered with colored tattoos. Without staring too much, I made out a tangle of tropical vines and flowers with either butterflies or monkey faces at the intersections. I'm okay with tattoos. I myself have a red rose in a very private place. But she also had three silver rings through the septum of her nose. They reminded me of big wet boogers hanging over her mouth. I kept expecting her to slurp them down. Every time she moved—and she twitched a lot—my stomach lurched.

She handed us menus. I focused on Jack's face while I gave my order. "I'd like a large salad of organic greens, oil and vinegar on the side."

"We ain't got no salad right now. Dinner don't start until seven." Her feet did a little jig bypassing orders from the mother ship.

"But surely you have the ingredients." I pointed to Jack. "Here's the guy who delivers your produce."

"You gotta order what's on the menu, but nothing green." Her pencil tapping became more urgent.

"Maybe the chef could make an exception just this once."

"Chef?"

I rolled my eyes at Jack. "Yeah, you know. The guy who cooks the food."

"The cook don't start 'til seven."

"We have to wait until seven to eat?"

"No, no, no." The pencil flipped faster than ever. "We don't serve much food before the cook comes on, but he saves everything from yesterday. I just stick it in the microwave and it's ready. But it's got to be something from the menu. And nothing that'll wilt. You see?"

I did see. So what leftovers from the menu would taste good reheated twenty-four hours later?

"I'll have a black bean burrito, hold the sour cream." I've seen what happens to sour cream in a microwave and it's not pretty.

"Right."

"Do you want something to drink?" Jack asked. "Beer, wine, margarita?"

"No thanks. I can't."

"What do you mean?"

"Tell you in a minute." I nodded at the waitress without looking higher than her jiggling elbows. She had a couple of pimples between her wrist and elbow. I sure hoped she'd wear gloves when she put my food in the microwave.

Jack finished ordering and the waitress rattled off, bouncing against a sculpture of welded stovepipes on her way to the kitchen.

Jack unfolded his napkin. "I'd say she's on meth. Good thing we're the only customers for dinner."

"Good thing we aren't paying."

"Yeah, there is that," Jack said. He leaned back and studied me. "So you don't drink?"

"I do, I mean, I used to drink, wine mostly, not beer, but, uh, right now I'm pregnant." So smooth.

"Right now?" Laughter crinkled the lines around Jack's eyes. "At this very moment?"

I smiled back. "Yeah, right now and for the next five months."

"That's terrific, Sunny. Do you know if it's a girl or boy?"

"Girl."

"Nice. Girls are cool."

"Yep." We grinned at each other in that sappy way I thought I'd be doing with Ken.

"So tell me about your son," I asked. "You seem like you'd make a great father." I blushed and added, "Not that I'm asking you to help raise this one."

"Got it. Anyway, my son, Rolf, is twenty."

I did the math. Jack had to be about ten years older than me, five years younger than Ken, a good age if we kept on dating. "And you said he doesn't live on your farm anymore. Is he still in the Puget Sound area?"

"In a manner of speaking. He's in Monroe." That's a small town about thirty minutes east of Seattle famous for the 4-H fairgrounds, flea markets, swap meets, and a correctional facility.

"Why Monroe? Is that where he works?"

"State pen." Jack sounded tense, but I plowed on anyway.

"He's a guard?"

"Naw. An inmate." Jack tilted his head back. His jaw muscles clenched, and his eyes blinked like he was fighting tears.

"I'm so sorry." I covered his hand with mine and held tight.

He looked down. I'd been right about the tears. "Rolf's scheduled for parole next month. I wanted him to be released to work on our farm."

"So good, he's getting out."

"Getting out, but it's not good, not really." Jack's chair thunked down on the brick floor. "Damn injustice system. Rolf was busted for intent to distribute. Marijuana. Nobody gives a fuck about marijuana anymore. Instead of serving three to five years, he got a death sentence."

"Death? What do you mean?"

"AIDS. He got AIDS at Monroe. I don't wanna know how.

Rolf's a good kid, a sweet kid, always has been. Teufel adored him. He raised lambs for 4-H. Lambs, dammit. He went into prison a lamb and he got slaughtered. The whole thing turns my stomach."

"Is there anything I can do to help? I have a friend who's a defense attorney. He's supposed to be pretty good. Maybe he could—"

"Goddamn lawyers. Don't get me started with lawyers. We had a lawyer. I mortgaged the farm to pay him. And for what? Rolf still landed in the can. The prosecutor came down hard because he wanted the names of the guys who controlled the West Coast operation. The kid wouldn't say a word. He knew what would happen if he ratted them out. So he went to prison. Three to five years. Damn. I thought he could handle it, do his time, survive, get out. But I was wrong."

"What about his mom?"

"She hasn't been part of the picture for years."

"Oh." I knew all about MMIA—Moms Missing In Action. I squeezed Jack's hand again. "What can I do to help?"

"The state department of corrections has to inspect my farm to see if it's a fit environment for a parolee."

"But what about that field? You know, the marijuana?"

"Yeah, that's a bitch."

"You didn't destroy the plants after Mac found them?"

"No, I couldn't. They're worth about fifty thousand. If I couldn't sell them, I couldn't make the payment on the mortgage I had to take out for that shithead attorney. And if I couldn't make the mortgage payments, there wouldn't be a farm for Rolf to come home to."

"I wish there was something I could do to help. But you might be better off if I stay far, far away. I mean, the cops are still trying to find out who killed the guy in my yard. I'm not a suspect. At least I don't think so, but I'm not as Jane Q. Citizen as I used to be."

Jack gripped my arm. "You're still as cute as a bug's ear."

I smiled and Jack continued. "Let's change the subject. I meant to ask you about those murders. Do the cops have any leads?"

I shook my head. "Not that I know about."

"Tell me more. What's happening?"

I thought about what Ace had said—don't talk to anyone about the investigation. I thought about what Mac had said—don't talk to Jack. But darn it, Jack was in pain and he had leveled with me about his son. Life could be so unfair. If JayJay got caught up in drugs—I couldn't even think about what I'd do.

And finally, I needed someone to talk to. Ever since I found Lank Lungstrom's body in my yard, I'd been hiding something from someone: the picture, the poker club, my brother Robbie, my illegal hens. I wanted to come clean.

So I told Jack everything.

CHAPTER THIRTY-TWO

When Mac heard the explosion inside his apartment, he banged past Ace and burst in through the front door. He scanned the living room but saw neither body parts hanging from the ceiling nor blood flecked across the walls. And the rapidly dissipating fumes were orange, not black and greasy with human fat.

That little jerkbutt. No fatalities this time but still a massive cock-up.

Mac took a deep breath to restore his blood pressure to its normal level of irritation and shouted, "Pete! Where are you?"

His grandson didn't answer. Of course.

Mac quickly searched the apartment. Other than the smoke and a badly singed couch, it was empty and undamaged. Above his head, he heard a wild shriek and the clattering of high-heeled sandals against polished wooden floors. "Pete! Pete!"

Oh lord, Nasreen. The Iranian lioness protecting her young.

Resigned to the inevitable sandstorm of motherly love, Mac grabbed a fortifying Belhaven from the fridge and popped the top. Seconds later Nasreen ran through the open door, sweeping Ace before her like a Kleenex in the wind.

"Where's Pete? Where's my baby?" Without waiting for an answer, she rushed around the apartment, flapping at the smoke and calling for her son.

Mac took another long pull on his Belhaven, and thought, *some days there's naught enough beer in the world to make life bearable.*

"What the hell is going on?" Ace asked. He had barricaded himself behind Mac's recliner as Nasreen swept past.

"The bathroom window's open. Pete's done a runner. He must have come up with something better to do than answer our questions."

"What caused the explosion?"

A clank of glass and a muffled curse from the bedroom suggested Nasreen had slipped on Mac's dirty underwear and crashed into the box of empties.

"Want a pint?" he asked Ace.

Ace shook his head. "Tell me—"

Mac held up a hand to quiet him. He set down his beer and started poking around the living room. Behind the couch, he found what he been searching for, a mass of two-inch paper tubes bound together with wire and attached to a small chunk of melted plastic. The end of each tube was charred and smelled of gunpowder. He held his prize aloft so Ace could see it.

"Firecrackers. Rigged to be detonated by a cell phone." Mac fought down a burst of pride. "It's not easy to do right the first time."

"If it is the first time. The kid's a terrorist in training."

"Terrorist? Nae. Pete's just a lad who likes to muck about."

Nasreen grabbed the string of spent firecrackers out of Mac's hand. She'd snuck up behind him, moving quietly as a prowling lion. "This is all your fault, Mac. You had to fill Pete's head with your stories about bombings. Now look what you've done. You've corrupted my son."

"You reckon?" Mac recaptured his beer. "After this little kerfuffle, there's some who might wonder if Pete set the bomb that blew up Ace's house."

"Ridiculous," Nasreen's bracelets clattered indignantly. "You have to find him. Maybe he has a concussion. Or—"

"Nae, lass. Calm down. Any pain he's feeling now is nothing

like what he's gonna experience when I catch up with him. He destroyed the back of my couch and it was three hundred dollars. He's going to make restitution if it takes every cent he has."

"Forget your couch." Nasreen whipped out her cell phone. "Go find Pete or I'll tell the police chief to organize a search party."

"Now, now." Mac gently pried her fingers away from the phone. "We don't really want the cops involved, do we?"

"I do." Ace strode into the center of the room. "That kid spied on Sunny, tried to humiliate Lank, and set off an explosion that could have killed us all. He should be in custody for his own good."

Nasreen's face darkened. She marched up to Ace. Her gold earrings jangled menacingly. She jabbed a finger at his nose. Mac glanced down, expecting to see another sharp-nailed finger slashing the lawyer's goolies. "You. Get out. This is a family matter, no business of yours. Out, out."

With more courage than Mac expected, Ace stood his ground. He was muttering something to himself. He stared at Mac over Nasreen's head. "Wait a minute. Right before the firecrackers went off, did you say Sunny went to dinner with a farmer who raises organic marijuana and free-range chickens?"

"Pay attention to me. Both of you." Nasreen stamped her feet and shook her bracelets.

"Aye, but so what?" Mac said. Nasreen was past civilized discourse. "Let the lass have her fun."

"I know a guy like that. I defended his son on drug charges. I lost. The kid was as guilty as hell. I need to find out what happened to him since. But how? Our tech guys don't work weekends."

"Search me, mate."

Ace shook his head and ground his teeth. Then he grabbed

Mac, "Where's Pete? He can find them."

"Pete?"

"Yeah, if anyone can hack his way through the NCIC database, it's Pete." Ace took Nasreen's phone from Mac and handed it back to her. "Text him. Tell him I'll pay. But he's got to show up right now."

"No. Pete is a good boy. I don't want him doing anything with you." Nasreen clutched the phone to her chest and bared her teeth at Ace. Mac thought he saw a snarl.

"Look here, Nasreen—" Ace began, but he was interrupted by a fierce banging on Mac's front door.

Mac sucked down another swallow of Belhaven, opened the door, and revealed Detective Sergeant Stanislaus. "What are you doing here?" he asked, although he was pretty sure he knew the answer.

"Your neighbors called the chief. Thought they heard an explosion inside here. Is everything okay?" She sniffed the air. "Stupid question. What's that you're holding, ma'am?"

Stanislaus pointed to the string of firecrackers.

Nasreen thrust them behind her back. "This is private property. You get out." She turned to Ace, her skirt swirling around her legs. "You tell that policeman to leave. Right now."

Ace stuck his hands in his pockets. "What about Pete? Is it okay if he helps me?"

"Okay, okay. Just get the cops out of here."

"Then call him."

But before Nasreen could turn on the phone, there was another knock at the door.

"You rang?" Pete sauntered inside like he owned the world.

Mebbe he does, Mac thought. *Mebbe he's what the world is coming to, God help us all.*

"Pete. Are you hurt?" Nasreen tried to engulf her son, but he neatly evaded her flashing bracelets and murmured endearments.

"It's all right, mom. Leave me alone." Pete glanced at Ace. "What's the job?"

"But Pete, you should rest," Nasreen insisted. "I'll get you something to eat and a pot of tea, hot, sweet tea."

"Mom, I'm okay. Really. Go back upstairs. I'll be there as soon as I take care of the job for Mr. Pennington." As he spoke, Pete walked his mother to Mac's front door, gently pushed her outside, and shut the door firmly in her face. It looked like a well-practiced maneuver.

"What's up?" he asked Ace.

Ace glanced at Stanislaus. "I think you should stay. I've got an idea."

"Do I get a beer?" she asked as she sat in Mac's recliner. "I was officially off duty ten minutes ago."

"Sure, lass."

Mac took care of refreshments while Ace said to Pete, "You've got to get online. We need a computer, but I don't know where to find one. The police confiscated Sunny's and mine. Should we go to your room?"

"No." Pete pulled his iPhone out of his pocket. "Just tell me what you need."

"Will that thing work?"

"Sure."

"Right." Ace collapsed on the couch. Mac got another Belhaven out of the fridge for himself, and Pete perched on the burned couch. "About three years ago I defended a man named Rolf Rabbit. He was convicted of possession of a Schedule 1 drug with intent to distribute. He was sentenced to five years and sent, I think, to the state pen in Monroe. With good behavior, he'd be eligible for parole right about now. I need to know if he's out."

"What do you care?" Pete asked as his fingers tapped the phone.

"Ms. Burnett is on a date with a guy named Jack Rabbit. I need to know if he's Rolf's father."

"I can do that. How much will you pay me?"

"Hell, I don't care. How much do you want?"

"Buy Grumps a new couch."

"Done."

Pete nodded, never lifting his gaze from the screen. A minute later, his face lit up. "Bingo." He glanced up and smiled like a fookin' Raphaelite angel. "I'll bet you another hundred bucks I can find out where Jack took her on their date. What do you say? Is it a deal?"

"How can you do that?" Ace asked.

"Her cell phone. I installed one of the GPS tracking devices for parents."

"Why?"

Pete shrugged. "Don't know. To see if I could?"

"Quit yer fussing, both of ya," Mac snarled. "Let's see if the blasted thing works."

CHAPTER THIRTY-THREE

While we picked at our dinners, I told Jack everything I knew or guessed about the Laurelmere murders. Talking to him, an objective bystander with no connection to the Cross-Dressing Poker Club, gave me hope that someday this whole mess would be nothing more than a depressing memory. As I finished, my cell phone chirped.

"Dead battery?" Jack asked.

"Yep." I said, and replaced the phone in my purse.

Jack gestured toward his pocket. "I've got mine if you need to make a call."

"Thanks, but no. I don't want to talk to anyone tonight. It's such a relief to get away from the craziness at home. I feel like I've escaped from jail."

Jack winced and so did I.

"I'm sorry," I said. "That was pretty darn insensitive."

"Don't worry about it. But that's some story about the murders and arson. It sounds like your friend Ace is a bad guy to know."

"What do you mean? You don't think he's the killer?"

"Nah. But he's the center of this thing, isn't he? Lank and Balls were his closest friends and now they're dead. Did they get killed because of him? Then his house blows up. What's that? A two-million-dollar loss? And he's probably next on the killer's hit list. He must feel like a sorry sack of shit about now."

Jack's words sounded okay, but I thought I glimpsed something mean in his eyes.

"You're right," I said slowly. "Ace does feel terrible. His life has fallen apart. I wish I could figure out what's going on. Do you really think someone would kill Ace and his friends because they liked to dress up? That seems a little farfetched."

"Men in women's clothes. I don't hold with that kind of perverted stuff." Jack's face darkened. I guessed he was thinking about his son getting AIDS in prison.

Well, damn. I hadn't meant to reopen Jack's wound. No wonder he couldn't conjure up much sympathy for Ace. I put my hand over Jack's and squeezed for a second.

"I'm not a fan of cross-dressing either," I said. "But it still doesn't seem like a reason to murder someone."

A trio of men swaggered past and sat at a nearby table. They were in their early thirties and aggressively well groomed. Unlike the working men at the bar, they wore tailored suits, flashy watches, loafers without socks, and a certain air of smug self-satisfaction. I recognized the type.

"Real-estate developers," I whispered to Jack as the waitress hurried to take their drink orders. "They're probably involved in the factory conversion across the street."

"I hate those kind of guys," he said. "They're just like your buddy, Horace L. Pennington the Third. The one-percenters. They think they own the world."

"Ace is not my buddy."

I suppose I should have said more to defend Ace, but I was tired of talking about the murders. Jack didn't have any new insights, and I didn't want to listen to another rant on the topic of "life is so unfair."

I pushed my plate away. Half a black bean burrito had been more than enough.

"If you're done, let's go," Jack said. "I don't want anymore either."

He signaled the waitress, but she was too busy jiggling for the suits to notice him. She flounced off to the bar and returned with a pitcher of beer without glancing our way. Jack glared at them and called out, "Miss, over here."

Flounce-jiggle, flounce-jiggle. She disappeared into the kitchen.

Jack scooted his chair back. "Come on, let's get out of here. It was supposed to be a free meal anyway."

"But what about her tip?"

"The only tip I'd give that bitch is 'watch your back.' "

I didn't like this side of Jack. Sure the food had been terrible, the service lousy, and the ambiance tragically city dump, but I'd worked enough dead-end jobs myself to know it wasn't the waitress's fault. Or at least not totally. She might be dropping belly bombs in the woman's bathroom during her shift, but she should still get a tip. No waitress can survive on wages alone.

I stood as she pushed through the kitchen doors. I gave her the queen's wave and she walked over to our table. "Hope you enjoyed your meal, folks." She tapped a faux leather folder against the table a couple of times before dropping it beside Jack's plate.

"What's this?"

"Your bill." She rolled her eyes in that you-must-not-get-out-very-much way and added, "Sir."

Jack flipped the folder back to her. "I'm not paying."

"Why not?" Her voice went up an octave. She attacked her leather-clad thigh with her pencil. "You ate your meal."

"Your boss offered me two crappy dinners gratis because he was late paying for his produce." As he spoke, Jack kicked back his chair and stood until he towered over the waitress. His butt still looked cute in his tight jeans, but he was way overreacting to a thirty-dollar tab.

"He ain't here, and I don't know nothing about free meals. Did he give you a chit?"

"No. It was a gentleman's agreement."

"I don't know nothing about gentlemen, neither. You shoulda said something when you ordered." One more flounce and the snot hanging from the waitress's nose rings flipped off. It landed on the table next to my hand. My stomach heaved. JayJay kicked in protest.

I hate confrontations, especially public confrontations about money. My father was a master of dine-and-dash. He'd been so proud the time I upchucked on the table while he argued with the waitress about our bill, a bill he never intended to pay. Afterward I dreaded going to restaurants because he always wanted me to try that little trick again.

"Jack," I said, "please, settle up. Let's get out of here. I think I'm going to be sick."

"I'm not going anywhere. They can't pull this crap on me."

"Arnold," the waitress hollered without moving. "Arnold, get your fat ass out here."

The bartender appeared in the doorway. I hadn't paid much attention to him when we entered, but now I saw he could have turned WWF pro if they added a Sumo division.

Jack didn't show any signs of relenting. Maybe he really couldn't afford to pay. I opened my wallet and dug out my last two twenties. "Let me deal with it. I've got to get home."

"No, ma'am. You're not paying and I'm not paying. No one is paying." He picked up my twenties, crushed them in his fist and folded his arms across his chest. His biceps flexed and the knot in my stomach swelled. I wondered if I'd seen the last of my cash.

By this time, the waitress had danced behind the stovepipe statue and the bartender had waddled six feet closer. Closer didn't improve his appearance. Plus, now I could smell him— sweat, booze, and something metallic.

Give me good clean chicken poop anytime.

Bile mounted in my throat. I put my hand over my mouth and mumbled, "Jack, I've got to get some fresh air."

He shook his head once without looking away from Arnold. JayJay kicked again, playing handball with my guts. I took a deep breath, smelled Arnold, and pulled my dress tight over my baby bump. "Watch out, I'm pregnant," I cried a second before my burrito made an encore appearance on my plate.

The waitress's face turned splotchy green, like zucchini infested with powdery mildew. Grabbing her stomach, she dashed out of the dining room and collided with a pierced and tattooed couple in the doorway. Seconds later, the sound of heartfelt retching filtered in from the bar. The inked couple vanished, the suits groaned loudly.

Arnold threw me a disgusted glance. He shouted to the waitress, "Get it cleaned up before we lose any more customers."

I spotted the emergency exit behind the kitchen. I yanked Jack's arm. "Let's get the hell out of here. Just give them the money."

"No," he said as he pocketed my two twenties. He draped his arm over my shoulder and steered me toward the exit. "You're really something, Sunny. Your timing was great. We should go out on the town."

On my forty dollars? No way.

Here's the thing. I couldn't be angry with Jack because he'd unknowingly morphed into my good-for-nothing father. But I wasn't a powerless eight-year-old anymore. I didn't have to put up with him. Tonight I had learned that Jack, for all of his good points as an organic farmer and concerned parent, was not the man for me.

I wanted Jack to drive me home so I could take off my shoes, drink some warm milk, and tell him to get lost. Even if dumping him meant losing my last forty dollars, it was cheap at twice the price.

CHAPTER THIRTY-FOUR

The alarm went off as we left the restaurant through the emergency exit, but no one chased after us. We hurried around the block to Jack's Beemer, not running exactly, but not wasting any time admiring the moon over the Olympic Mountains either.

Jack turned on the engine and the car door locks clicked into place with a sound like shelled peas dropping into a metal bowl.

"Some date," Jack said as he drove. "Not real romantic. I'm sorry about that." He reached over and squeezed my hand. "But boy, you were great. There aren't many women who can upchuck and still look terrific."

I'd forgotten one important thing about dating. It's as hard to get rid of a bad date as it is to find a good one. I had a horrible feeling we were in for some meaningful conversation before Jack realized we didn't have a future. At least not together.

Jack merged onto I-5 northbound. The Beemer took the turns smoothly, lulling JayJay to sleep. I relaxed and said, "I can't believe I threw up. The poor waitress. I hope she doesn't have to pay for our meal."

"I'll call the owner tomorrow and straighten things out. Tell him to give her twenty percent. She earned it."

"Thanks."

Jack reached across the console and brushed my thigh with his fingertips. "You're a softie, aren't you, babe?"

He'd touched my leg and called me babe. Dumping him might be harder than I thought.

"I know what it's like to waitress. No one respects you." As I spoke, I pointed my knees toward the passenger door and pretended to study the passing scenery. I wanted to get home before we had the whole this-relationship-isn't-going-anywhere discussion, especially since my cell phone was dead and my wallet was empty.

Something was bothering me though, something besides Jack's wandering hands. What was it? Something he had said in the restaurant.

"You'll help me out, won't you?" Jack asked. "You understand what I'm dealing with, don't you?"

"What?" Then it hit me. "You referred to Ace as Horace L. Pennington the Third while we were having dinner. How did you know Ace's full name?"

"It was in the paper. When his house blew up."

"No, it wasn't. Ace noticed. He's very sensitive to adverse publicity."

Jack thumped the steering wheel. "Should have known I couldn't put something past a smart woman like you. I know your ol' buddy Ace from way back. He's the lawyer who defended my son."

"Unsuccessfully."

"Yep, that's the bastard who screwed me over but good. I mortgaged my farm to pay his bill and then he lost the case anyway. Now I've got a bank loan I can never hope to pay off."

"Why didn't you sell your farm instead of mortgaging it?"

"That place is my identity, Sunny. I'm the fourth generation in my family to farm there. My great-great-grandfather bought the land from the Indians and built the house with his own two hands. Without that farm I'm nothing."

I felt an unwelcome wave of sympathy. That was just how I reacted when Jessica told me to sell my house and move into a nice little apartment where I could grow herbs in a window box. No way.

"I understand what you mean," I told Jack. "You're in a horrible spot."

"Yeah, well. After Ace lost the appeal, Rolf was thrown into Monroe with all those perverts."

"And now?"

"Now I'm getting even. What goes around, comes around. Ace destroyed my life. I'm destroying his. And you, babe—"

"Me? I'm not part of this."

"Yes, you are. You understand what I'm up against. I knew you would. So you're the logical person to help me."

Unspoken words hovered between us: *Whether you want to or not.*

Without meaning to, I'd stepped in a swamp and now I was sinking deeper and deeper. But what could I do? I couldn't leap from a car going sixty-five on the freeway. Especially not in my condition.

I had to play along.

"How do you want me to help?" I asked, striving for nonchalance. As if helping killers was something I did every day of the week.

Jack smiled at me, his teeth straight and white in the headlights of the oncoming cars. He had a great smile. Weren't bad guys supposed to have acne and sweaty palms, beer guts and insolent smirks? I felt doubly deceived.

"It's easy." Jack's voice was relaxed and confident. "When we get to your house, you phone Ace and tell him to come over right away. You have a basement, don't you?"

"A basement?" A plan sprouted in my mind. My gun safe was in the basement. Maybe I could—

"You stay down there until it's all over. I'll take care of everything."

"Everything?" I didn't sound nonchalant any more.

"Yeah."

"But I thought your son was getting out of prison on parole. I thought he was going to work on the farm with you. Why would you give that up to get even with Ace?"

"The parole board said no."

"Said no to what?"

"Said no to Rolf working on my farm. They found the marijuana. They burned the field and arrested me. I'm out on bail right now."

"Did Mac turn you in?"

"No, they brought drug-sniffing dogs when they turned up to inspect the farm for work-release. Teufel tried to fight them off, but we didn't have a chance."

"What's going to happen when the police come to my house to get you?" I asked. "Because they will, you know."

Jack exited I-5. We were less than ten minutes from Laurelmere. He shook his head. "I'm not getting out of this alive, babe, anymore than Rolf is. But you can. You should." He reached over and took my hand. "I want you to stay in the basement until it's all over. Okay?"

I tried to nod but my head wouldn't move.

Jack squeezed hard. "Promise me you'll behave. You and that little girl of yours deserve a chance."

I blinked and realized tears were streaming down my face. And my nose was running. I didn't want to let go of Jack's hand. As long as I held on, I had a chance to talk him down. Maybe I could alert George, the security guard at the gate, that something was wrong. How could I tell George to call the police without making Jack think I posed a threat?

That JayJay and I posed a threat?

For a second, I couldn't breathe.

I was still trying to formulate a plan when Jack approached the gate to Laurelmere. But as it turned out, having a plan didn't matter. George saluted and waved us through. We didn't even slow down.

I shook off Jack's hand and wiped my nose. "You served in the army with George, didn't you?" I asked. It wasn't really a question.

"Yeah. I was his commanding officer in Iraq. It was a pretty tight unit."

"That's why he always waves you through the security checkpoint, right? Without ever putting your name on the list."

"Yeah, George is a straight-up guy. Very loyal. Not smart maybe, but very loyal. He didn't connect me with the murders at all."

I'd finally found someone who didn't put the gilt-edged sanctity of Laurelmere before everything else. Too bad it was the security guard.

We turned into my street. Still and peaceful in the moonlight, the houses were filled with people totally unprepared for the bloodbath brewing in Jack's brain. I could see Pete's monitor through his bedroom window. The pneumatic breasts were back, bouncing merrily across the screen. The remnants of Ace's house looked like the Haunted Mansion at an amusement park—too gothic and creepy to be real. My house, my grandmother's house, glowed softly. Drat, I must have left the lights on. Or maybe Ace had. I fretted about the wasted electricity for a second then came to my senses.

It didn't matter.

Jack parked at the curb. He got out and walked around the front of the car. I unfastened my seatbelt and heard a click. He'd locked the Beemer with me inside. I thought about screaming. But no one would hear me. And I needed to keep Jack calm while I figured out what to do.

He unlocked my door and helped me out. I said, "Thank you," like we were still on a real date. He gripped my elbow and took a revolver out of the glove compartment. With his free hand, he clicked off the safety. He pressed the barrel against my stomach.

"Just in case," he whispered against my ear. "You might survive, but the baby won't."

"But you said—"

He jabbed me harder.

"Okay, I understand."

The full moon illuminated my front yard. We walked to my porch, easily navigating around the cherry trees and strawberry beds. It was the same front porch: wooden swing, arbor of ripe grapes, and the wrought-iron hose reel decorated with a rooster.

"Give me your key." Jack's gun nudged my baby bump.

I rummaged in my bag and found my key ring. I had a fierce urge to jab him in the eye, but he could shoot faster than I could jab.

I handed him the ring with Mac's key on top. Maybe the wrong key would buy me a few more seconds. I wished I knew what to do with them.

Pray? Or faint?

I did neither. Jack held me with his left arm around my waist, the gun barrel pressing into my baby bump. With his right hand, he inserted Mac's key into the lock and turned.

The key balked.

"Sometimes it sticks," I said. "Do you want me to try?"

He growled and tried again. "Goddamn it. Are you sure it's the right one?"

"Let me see." I leaned closer to him and pretended to study the keys. "Oh, sorry. It's the other one."

He growled and put the correct key in. He turned it. The lock clicked. He turned the doorknob. The door didn't open.

"You have to turn the key and the knob at the same time." I tried to sound helpful, nothing more. Out of the corner of my eye, I checked the position of the hose on its reel.

A third growl. Jack turned the key with his right hand and

gripped the doorknob with the fingertips of his left hand, the gun hand.

I ducked under his arm and grabbed the nozzle of the hose.

Jack pushed me against the siding. "Stop moving, bitch!"

I kicked his shin as hard as I could with my strappy sandal. My foot hurt like hell.

He yanked on my arm. "I'm going to kill you for that."

I pointed the nozzle at his face and flicked the release lever.

Chicken manure tea gushed straight into his mouth. He fell back and dropped the gun.

I kicked it into the grapevines surrounding the porch.

He lunged for me, but I took off. I ran down the steps toward Mac's apartment, screaming at the top of my lungs.

Lights flicked on in the houses around me.

Still running, I looked back to check on Jack. He was gaining on me. I ran full-tilt into a tree.

No, make that Detective Sergeant Stanislaus.

She pushed me to the ground, drew her gun, and shouted, "It's all over, Jack Rabbit. You're under arrest."

With a roar, Jack leaped straight at Stanislaus, arms raised, my key ring glinting in his right hand.

She fired. He fell to the ground. He kicked once and it was over.

Chapter Thirty-Five

"This isn't a good idea," Ace said for about the twentieth time. He'd been bitching at me ever since Mac agreed to drive us to the animal shelter the morning after Jack died.

The night before Ace had been a rock, an absolute rock. He held me during the terrible formalities of suicide by cop: sirens, ambulances, officers swarming my house and yard, media attacking us like howling coyotes, and endless questions from the police.

Wilson relieved Stanislaus of her weapon as soon as he arrived on the scene, and Vanderhorn hustled her into an unmarked car. My last glimpse of the detective was her ashen face staring out the window as they drove away.

"What can I do to help Stanislaus?" I asked Ace. "She had to defend herself."

"Tell the truth," Ace said and of course he was right. Jack had told me he wouldn't survive the evening and he did everything he could to make his prophesy come true.

To cap the evening, Jessica showed up and bullied her way through the police barricade. She rushed into the house, crying hysterically. "It's all my fault, it's all my fault."

"What are you talking about?" I asked.

"The picture." She reached into her purse and pulled out the photograph of Ken and Lank that I'd snatched from Lank's fingers. "Do you remember asking me to measure the guestroom so we could fix it up as a nursery? I was searching for something to write on and grabbed *Urban Homesteading* from your cookbook shelf. The picture fell out. I didn't know what to do with it, so I took it home with me. I didn't want Jessica Junior to find it some day. Who knows what effect it would have on her psyche?"

I started to tell her it didn't matter, but stopped and bit my lip. I'd be a fool to give up any leverage over Jessica. Instead I burst into hysterical sobs. Ace told Jessica to go home. He helped me upstairs and chastely tucked me into bed.

The next morning, however, Ace was back to being his normal bossy self. He ordered scrambled eggs, toast, and coffee for breakfast like I was a short-order cook and forbid me to go to the animal shelter.

"Forbid? I don't think so." I slammed the skillet into the sink and poured myself another cup of coffee. "The thing you need to learn about me, Ace, is that I am perfectly capable of making my own decisions. You can't forbid me, you can't order me around, and you can't cajole or trick me into doing what you want. Have you got that?"

"Don't get so damn emotional. You're not thinking straight. You need to calm down."

"So what? I make my own decisions whether I'm thinking straight or not. And if they turn out terrible, I'll deal with the consequences. Okay?"

"But I still think—"

"Okay?"

"Okay." He sighed like he'd just sliced a golf ball into the ocean below Pebble Beach.

Of course with Ace, an agreement was just the beginning of negotiations. By the time we got to the animal shelter, he'd started haranguing me again. "This is another terrible idea, Sunny."

Mac and I ignored him while we talked with the attendant.

Outside, the temperature had hit ninety-five degrees and Seattle was wilting after four weeks without rain. Inside, the shelter was about ten degrees cooler and one hundred percent smellier. The attendant rolled his eyes when he saw me wrinkle my nose.

"Our air-conditioning system is on its last legs," he said. "We haven't figured out how to finance a replacement. Donations are way down this year, and we have more animals than ever. With the recession, people decide they can't afford to take care of their pets. They drop them off even when we're closed."

I nodded sympathetically. He opened the steel door into a chaos of caged dogs barking, yipping, and whining, all pleading to go home with me. My heart lurched. That settled the question of what to do with my reward for finding the Cross-Dressing Poker Club Killer. And maybe I could talk Ace into matching my donation to the shelter.

The attendant checked his clipboard, and Ace shouted at the back of my head. "Forget this crazy idea. I'll pay for a security system at your house until you get on your feet."

"No," I shouted back. "I don't need charity, I need a dog."

Mac stayed out of the fray. I sensed he was making his own calculations.

The attendant glanced back at me. "In the next room," he said. "Are you ready?"

"Sure." Mac and I followed him through the barrage of noise. Ace trailed behind. We went through another steel door which was plastered with signs: NO ADMITTANCE WITHOUT STAFF. NO CHILDREN ALLOWED. ENTER AT YOUR OWN RISK. CLOSED-TOE SHOES MANDATORY.

This room was dark, stuffy, and profoundly quiet. The attendant switched on an overhead light. The silence was broken by one bark, a deep, sonorous bellow. It came from a steel mesh cage in the corner, the only occupied cell on death row.

The attendant stopped and turned to me. His gaze dropped

to my baby bump. "You're sure?" he said. "This guy was a guard dog for a killer. I can't guarantee how he's going to be around a baby."

I nodded at Mac. "Mr. MacDougall was responsible for a K-9 unit before he retired. He's going to handle the training."

"You'll have to learn German," Ace said, coming up behind us. He put his hand on my shoulder and squeezed. "Sunny, you don't have time to learn a new language on top of everything else. You know what 'Teufel' means in German, don't you? 'Devil.' If you take this dog, you're making a deal with the devil."

"German isn't such a big deal," I countered. "I don't have to be able to read Wittgenstein in the original. Besides, Teufel is half-poodle. Mac's going to appeal to his poodle side and train him in French."

"Nae, lass. The Queen's English is what the sodding beast gotta learn. The Queen's English and naught else."

Ace snorted. "Teufel will never understand English if he has to listen to you."

"Shove it, Ace," I said. "I know a little doggy German. Watch this."

I stepped closer to the cage. The black mutt inside pushed his enormous tongue through the bars and licked my hand. "*Welkommen zu Laurelmere,* Teufel," I said.

He wagged his tail joyously.

I wagged back.

ABOUT THE AUTHOR

Judy Dailey grew up on a small organic farm in Indiana. She graduated from Bryn Mawr College (PA) and received a MBA from the University of Washington. She and her husband live on an urban farm and raise chickens in a not-so-exclusive neighborhood in Seattle. Please visit her website at www.JudyDailey .com.